Also by Shane Maloney

The Brush-Off
Nice Try
The Big Ask

A
MURRAY
WHELAN
MYSTERY

STIFF

SHANE MALONEY

Arcade Publishing • New York

Arcade Publishing books may be purchased in bulk at special discounts for sales promotion, corporate gifts, fund-raising, or educational purposes. Special editions can also be created to specifications. For details, contact the Special Sales Department, Arcade Publishing, 307 West 36th Street, 11th Floor, New York, NY 10018 or arcade@skyhorsepublishing.com.

Arcade Publishing® is a registered trademark of Skyhorse Publishing, Inc.®, a Delaware corporation.

Visit our website at www.arcadepub.com.

10 9 8 7 6 5 4 3 2 1

Library of Congress Cataloging-in-Publication Data is available on file.

ISBN: 978-1-61145-809-1

Printed in the United States of America

For Christine
my kind of funding body

STIFF

The fiddle at the Pacific Pastoral meat-packing works was neither particularly original nor fabulously lucrative. But it was a nice little earner for all concerned while it lasted, and probably harmless enough. All that changed when Herb Gardiner reported finding a body in Number 3 chiller.

There it was, jammed between a pallet load of best export boneless beef and half a ton of spring lamb. It was a Friday afternoon so, if Gardiner hadn't found it when he did, the corpse would have spent the weekend locked in with the rest of the dead meat, carcasses parked halfway between paddock and dinner plate.

According to the statement Gardiner gave to the department of labor investigators and the police, the Number 3 unit had a history of playing up. He had unlocked the door and gone inside to read the gauge when he saw the body squeezed into the aisle running through to the emergency exit hatch. He recognised it immediately as a leading hand with one of the casual work crews, later identified as Ekrem Bayraktar. He didn't need to feel for Bayraktar's pulse to know that he was dead. He could tell by the waxy pallor of the man's face, by the dusting of fine sugar on his lips where his last breath had turned to frost.

The body was sandwiched into a tight space between roof-high stacks of boxes. It was a narrow gap, but it was just wide enough for most men to pass along sideways even in protective clothing — obstruction of access to the emergency hatch was illegal. But Bayraktar was big, even by the standards of a place where men were hired to hump heavy loads around. Later at the morgue his naked corpse weighed in at close to 300 pounds, big doughy rolls of flesh, soft obese bulk, like a weight-lifter gone to seed.

He was squeezed in so tight that they had to bring in one of of the forklifts to move the loaded pallets around him before they could remove the body. Even without the boxes there to support him he remained upright, balanced like a great big stalagmite. It was hard to imagine how he had gotten himself that far down the passage, or why.

In the business that followed — the calling of the ambulance, the notification of the police and the department of labor, the removal of the body, the taking of photographs and statements — it never occurred to anyone to look for the small zip-lock plastic bag of folded fifties and twenties that Bayraktar had taken into the freezer with him. And even if they had known to look, and where, they would not have found anything. There were quite a few little details about that afternoon that seemed to have been missed.

With Bayraktar gone, everything might have ended then and there and no one would have the wiser. It was just bad luck really that his untimely demise coincided with a delicate readjustment then taking place within certain echelons of the Australian Labor Party, an organisation founded to further the aspirations of those who toil unseen in dark and dangerous places. An organisation which, next to itself, loves the working man best.

1

PERHAPS I SHOULD BEGIN by saying that this is not a sob story. It's a cruel world, I know, and even in the just city a man can be stiff. Bad luck happens. And it's not like bad luck was something I didn't already know a bit about. Damage control was part of my job, after all. But up until then it had been other people's bad luck, not my own, that exercised my professional interest. Maybe that's why I was so unprepared for what happened over those four October days. So I'm not doing any special pleading, you understand. Considering what happened to others I could name, I got off pretty lightly.

It all started on one of those miserable wet Monday mornings when, come nine o'clock, half of Melbourne is still strung out bumper-to-bumper along the South-eastern Freeway. I had just dropped my son Red at school, and as I swung my clapped-out old Renault into Sydney Road the thought of all those Volvo and Camira drivers stewing away behind their windscreen wipers brought a quiet smile to my lips. Not that I bore them any personal animosity, you understand. It was just that if God wanted to punish the eastern suburbs for voting Liberal, She wouldn't hear me complaining.

I could afford to feel like that because the Brunton Avenue log-jam was miles away. Where I lived, north of town, the toiling masses tended to start their toiling a little earlier in the day, and most of those that still had jobs were already at work. By nine the rush hour had already come and gone. Apart from a few hundred light industrial vehicles and the occasional tram disgorging early shoppers, women in head-scarfs mainly, I had the northbound lane to myself.

Not that I was busting a gut to get to work. No clock was waiting for me to punch it, and I couldn't see the pile of paper on my desk bursting into flames if left undisturbed a little longer. The fifteen minutes it took me to drive to work provided one of my few moments of solitude all day and I liked to make the most of it. As I drove I read the paper.

This was less dangerous than it sounds. I'd already studied the broadsheets over breakfast, and the *Sun* was the kind of tabloid easily absorbed while doing something else — shelling peas, for instance, or operating a lathe. I had it spread open on the passenger seat beside me, and whenever I hit a red light or got stuck behind a slow-moving tram I skimmed a couple of pages. The spring racing carnival had just begun, so the emphasis was on horseflesh, fashion and catering. Just A Dash was favourite, black was big, and interesting things were being done with asparagus. Agreement was unanimous — four years in and the eighties were holding firm as the most exciting decade ever.

The Bell Street lights had changed and I was halfway across the intersection when my eye caught a name buried in a two-paragraph news brief at the bottom of page seventeen. That was when I first encountered the name Ekrem Bayraktar. Not that it meant anything to me at the time. It was the other name that got my attention. I snatched up the page, draped it over the steering wheel and turned my concentration away from the road long enough to constitute a serious threat to public safety. This is what I read:

> Police have identified a man found dead last Friday in a freezer at the Pacific Pastoral meat-packing works at Coolaroo in Melbourne's outer north as Ekrem Bayraktar, 42, a shift supervisor at the works. It is believed that he suffered a heart attack and was overcome by cold while conducting a routine stocktake.

Pacific Pastoral has announced an immediate review of its procedures in light of the incident which coincides with the state government's attempts to gain Upper House approval for its controversial industrial health and safety legislation. Informed sources at Trades Hall believe the matter will be considered when the THC Executive meets late next week. The Minister for Industry, Charlene Wills, was unavailable for comment.

I liked the way a whiff of Labor intrigue had been slipped into an account of some poor bastard's cardiac arrest. But that wasn't what interested me. What had pushed my button was mention of the Minister for Industry. Charlene Wills was a person whose reputation was a matter very close to my heart.

Up ahead I could see Pentridge, the razor ribbon atop its bluestone walls dripping dismally in the drizzle. On my left was an Italian coffee shop and a row of old single-storey terraces that had been tarted up into offices and professional suites. I pulled into the curb, tucked the *Sun* under my arm and pushed open the glass door of one of the shops, the one with the letters on the window saying "Charlene Wills: Member of the Legislative Council for the Province of Melbourne Upper."

With a bit of luck, I thought, I'd have just enough time to call Charlene's parliamentary office and get the lowdown on this piece of tabloid crap before the business of the day wrapped its tentacles around me.

Too late. The daily grind had already walked in off the street and was standing at the desk just inside the front door. He was solidly built, in a knockabout sort of way, anywhere between thirty and forty-five, with a duck's bum haircut and hands like baseball mitts. When I walked in, he shifted irritably and shot me a glance that told me he'd got there first and I could fucking well wait my turn.

All his weight was balanced on the balls of his feet, and the tips of his fingers were pressed down hard on the desk. He was glowering across it at Trish, who was in charge of office admin. "I've had a gutful," he said.

Statements like that, half-threat, half-plea, weren't unusual at the electorate office. But this fellow's tone was tending more to the threat end of the octave, and as he spoke he began tugging his khaki work shirt out of his pants and fiddling with the buttons. "I pay my taxes," he said. "I know my rights."

Trish nodded at the bloke sympathetically and, without moving her eyes, casually bent forward as if to better hear him out. Trish was big in the chassis and not afraid to use it, but just in case push ever came to shove she kept the butt end of a sawn-down pool cue sitting in her wastepaper basket. As far as I knew she'd never had cause to use it, but on the odd occasion its mere presence could be a comfort. If this dickhead's manner didn't rapidly begin to improve, we'd all have a very unpleasant start to the working week.

"May I help you, sir?" I said, stepping forward. "I'm Murray Whelan, Charlene Wills' electorate officer."

As I spoke the man turned towards me and threw his shirt open, like he was performing a magic trick or unveiling the foundation stone of a major civic monument. Underneath, he was wearing what appeared to be a paisley-patterned t-shirt. As I got closer I realised that he was one of the most comprehensively tattooed human beings I had ever seen. Which, in that part of the world, was no mean achievement.

I tried to look unimpressed as I accepted his tacit invitation to inspect his pecs. He was certainly toting some artistry about. Fire-breathing dragons, dagger-pierced hearts, tiger-mounted she-devils, flame-licked skulls, Huey, Dewey and Louie, you name it, he had it. Innumerable little pictures exploded out of his pants, ran up over his flaccid paunch, covered his torso, and curled back across his shoulders.

The mad swirls of colour stopped abruptly, however, at the V of the man's collar line and, I was prepared to bet, at the point in mid-bicep where the sleeves of a summer work shirt would run out. His hands, neck and face were unadorned. No spider webs embellished his earlobes, no intertwined bluebirds flew up his neck. This was a good sign. Here was a man who knew that some people tended to jump to the wrong conclusion about tatts, a man who had the brains not to let his passion for self-decoration get in the way of his employability. Someone you could talk sense to.

And now that he was dealing with a fellow male, he became a little less highly strung. "I want this bloke put out of business." He jabbed his finger at the place right above his heart where a freshly laid-on pair of baroque cherubs, beautiful work, were holding aloft an ornate scroll. I moved his shoulder sideways so I had better light to read by. Inside the scroll were the words "Gial For Ever."

"Gial?" I said.

He nodded morosely. "Gail took one look and shot through," he said. "Reckoned if I couldn't even spell her name properly, she certainly wasn't gunna marry me." Then he brightened up. "I told that fucken prick of a tattooist I'd have his licence. And I'm not leaving here until I do. Dead set. I'm adam-fucken-ant."

Three years before, when Charlene had offered me the job of looking after her constituents, a Labor MP's electorate office was, by definition, a backwater. Then the tide had turned and swept Labor into office, first at state, then federal level. The drover's dog was in the Lodge. We were the power in the land. And that sign on the door had become a homing beacon for every dingbat within a ten-mile radius.

When I began at the electorate office, our only customers were ordinary voters desperately seeking redress from bureaucratic inanity or government indifference. Or the harmlessly wan and smelly looking for somewhere out of the cold. But by late 1984 we were attracting such a daily barrage of basket cases and snake-oil salesmen that the sign out front might as well have read "Axes Ground Here."

Surely, I was beginning to think, the cause of social progress could be deploying my skills more effectively. Could I not perhaps be managing a small lake or pine plantation for the Department of Conservation, Forests and Lands? A modestly demanding range of foothills even? Something with a little less interface.

"Okay, Mr. Adam fucking Ant," I shrugged. "Let's see what we can do." Behind the man's back, Trish had relaxed and was grinning like an ape. I discreetly flashed her a splayed handful of digits and led off towards the back of the office. Five minutes of deeply concerned bullshit should, I figured, be enough to see this particular dipstick safely off the premises. "Walk this way."

Adam Ant, or whatever his name was, tucked his shirt back into his pants and slouched after me. "It's not right," he mumbled under his breath.

What passed for my office was a partitioned cubicle tucked into a back corner behind the stationery cupboard. Before the election had transformed Charlene into a Minister of the Crown, it had been hers. Back in those days, I'd shared the reception area with Trish and whoever else happened to wander in. But I was fast to grasp the perquisites of political power and had quickly taken advantage of Charlene's increasing frequent absence to commandeer her privileges.

I snapped on the flickering fluorescent light, parked myself behind the laminated plywood desk and indicated the orange plastic of the visitor's chair. As Ant lowered his backside into place, obscuring my Tourism Commission poster of Wilson's Promontory, I squared off my blotter, uncapped my pen with a bureaucratic flourish and tried to look like I gave a shit.

"I'd like to help you, mate. I really would," I said. "But you've got the wrong department."

Ant finished buttoning up the National Gallery, ran his hand through his greasy pompadour and looked deeply wronged. "I rung up Consumer Protection. They said I should try my local member."

Typical. Consumer Protection took the cake at pass-the-parcel. I nodded understandingly and went through the motions of taking down the particulars. This was the first instance of a dyslexic tattooist that Mrs. Wills' office had ever been called upon to address, I explained. And while the Minister would undoubtedly be sympathetic, in a case like this the powers of an elected member of the state's legislative chamber of review might be somewhat circumscribed.

The *Sun* lay between us on top of my overflowing in-tray, still folded open at page seventeen. If I don't piss this joker off soon, I thought, Parliament will begin sitting and Charlene will be unreachable for the rest of the day.

"I'm not going anywhere, pal," said Ant. "Until this thing is fixed."

"This is a legal matter," I said. "Restitution. Punitive damages." These were words he liked. "You need the Community Legal Service." The Family Law Act surely included provisions for the irretrievable breakdown of the relationship between a man, his tattooist, and his intended.

Looking like the height of efficiency, I dialled the CLS and made an appointment, skipping the details in case they thought I was pulling their collective leg. Friday was the earliest the slack-arses could squeeze him in. "This lot will look after you," I told Ant. "Top people."

The CLS was half a mile down the road. I drew a map, wrote the appointment details underneath, and slid it across the desk.

Ant folded his arms across his chest. "You're just trying to give me the bounce."

True. But it wasn't as though I hadn't given it my best shot first. "Look mate," I said, marginally more firmly, "there's nothing else I can do. The legal service will handle it from now on. Good luck. Let us know how you go. I'll keep Charlene informed. But in the meantime my hands are tied."

He shook his head and settled his Technicolor mass even more firmly into the moulded plastic cup of the seat. I opened Charlene's correspondence file and buried my face in it, wondering how long it would take Trish to burst in with an urgent pretext. "Dear Madam," the top letter began. "You are a pinko ratbag bitch."

Five minutes later I was still pretending to read and Ant was continuing to glare. What did he want me to do? Whip out a bottle of correcting fluid and a blue ballpoint and personally amend his faulty chest? "I'll call the cops," I said, lamely.

He snorted derisively. Quite right, too. For a start, we could hardly be seen having someone dragged away merely for demanding that the government do something about their problems. That, after all, was what we were there for.

Also, I found it hard to sound convincing. If I called the coppers on every cantankerous customer we had, they'd have to start running a shuttle bus. And given the ongoing budgetary constraints faced by the various agencies under the jurisdiction of the Minister for Police and Emergency Services, a factional ally of Charlene, that was a poor prospect.

Mainly, however, I couldn't call the coppers on some love-struck dumb-bum with Cupid engraved on his left tit because such an encounter was unlikely to be conducive to an outcome of social equity. Let the coppers catch who they could. I'd gone to school with blokes like Ant, and having to resort to the wallopers in my dealings with them would have been an affront to both my personal morality and my professional pride. Quarrels should be kept in the family. "Do us a favour," I suggested courteously. "Fuck off."

Ant smiled maliciously and leaned back like he had all the time in the world. Fortunately, at exactly that moment the phone rang. It wasn't Trish but Greg Coates, a deputy director in the Melbourne office of the Department of Immigration and Ethnic Affairs.

Nearly a quarter of the electors of the Province of Melbourne Upper had been born overseas and it wasn't uncommon for constituents with an immigration problem to turn up on our doorstep. No problem. Immigration is a Commonwealth matter, so all we had to do was steer them over to the local federal member.

But, as often as not, the problems were little more than language mix-ups, and it would have been criminal of me to allow an important federal politician to be burdened with such trifling matters. Especially if Charlene could get the credit for fixing them. Which wasn't difficult to arrange since Greg Coates had been a mate since university, and was both a fellow spear-carrier in my faction and a member of the same party branch. So about once a week Greg gave me a call and we cut a bit of red tape together and swapped political gossip.

I swivelled my seat around, pointedly turning my back on the tattooed wonder, and spent fifteen minutes firming up a batch of family reunion applications. Eventually Coates made his way, as if in passing, to the prospect of an early election. There was a lot of speculation about, and what with Charlene being in Cabinet, Coates was always trying to weasel the latest inside info out of me.

I told him what I knew, which was exactly zip, and we finished off with the customary exchange of promises to get together for a drink. When I spun my seat around to hang up, Ant had helped himself to my *Sun* and was pretending to read it, something he wouldn't really be able to do until he developed the intellectual capacity of an eight-year-old.

I was about to get seriously snaky when the phone rang again. This time it was a nice old Greek pensioner whose plumbing difficulties I had been shepherding through the maintenance division of the Housing Ministry. In comparison with the idiocy incarnate sitting opposite me, the institutional oddities at Housing were child's play. I made a couple of quick calls to the appropriate authorities, threw my weight about in a minor way, and called the old bat to reassure her that she'd be flushing again before she knew it.

By that stage, it was too late to call Charlene. Besides which, the day had kicked in with its customary vigour. In rapid succession I had a branch treasurer ring to fish for his postage costs to be reimbursed, a school wanting Charlene for its prize night, and a personal visit from a guy with a Ned Kelly beard describing himself as Citizens For A Freeway Free Future. I took him out to the waiting area and spent half an hour outlining the intricacies of the Western Ring-Road community consultative process. He kept his helmet on for the entire conversation, so I'm not sure if he understood everything I told him.

Just after eleven Agnelli rang.

Angelo Agnelli was Charlene Wills' ministerial adviser at Industry. The Industry Ministry was where government policy rubbed noses with the big end of town. The nose was Ange's weapon of choice and Charlene paid him a princely sum to implement initiatives, expedite the legislative process, keep the mandarins on their toes, and God knew what else. Recently, he'd been making the effort to find the time to look over my shoulder and make tut-tutting noises.

That day, the big bee in Agnelli's bonnet was Joe Lollicato. A couple of years previously, Joe had been elected to one of the municipal councils in the area. And in the last round of local government polls he'd been returned with a handsomely increased majority. To Agnelli, who'd never been elected to anything in his life, this sort of personal popularity was both a personal affront and evidence that Lollicato was positioning himself to seize the party's endorsement away from Charlene.

"Forget Lolly," I told him. "Parliamentary ambitions are a fact of life around here. Lolly wouldn't be the first person in local government to start thinking he's on the up-escalator to Canberra. But if Lollicato wants a stab at Charlene's job, and that's a debatable point, he'll have to wait until she decides to go, then take his chances along with everyone else. If he tries anything sooner, he'll find out that a stretch at a suburban town hall, a few half-baked factional connections, and an Italian surname won't be enough to convince a pre-selection panel to dump a sitting member. A minister at that."

Agnelli refused to be mollified. "There are plenty of people in the party who'd like to see Charlene taken down a peg or two. Lollicato's a sneaky little prick. It wouldn't pay to underestimate his deviousness. He's got more friends than you'd suspect."

These were facts that could not be disputed, but they were hardly very specific, just the usual Labor Party love talk. The real reason for Agnelli's antagonism towards Lollicato, I suspected, was cultural. I thought this because sensitivity to ethnic cultural nuances was an essential aspect of my professional capabilities.

Charlene's electorate, the whole area in fact, had Italians coming out of its armpits. Fully a quarter of all the Italians in the entire country lived in Melbourne's northern suburbs, not counting their second and third generation descendants. This was apart from the Greeks, Lebanese, Maltese, Macedonians, Turks and Maoris. All things considered, Melbourne Upper should have been called

Wogolopolis. A high level of skill in multiculturalism was, therefore, an indispensable aspect of my job.

It was, I believed, a requirement I fulfilled as reasonably as could be expected for the descendant of three generations of Irish publicans. I had been handing out how-to-vote cards in Italian since I was a teenager. I knew better than to confuse the Federazione Italiana Lavoratori e Famigli with the Comitato d'Assistenza Italiano. I knew who could be relied on at the vegetable market to buy a book of raffle tickets at election time, and whose brother-in-law was private secretary to the Christian Democrat mayor of San Benedetto del Tronto. And while I would have been the first to admit to having trouble picking a Guelph from a Ghibelline in a dappled olive grove in the Tuscan twilight, I could, to the extent required by profession, reasonably claim to know my tortellini from my tartufo. "This isn't some sort of Italian crap, is it Ange?" I said.

Agnelli was obsessed. "That little shit Lollicato is capable of doing any amount of damage if he thinks he can use it to his own advantage. You see the newspaper this morning?"

"Minister in Pre-Selection Wrangle?"

"Jesus, where was that?" There was real panic in Agnelli's voice.

"Relax, Ange. You mean the dead guy at the meatworks in Coolaroo? I've been wondering about that. What's the story?"

Agnelli's voice took on a gossipy conspiratorial hiss. "What are you doing for lunch?"

"I was thinking of having a pie," I whispered back. "You reckon it's safe?"

"Be serious for a minute, can't you, Murray? I'm trying to put something useful your way. Come into town."

I swung my chair around. The amazing tattooed nuisance had his boots on my desk, right on top of the in-tray. "I dunno," I told Agnelli. "I've got a lot in front of me at the moment."

"I'll buy." Agnelli's salary was nearly double mine and this was his first gesture of generosity with anything but unsolicited advice. Clearly, something was going on.

"Ministry or House?"

"House. And since you're coming in, can you do us a favour and give old Picone a lift. He's having lunch with Charlene and I want to pick a bone with the old bugger first. Give him the two dollar tour and bring him downstairs."

I took my umbrella off the filing cabinet, turned off the two-bar radiator and gently moved Ant's feet over to the out-tray.

"Anyone calls," I said, "I'll be out for the rest of the day."

2

OCTOBER WAS SHAPING UP as the customary disappointment, dithering between erupting into spring or pissing down all the way to Christmas. For the second week in a row, the predicted break in the damp had failed to materialise and rumour had it that the smart money was out the back sawing gopher wood into cubits and collecting matched pairs of animals.

In the rare intervals between showers, masses of frigid air fleeing north from Tasmania or some similarly dismal polar region swept into town and did their best to give spring a bad name. An hour after Agnelli's call I was copping the full brunt of one of these tornadoes as I trudged my way up the terrace of Parliament House.

Our glorious forebears, febrile with easy money and puffed up with Victorian self-aggrandisement, had built the House on a hill and modelled it on classical lines, all monumental portico and reiterated horizontal emphasis. The result was considered by some to be a commanding vista. Personally, with nothing to deflect the nut-numbing elements but a two-piece ninety-nine-dollar del Monaco special, and my pace slowed by the company of a wheezing geriatric, I found it all a trifle overstated. When Ennio Picone stopped for the third time for a bit of a breather, I grabbed his arm and all but frog-marched him up the last dozen steps and into the shelter of the foyer.

Gentleman that he was, Picone took it for a courtesy. Gentleman that I was, I let him.

Ennio Picone was one of Charlene Wills' prize constituents, an elegant seventy-seven-year-old with fine hands and a matinee moustache. At one time the leader of a dance band, he had spent thirty years tirelessly orchestrating the social life of the electorate's Italians. He had played at their weddings. He had taught music to their children and grandchildren. And now that they were retired, he organised their leisure — for which their grown-up children were profoundly grateful.

Those of us who conducted Charlene's affairs knew that we ignored this little old man's ceaseless vitality at our peril. He warranted special attention. It was my job to see that he got it. I wondered what Agnelli wanted with him.

I walked Picone across the coat-of-arms inlaid in the foyer floor and led him into a spacious, high-ceilinged hall with an iceberg of white marble shaped like the young Queen Victoria embedded in the carpet. Leading off to one side was a corridor and a high double doorway. "Charlene will be with you as soon as possible, Maestro Picone," I said. "She's a bit busy right now."

I shouldered one of the doors open and casually displayed the interior of the parliamentary chamber. It was quite small, hardly more than twenty paces deep, but utterly fantastic, the plaster and gilt hallucination of an imagination overdosed on allegory. Not a surface in the entire room had escaped being moulded, embossed, inlaid, fluted, scalloped, gilded or engraved. Ant's tattoos had nothing on this joint.

An arcade of ivory columns flanked the walls. Above, a squadron of bare-bosomed Amazons brandished symbolic artefacts — the Spear of Boadicea, the Laurels of Victory, the Sheathed Sword of Mercy, the Chain of — what, of Command? Unicorns capered down the walls, and eagles fluttered on high. Heraldic waffle-work of every description abounded unbound, cascading downwards to the rows of padded leather upon which the Honourable Members of the

Legislative Council lounged like so many bull seals on a rocky headland.

Best of all, and this was even more than I could have hoped for, Charlene Wills herself was holding the floor.

Charlene was in her mid-fifties, at the height of her powers and, apparently, enjoying herself immensely. When the Cabinet posts had been dished out after the election, there had never been any doubt that Charlene would make the cut. For a start she had the factional support, but on top of that she was popular, visible and had a tone of voice that scared the living shit out of the boys in caucus.

She was using it now, a relentless, piercing monotone capable of reducing even the most fractious party conference to numbed compliance. Her topic was obscure — some amendment to some paragraph of some sub-section of some Act — but she was giving it her usual all. You could tell straight off that she knew her stuff and would waste no opportunity to bore it right up the Opposition first chance she got. She was loyal, conscientious, devoted to her constituents, and I loved her like a mother, which was convenient as I no longer had one of my own. Her colostomy bag you couldn't notice, even if you were one of the very few who knew about it.

Unfortunately I'd seen less and less of her in the previous two years. What with being a senior minister and Leader of the Government in the Upper House, she found it hard to make time for electorate matters and had been forced to leave me more or less to my own devices. It was getting so that I virtually had to fight my way through a phalanx of bureaucrats and ministerial advisers just to talk to her, apart from our regular fortnightly meetings. And she'd cancelled the last two of those.

Which reminded me of Agnelli. I allowed Picone a lingering moment to fully register the sumptuousness of his surroundings, and Charlene's central place in them, then tapped him on the shoulder. "This way, Maestro." I made a courtly sweep of the arm. Ostentation is never wasted on Italians.

Parliament, we both knew, was a pantomime. Real power was

exercised across the road in the Department of Premier and Cabinet, in Management and Budget, in offices with whiteboards and synthetic carpet tiles. But you could hardly impress a constituent with an open plan office and an ergonomic typist's chair, however artfully constructed.

I led Picone along the oak-panelled corridor and down a narrow staircase into a vaulted chamber of bluestone and exposed brick, the law's subterranean forge. Charlene's parliamentary office was a glassed-in alcove tucked under one of the supporting arches. Two desks took up most of it, each buried under piles of well-thumbed papers, sheaves of documents bound in manila folders thick with registry notations. Shelves crowded with green-bound volumes of Hansard and glossy policy proclamations ran up the walls. What little space remained was occupied by a heavy leather chesterfield and a cheap glass-topped coffee table littered with government brochures and the day's newspapers.

A tinny speaker on the wall was broadcasting Charlene's oration from the chamber above. Underneath it, sitting on a corner of one of the desks like he could think of nothing more deserving of his time than greeting the Minister's visitors, was Angelo Agnelli. It was novel to see him sitting somewhere other than on a fence.

Ange was pushing forty just a tad harder than it was pushing back. He had a full head of photogenic black hair, a chubby boyish face skin-deep in conviviality, and a manner calculated to make people feel that he had their number. Angelo Agnelli collected numbers. Sometimes they even added up.

As we entered he tugged at the cuffs of his expensive shirt and reached up to turn off the speaker. He shook hands with Picone and seated him on the chesterfield with the courtesy of a world-weary Venetian diplomat. Then he took a copy of that morning's *Coburg Courier* out of his jacket pocket and dropped it onto the coffee table. It was folded open at a photograph of a group of old men standing at the end of a bocce pitch trying hard to look sorry for themselves, Picone at their centre. The picture took up the bottom half of page three. Most of the top half was taken up by a banner headline reading GOVT STALLS ON ITALIAN PENSIONER CENTRE.

I could have kicked myself. Timely monitoring of the local press was one of my jobs. I'd only been in the room ten seconds and Agnelli was already one up on me.

"What's this fucking shit, Picone?" he said.

Picone, unoffended, showed his palms and shrugged. "Ten months we already wait. People, they say maybe you not so fair dinkum on your promise."

This explanation seemed to please Agnelli. "What people? Joe Lollicato you mean! Offered to help give us a little nudge in the right direction, did he? Have a word with the local paper, remind us of our obligations, eh? Nothing to do with wanting Charlene's seat upstairs, of course." He pointed at the ceiling. "You want Charlene's help, you better watch yourself, Picone." Evidently Agnelli had not enjoyed his piano accordion lessons. He could always be relied on to put on a good show, but voter relations were not his strong suit.

Picone knew what was expected of him. He shrugged resignedly and mimed the look of a chastened man. But you could see that he didn't mean it. Why should he? In taking his grievance to the local rag he was merely observing the cardinal rule of those who live in a safe seat: never allow yourself to be taken for granted. If the government drags its heels delivering on a promise, scream like a scalded cat.

Charlene had long since promised her electorate's Italian senior citizenry that the government would build them new clubrooms. And old Ennio knew her well enough to know that she would deliver. Eventually. He just wanted to make sure that he'd be still around to take the credit the day the brand new Carboni Club opened its doors.

And so what if Lollicato had been urging the old farts on from behind the scenes, as Agnelli seemed convinced? Lolly was as entitled to cultivate his garden as any other local politician. Picone was merely playing his little part in the game. A man is never too old for that.

So Picone folded his hands in his lap and humoured Agnelli by not interrupting him while he played the minister's hard man. What more could he be expected do? his face seemed to say. Hadn't he come all the way into town in Murray Whelan's decrepit Renault, walked up all those steps in the freezing wind, pretended to be impressed by this overblown colonial copy of some Palladian palazzo?

"Charlene is very disappointed," Agnelli was saying. "She's a good friend of the community. You should be ashamed."

Then Charlene Wills herself came through the door, her plump frame rounded off by the shoulder pads of her knit suit.

"Maestro Picone was wondering if you would be available to be guest of honour at the Carboni Club annual dinner dance," I said. "He thinks it would be an ideal opportunity for the community to thank you for your work in securing funding for the new senior citizens' centre. Isn't that right, Maestro?"

Charlene tossed a bulky buff envelope onto the desk in front of Agnelli. "Lovely. Delighted. Check the calendar, Angelo. You'll stay for lunch of course, Ennio? Hello, Murray. You'll have the file back on my desk first thing in the morning, won't you Angelo? Or my life won't be worth living." She was already out the door, her constituency on her arm.

The envelope landed with a thud. It carried the logo of the Office of the Coroner and had something scrawled across the front in heavy felt-tipped pen. Upside down I could read the words "Pacific Pastoral/Ekrem Bayraktar."

As God is my witness, I should have got up and walked away then and there.

3

AGNELLI SCOOPED UP the envelope, flourished it triumphantly, and took off up the stairs like he either had an appointment with destiny or a very full bladder. Once outside, he braced himself against the squall blowing along Spring Street, hurtled down the parliamentary declivity and led me onwards into the city.

Since Agnelli was buying, I was content to let him lead. Especially since his destination appeared to be The Society, where a free lunch was worth having. But he didn't falter as he tore past its tinted windows, and I caught only the barest sparkle of silver cutlery before he darted across the road and headed up a lane.

Conversation was impossible. Apart from maintaining a blistering pace, we were both fully occupied negotiating a passage through mountains of old cobblestones and untidy hillocks of sand. What had been a mere footpath for the previous hundred years was in the process of being converted into a pedestrian access facility harmonised to the heritage aspects of the built-form environment. And judging by the amount of excavation going on, it was putting up quite a bit of resistance. Either that or the city council was financing the exercise by strip-mining the entire precinct for minerals.

This kind of obstacle course was something we were all getting used to. Ever since Labor's arrival in power the city had taken on the aspect of a vast construction site. The leadership had wasted no time making it abundantly clear to both the business end of town and its own membership that the party's historical antagonism to speculation was a thing of the past. A government that couldn't come up with jobs wouldn't last five minutes. Property development equalled jobs, and no sentiment was to be wasted on sentiment. Overnight, ancient landmarks became vast pits filled with tip-trucks and management types in business shirts and hard hats.

In keeping with its resolve on the issue, the government had just given some of the more boisterous elements in the building unions a severe judicial crutching. As a result, there were so many construction hoardings and concrete trucks in the city it was impossible to find anywhere to park. And deep festering pools of bad blood awaited the unwary at the Trades Hall.

So far none of those juicy new jobs had come my way. Meanwhile my sense of historical geography was having the shit shot out of it. The old familiar shape of things was changing so fast that it was sometimes hard to know exactly where I stood.

I had no such problem that day, however. Our objective was clearly Chinatown. The pavers beneath our feet had taken on a decidedly oriental motif and all around us gaggles of almond-eyed citizens nicked in and out of eating houses with dead ducks in their windows and names like Good Luck Village and New Dynasty. At a dragon-entwined archway Agnelli abruptly stopped and pushed open a black lacquered portal encrusted with brass studs the size of the hub caps on a Honda Civic.

I was pleasantly surprised and immediately suspicious. My initial assumption when we entered Chinatown was that Agnelli's generosity would run no further than a cheap dim sum, hardly worth my ten-kilometre drive into town. Instead, I found myself being ushered through a grove of bamboo into the Mandarin Palace, winner for three years in succession of the Golden Chopsticks Award in the *Age* Good Gourmet Guide. Judging by the high standard of grovelling we got from the smoothie in the Chou En-lai suit who handed us the menus, Agnelli was a regular.

It was hard to credit that this Agnelli was the same nervy solicitor who had come tentatively tapping on my door at the Municipal Workers' Union ten years earlier, asking to be introduced around the traps. The legal firm that looked after our workers' compensation cases had just taken him on. He joked that he'd probably only got the job because the senior partners assumed he could speak to some of the plaintiffs in their own language.

In reality, his language skills consisted essentially of what he had managed to pick up in his mother's kitchen in Mitcham. His Italian was dialect, secondhand, and unintelligible to most of his clients, especially the Italians. On top of which, he was an indifferent litigator, not that that's ever been an impediment to a successful legal career. But he took to industrial law like a duck to water. For the following three years he pursued it so avidly that he eventually caught enough to hang out his own shingle.

Poaching the best of his old firm's clients and spreading his briefs generously around the barristers' chambers, he steadily built an impressive network in the law and the unions. Now here he was, factional heavyweight, member of the state executive of the Socialist Left, and if not the architect then at least the master builder of some of the government's most ambitious reforms. Self-approbation burst from him like a fountain from a ruptured pipe.

He sat the coroner's envelope face-down on the floor beside his chair, murmured something in the waiter's ear, and pressed a steaming white hand towel to his florid cheeks. "How's Wendy?" he said. "Still enjoying Canberra?"

The family small talk was to demonstrate that he hadn't lost the common touch. "Fine. She's fine." I hoped I didn't sound too unconvincing. The truth was I hadn't spoken to my wife in over two weeks and hoped it stayed that way.

"You two certainly make an odd couple," Agnelli went on. "There she is, flying about the country in her power suit, shouldering bureaucrats aside, writing policy for the PM's department. Here you are, sitting in a three-metre-square cubicle, doing Charlene's housework."

Agnelli's line on my personal life wasn't so much tactless as simply out of date. The fact was, Wendy and I were over in everything but name. All that remained was the inevitable public brawl over custody of our child, Redmond. As Agnelli might have put it, Wendy was out of my league. And she'd worked so hard getting there I was relieved to see her go.

Wendy had been in Canberra for nearly a year on secondment from the Women's Information Referral Exchange to the Office of the Status of Women Industrial and Technological Change Secretariat. Originally the job had been temporary, four months tops. But life with OSWITCS had proven infinitely more personally empowering than WIRE and her contract kept being extended.

When the offer had first come up, a tribute to Wendy's professional standing, I could hardly have stood in the way of her career, could I? Red would miss her but, now that he was settled into school, it was my turn to experience a stint of prime parenting. It was only for a few months, after all, and she would be commuting back to Melbourne two weekends a month. Sure, I said, go.

Ten months later, the so-far-undeclared reality was self-evident. The weekends at home had become more infrequent, what with the conferences in Darwin and Perth, the in-service skills-enhancement seminars in Cairns, and Wendy's ongoing professional need to piss in every pocket within a bull's roar of Lake Burley Griffin. Separation had merely confirmed what we had probably long suspected anyway. Our lives were going in opposite directions.

Not that anything had been spelt out yet. It didn't need to be. We were both old hands at reading which way the wind was blowing. Wendy still phoned Red most nights. She could never be accused of being an uncaring mother. Absent yes, negligent no. Sometimes it was me who picked up the phone when it rang and we exchanged banalities, but there was little the two of us could find to say to each other anymore.

I took it for granted there was someone else. Bound to be. I even had a mental picture — Senior Executive Service, fleet vehicle, desktop computer, divorced, weekender at Batemans Bay, beard. Not that

I minded. I felt no rancour. I just didn't want to know about it. And if Wendy had any ideas about getting Red, she and the Family Court had another thing coming.

"So," Agnelli was saying, "she still funding long-term unemployed Tasmanian lesbians to build mud-brick whale refuges?"

What a jerk. You had to laugh. A platter of minced pigeon breast arrived, too pricey a dish to be paid for with domestic chit-chat. While the waiter was shovelling a load onto my plate I fed Agnelli his cue. "If you want someone killed," I said, "it'll cost you more than a feed of sang choi bao."

Agnelli smiled the thinnest of thin smiles. Ministerial advisers were part of the new breed, technical experts who did not like to be reminded, even in jest, of the sometimes rough and tumble reality of political life in the branches and the machine. Politics for them was just another career option. These guys hadn't got where they were without at least some political credentials — Agnelli's ticket had been punched by Labor lawyers and his clients in the unions — but their personal writ ran no further than the distance between their ministers' ears.

Top-level access and plush salary packages made them feel important, but they were uncomfortable and sometimes even a little fearful in the rough company of party organisers from down the line. And they never really knew where they were with battlefield sergeants like me, crude types who came fully equipped with invisible networks, tacit alliances, and uncertain ambitions. We who could fill halls with a single phone call. Jokes about having people knocked off and knowing where the bodies were buried made the likes of Agnelli nervous. And he didn't need any reminding that it would take more than a free lunch to get me where he wanted me. Or so I thought.

Agnelli launched his spiel. "Let's contextualise. Then we can parameter the specifics."

It was getting so I couldn't tell if people were joking when they talked like that. I gave Agnelli the benefit of the doubt.

"Charlene's held her seat for what, ten years?" he asked blandly.

I plucked a figure out of the air. "Eleven years, two months, five days."

The sarcasm was wasted. Agnelli was winding himself up to something. "Amazing, isn't it?" he said. "To think that all but two and a half years of that was spent in Opposition. What a waste of talent."

"I'll tell her you said that," I said. "Sucking up to the boss on your own time."

Agnelli made a self-deprecating gesture. "I'm like you, Murray. Strictly an idealist. Goes without saying. It's the others I worry about. The ones who can't wait to get their snouts into the trough."

Lollicato again, I thought. Boring. When were we going to get to the envelope and, with luck, the story behind the report in the *Sun*?

"Ah, but think how useful a bit of general ambition is to a reforming government like ours," I said. "Everybody out there, beavering away, racking up brownie points, hoping to be given the nod."

"Granted." Agnelli was working overtime at being agreeable. "But all that nervous energy needs to be managed, directed, channelled. Problem is, the collective memory is short. Even some of our own people seem to have forgotten that no Labor government has ever been re-elected in this state. Three years ago nobody under forty could remember the last time there was a Labor government here. Now half the reporters in town can't remember when there wasn't one. And the way some people are carrying on, there won't be one for much longer."

Unbidden, steaming platters arrived, glistening and fragrant. I should have held on to my suspicions more firmly. Instead, I picked up my chopsticks and waded in. "Not Lollicato again?"

The ma-po beancurd was ravishing. Pungent and slimy. I decided to let Agnelli do all the talking.

"If I was him," he said, referring to Lollicato, "I'd be thinking that my best chance of knocking off Charlene would be to undermine her credibility as Minister for Industry. Quietly stir up some sort of business-union conflict then step back and watch the fireworks. Do it all at a distance. That way I wouldn't have her blood on my hands when I get reluctantly drafted to replace her after she's become a liability to the party."

It wasn't a bad plan, but I couldn't see Lollicato pulling it off. "Bit ambitious for Lolly, isn't it? He'd be lucky if he could knock the head off a beer."

Agnelli drew his chair closer to the table, squared off his chopsticks, picked up a fat ginger scallop and dropped it into my bowl. "Joe Lollicato's very well connected at Trades Hall, don't forget. His brother used to be an organiser with the Meat Packers' Union. And there are plenty in the union movement who are still dirty on the government over those building-union prosecutions. They might be on the back foot at the moment, but setting Charlene up for a fall would be a good way of telling the government to stay out of union business."

It was all quite plausible. "That's the greatest load of shit I've ever heard, Ange," I said. "That rarefied air you've been breathing has gone to your head."

"Yeah?" he said. "Where do you reckon that story in the *Sun* today came from? That 'informed sources at Trades Hall' crap doesn't seem suspicious to you?"

So this was Agnelli's great revelation. He was buying me this splendid luncheon so I could massage his petty paranoia. "Typical *Sun* beat up, Ange. Anything to slag the government. They've been churning out that 'War Drums at Union HQ' stuff for a hundred years."

"Notice it wasn't signed?"

"So?" As far as I was concerned, no self-respecting journalist would want their name associated with anything in that awful little rag.

"Anyone at the journalists' association will tell you that's a clear signal the piece was cooked up in the editor's office." Agnelli suddenly leaned forward, beckoning across the hot and sour sauce. "Truth is," he muttered, "it's not just Charlene we're talking about here. There are bigger things at stake than a one-sided pre-selection brawl. Word is, and mum's the word, the chief has decided not to go to full term. There'll definitely be an election before the end of the year."

My mind raced, but I merely nodded noncommittally and poured myself a thimble of tea, letting the news germinate, take root, send out branches, bear fruit. If Agnelli was right, and it was just the sort of thing Agnelli made it his business to be right about, then I had no choice. As of now, like it or not, I was on the Lollicato case. Shake the Agnelli family tree, I thought, and out would fall a crop of papal nuncios' bastards.

Lollicato was yet another lawyer, working out of the Broadmeadows Legal Service. A tribune of the people, big on street cred. Years of fronting for first offenders in shitbag cases had given him a sanctimonious edge. And now that I thought about it I could see the signs of creeping ambition. Young Lolly was changing his look. The earrings were disappearing, one by one. Ties were in evidence, even out of court. Such a transformation was not inconsistent with parliamentary aspirations.

If Lollicato wanted a seat, fine. So did half the party. When the time came, he was entitled to make a run, even to play a little rough if that was his style. But if he and his disgruntled union mates were sour enough to run a dirty tricks campaign in the *Sun*, and there was an surprise election in the offing, it wouldn't matter whether his shot at Charlene hit home or not. The *Sun* was the biggest selling paper in the state, pitched well under the lowest common denominator. Kicking Labor was its second nature, and it would jump at any chance to bag us as an in-fighting rabble of intriguers. Not that this was necessarily an inaccurate picture, but it was one we preferred not to be bandied about in the lead up to the polls. Talk about frightening the horses.

"Get the executive committee to haul him in, clip his wings," I eventually said.

"Based on what?" said Agnelli. "We need to make a case first. So far all we've got is a bit of gossip and a plausible hypothesis. Lollicato could just be flying a kite. The real question is whether he and his union mates have got enough clout at Pacific Pastoral to make serious mischief."

"What's Charlene think about all of this?" I asked.

"Put it this way," said Agnelli. "It's your job to see that Charlene knows what she should know. It's my job to see that she doesn't know about things she shouldn't know about."

He was right. Charlene had to be kept out of the picture, at least for the time being, or we really would have headlines reading "Minister in Pre-Selection Wrangle." It was also clear that Agnelli was expecting me to do all the leg work. But I was not about to volunteer for any cowboy reconnaissance mission.

"I see," I said, and turned my attention back to the table. Those Golden Chopsticks were indeed richly deserved. It was a pity to spoil a lunch like this with politics. But politics was paying and the bill had just been presented.

When Agnelli eventually broke the silence, he seemed to have changed the subject. "MACWAM met this morning. They were shitting themselves."

The Ministerial Advisory Committee on Ways And Means had started off as Charlene's private brains trust, a half-dozen old pals from the universities and the career civil service. After the election it was beefed up to an official body and given the job of overseeing smooth passage of Charlene's raft of reforms. Agnelli's official title was MACWAM Executive Officer. MACWAM presided, but Agnelli executed.

"You know what a pack of nervous nellies they are," he went on. "It's taken me two years to get them this far. Now, less than a week before the final vote on the new industrial health and safety bill, they've broken out in a cold sweat. The *Sun* runs a story about some silly dago turning himself into a Paddle Pop and now they think the whole legislative process is about to jump off the rails." For a former defender of the industrially maimed, Agnelli could seem remarkably insensitive to the fate of individual members of the working class.

I could see where all this was heading, and was surprised at how soon I had resigned myself to it. I clicked my tongue sympathetically, feeding Agnelli his lines. "So you told them that you wouldn't rest until you were sure that some feral shop steward was not about to declare class war at such an inconvenient juncture in the imminent legislative process."

Agnelli grinned. He liked having his cleverness appreciated. "Naturally they felt better immediately. And just to formalise matters, I got them to ask me to commission a full and detailed report before the final reading of the bill on Friday."

Agnelli was full of more than just fried rice, but he could play a committee like Rostropovich played Shostakovich. Now he was sawing away at my strings. "You can do it on your ear, Murray," he said. "You know the drill. Nothing fancy, couple of pages, max. As long as it's in by Thursday it's all the official sanction we need to cruel Lolly's pitch. How soon do you think you can get out to Pacific Pastoral and take a look around?"

I put up a last, half-hearted line of resistance. "A big firm like that won't take too well to me waltzing in off the street and grilling the workforce."

"Leave them to me, Murray. Relations with the business community are my forte. And take a squiz at this."

Agnelli was really enjoying himself now. Charlene's buff envelope materialised in his hand and skidded across the table. "If the deceased happened to have any shit on him, the high moral ground would tend to be cut from underneath Lollicato somewhat, don't you think?"

Inside the envelope was a file containing a sheaf of papers and some photographs. One spilled out. It was of a very fat, very dead body with white stuff around its lips.

"Go ahead, Murray," said Agnelli. "Finish the duck."

4

IT HAD ALREADY GONE three when I tossed the coroner's envelope onto the passenger seat, shoved Joan Armatrading into the tape deck and headed north. The sky had cleared to a pearly luminescence but the wind was still keen, entertaining itself by stripping the last of the blossoms off the flowering cherries in Princes Park.

Agnelli was probably being over-paranoid about Lollicato, I decided, but there would be no harm in giving his conspiracy theory the quick once-over. His inference that the fate of the government now rested on my shoulders was a bit rich, but any potential threat to Charlene, however unlikely, warranted a closer look. Guarding Charlene's back was, after all, the prime part of my job. And a couple of days' break from old ladies' plumbing and demented tattooees would be a welcome change of pace.

By some obscure culinary demarcation agreement, Chinese restaurants are prohibited from serving decent coffee. So by the time the stately boulevard of Royal Parade became the narrow funnel of Sydney Road, I was in desperate need of a caffeine fix. And I was in just the right place to find one.

Melbourne's main north-south axis is a clotted artery of souvlaki joints and low-margin high-turnover business. Half the Mediterranean basin had been depopulated of its optimists in order to line Sydney Road with free-wheeling enterprise. Bakeries and furniture shops run by Abruzzesi and Calabresi sat cheek by jowl with the delicatessens of Peloponnesian Greeks and the bridal boutiques of Maronite Lebanese. Signs in Arabic announced halal butchers and video shops displayed soap operas freshly pirated in Damascus and Nicosia. The promise of strong black coffee loitered in the air, and through the windows of the Café de la Paix, the Tivoli and the Lakonia I could see men bent over tiny cups of bracing black nectar. But parking spots were few and far between, and it wasn't long before I found myself stuck in a half-mile-long snaggle of mid-afternoon traffic with no option but to go with the flow.

At the traffic lights beside Brunswick Town Hall, a Rod Stewart haircut at the wheel of a customised panel van was taking the time to pass encouraging recommendations to a poor cow in skin-tight denims wheeling a yowling brat across the road. Further on, the windows of empty shops had been spray painted with hammers and sickles and plastered with initials and slogans in languages I couldn't identify. PKK. KSP. KOMKAR. Def Leppard.

At the top of a slight rise, a sandwich board outside the Mighty Ten hardware store read "Pink Batts Must Go." I parked illegally in a loading zone and stuffed the back of the Renault with bulky packages of the fibreglass insulation, paid for with a card already well over the limit.

Five minutes further up the road and I was back at the electorate office. I parked in a side street, and nicked into Ciccio's Cafe Sportivo, the Italian coffee bar next door. I was standing at the zinc counter, downing an espresso and considering my next step, when the vanguard of the proletariat marched through the door.

Her name was Ayisha Celik. She was a community development worker at the Australian Turkish Welfare League. Exactly what she developed in the Turkish community I wasn't sure. I knew what she developed in me, and I hoped it didn't show enough to cause embarrassment.

She had skin the colour of honey and her lips were like ripe pomegranates. Her eyes, ringed in black, were as dark and wilful as a peregrine falcon's. Her bosom spoke of silk cushions, fretted screens and tinkling fountains. Inspired by such a vision the Ancients had crossed the Bosphorus and pitched their tents beneath the crenellated walls of Troy. All in all, Ayisha Celik had the kind of looks that make veils seem like a sensible idea in places where hot-blooded men go around armed to the teeth. She made a bee-line for the counter and slapped a clipboard down in front of me. "Slackin' off as usual I see, comrade," she accused cheerfully.

Ayisha had arrived in Australia at the age of eight and spoke with the teasing upward-rising inflection the kids taught each other in schools where only the teachers spoke English at home. "Do us a favour, will ya?" she said. "Sign this." The clipboard displayed a ragged column of signatures.

Her words wafted towards me on a warm zephyr of spearmint gum, triggering primal erotic associations connected with Saturday afternoons in the back row of the Liberty Cinema. I wondered, not for the first time, what it might take to arouse reciprocal feelings in her. As usual, nothing presented itself. According to Trish, who specialised in such topics, Ayisha was unlucky in love. I was much heartened by this information. And although she was still in her twenties, a good five or six years younger than me, I liked to think that she at least found me interesting. Not that she gave any sign of that being the case.

Still, it's a free country. I could think what I liked.

I picked up the clipboard and tried to look fascinated by the petition. The Australian Turkish Welfare League was big on petitions. "Who is it this time? The United Nations? The International Court of Justice? The Water Supply Board?"

Ayisha was in no mood. She had news. "You know Sivan, our welfare worker?"

Everyone knew Sivan, a laughing beetle-browed man with thick English, another collector of signatures. "They've arrested his brother."

"They" could only mean the Turkish military, a regime whose taste for terror had driven thousands into exile. Some, Sivan among them, had ended up in the local Turkish community. Many were professionals and artists, progressives and liberals who were putting their skills to work for the benefit of their fellow expatriates. Others, I suspected, had been quite keen on the idea of armed struggle until an even keener crew of nasties had got the drop on them.

Up until that time, I hadn't had a great deal to do with Charlene's Turkish constituents, but they seemed a sociable enough mob. For Muslims, most of them were about as fundamentalist as the C of E. And if it wasn't for their kebab shops, every Friday night the streets of the northern suburbs would have been awash with gangs of half-plastered school teachers looking for somewhere cheap to eat. All I knew, and all I needed to know, was that they could pretty well be relied upon to turn out en masse for Labor.

"We think it's because Sivan works for a subversive organisation," Ayisha was saying.

"The League?"

The Australian Turkish Welfare League was two rooms and a secondhand coffee dispenser a couple of blocks up the road from the electorate office. Ayisha, Sivan and a clutch of volunteer social workers ran information programs and cultural activities there for newly arrived migrants, partly paid for by grants from the Ethnic Affairs Commission. If pressed for an adjective to describe the League, subversive would not have sprung to mind. Charlene called it cost-effective service delivery in an area of perceived need. What I called it was damned convenient. If ever I needed translation for the odd Turkish customer that walked in the door, all I had to do was get one of the League people on the blower and have them sort it out in the vernacular.

Naturally, in keeping with their advocacy role, the folks at the League went in for the customary amount of third-worldish polemic. Ayisha, for instance, tended to get about in a red keffiyeh, sounding like Vanessa Redgrave. But nobody in their right mind could seriously believe the League posed a threat to anyone, let alone a fully tooled-up fascist oligarchy twenty thousand kilometres away.

Well, at the time I didn't think so. "You're petitioning the junta?" It seemed a little optimistic even for the League.

"Not them, you dickhead. Canberra. The Minister for Foreign Affairs. We want something done about the consulate." She signalled Ciccio for a coffee. He pretended not to see her. Women were not encouraged at the Cafe Sportivo, especially not a houri in jeans and half a ton of kohl.

The idea that the generals in Ankara kept a close eye on Turkish migrants and refugees in Australia was one of Ayisha's big bugbears. Even allowing for Sivan's emigré paranoia and Ayisha's marked list to the left, I assumed there was an element of truth in it. Dictatorships can be funny that way.

I'd heard other rumours, too. For years there'd been talk that neo-fascist groups with names like the Grey Wolves or the Black Ghosts or the Pink Panthers were active in the area. One time you used to hear the same thing about the Lebanese Tigers. They must have been related to the Tasmanian Tigers, because nobody had ever seen a real one.

The spooks in one of the intelligence outfits probably knew what was going on, or should have, if they were doing what they got paid for, but I couldn't see them losing any sleep over the civil liberties of a bunch of left-wing Arab types. The only time that lot ever came out of the woodwork was when some demented Armenian lobbed a bomb at the Turkish ambassador.

I ran my eye down Ayisha's petition, recognising names from the Community Health Centre and the council depot. Not too many of the blokes at the depot had said no to Ayisha. I borrowed her pen and added my name to the list. As far as I was concerned, all Australian residents were equally entitled to freedom of association and assembly. This was Coburg, not Queensland.

Mainly, however, I signed because of Ayisha. Frankly, if she'd invited me to stick my bum in the boiler of Ciccio's cappuccino machine I'd just as happily have agreed.

That probably sounds fairly wet, but you've got to keep in mind that at that point my conjugals hadn't had an airing in six months. If truth be known, they were beginning to develop a somewhat strident attitude. In fact, from here on in, you might as well take it for granted that my loins were pretty well in the driver's seat, although I wasn't necessarily aware of the fact except when they were shouting in my ear.

"The Kurds are getting the worst of it," Ayisha was saying. "Sivan's a Kurd, y'know." She had a full head of steam up by now, which went well with the full head of raven black hair. "Torture. Murder. Makes *Midnight Express* look like Club Med. Y' can't imagine."

I probably could, but it didn't bear dwelling on. "Petitions aren't going to do much good," I said.

"Maybe not," she conceded, stepping down off the high moral ground. "You got any better ideas? Some fascist bastards are going around spying on us. Either we convince the government to put a stop to it, or we take measures to defend ourselves." She made a pistol with her fingers and cocked one eye. "We can't just take it lying down, can we?"

Come the revolution I would flee with her to the mountains, impress her with my ardour. She would lie down with me in a cave on a bed of sheepskins. Then either Wendy or some swarthy Abdul would cut my nuts off with a blunt scimitar. Both of them. Both Wendy and Abdul. Both nuts.

Until then, putting my name on her useless petition looked like it was as close as I'd get. International intrigue was not yet on my agenda. As we spoke she pulled out a pouch of Drum and rolled herself a cigarette. When she lit it, a tiny strand of tobacco stuck to her bottom lip. Only the greatest effort of will stopped me reaching over and pinching it away. I could ask her out, I thought. I could get a baby-sitter for Red and the two of us could go to one of those places where they put a piece of fruit down the neck of your beer bottle. Perhaps not.

She put the petition back under her arm. "Doesn't look like I'm gunna get any coffee round here, does it?"

"Before you go," I said quickly, grasping the first available conversational gambit. "Ever heard of someone called Ekrem Bayraktar?"

Either my pronunciation was appalling or she hadn't. She shook her head.

"Turkish name, though, isn't it?"

"Thousands of people in this city have Turkish names," she said archly. "In case you haven't noticed."

"No need to get snaky," I said. "I just thought maybe he was one of your clients at the League."

"Could be," she shrugged. "We get so many people through the doors it's hard to keep track. Especially considering how little help we get from the government." Ayisha was never one to pass up a chance for a bit of lobbying. "So who is he?"

It was my turn to shrug. I could have told her, I suppose, but the last thing I needed was a diatribe about downtrodden workers being sweated to an early grave by the heartless bourgeoisie. "Just a name in some paperwork I've been lumbered with," I said.

Playing the beleaguered bureaucrat was no way to Ayisha's heart. She stuffed her tobacco in her bag and eyed the door.

"Tell you what," I suggested, like it was the best idea since the withering away of the state. "Why don't I drop into the League to-morrow. I can ask Sivan. Then the two of us can get our heads together on some funding ideas. There're some Commonwealth job creation dollars coming down the pipeline you might be eligible for."

She put her hand on my arm. "Murray," she said. "You're a brick."

Pathetic, I told myself. Trying to buy the woman's affections with taxpayers' dollars. Even if I could get her interested, the last thing I needed right now was an entanglement. Not that I stood a chance. And even if I did, I could already hear Wendy. *Murray's got himself a nice Turkish girl. Bit of a Maoist, but he likes them old-fashioned. Sings the "Internationale" while she does the dishes.*

I was watching the back pocket of Ayisha's jeans disappear through the open door and telling myself to get real when two plain-clothed coppers blew in with the breeze. What with the Hardcase Hilton across the road, dicks weren't an unusual sight in the neighbourhood. The major crime squad guys tended to the handy, all-weather look of well-off tradesmen and you had to be sharp to spot them. But these two were local CIB in three-piece suits that might as well have been uniforms.

They looked me over like I wasn't there and swaggered down the back to the two green baize tables where the same dozen old *paesani* sat day after day drinking coffee and shouting at each other over hands of cards. I had never seen any money on the tables and there was none there now, just a sudden, un-Italian silence and the hissing of the espresso machine. The coppers looked. The old men looked back. Something half forgotten surfaced in my memory, a blue sleeve with sergeant's stripes, the taste of blood.

Then, as suddenly as they had arrived, the forces of law and order were gone, trailing the knuckles of their authority. Ciccio said something that sent a ripple of quiet laughter running through the card players. The cards swished again. I washed my mouth out with cold coffee dregs and went next door to the office.

Adam F. Ant was still lounging around my cubicle like he owned the joint, his head buried in a copy of *Labor Star*. Who did he think he was kidding? Not even its own editors pretended to read the *Labor Star*. I shoved his feet off the desk and rang Bernice Kaufman, an industrial officer on the top floor at the Trades Hall. Bernice had done me the big favour once, just the once, back at university. Ever since she could be relied on to never pass up an opportunity to patronise me.

"It's about that thing in this morning's paper," I said. "The bloke dead at the meatworks."

True to form, Bernice launched straight into a rave about how only a halfwit would believe what he read in the *Sun*. The halfwit I took to be me. Shorn of its sarcasm, the rest of what she said merely confirmed that there was no truth at all to the alleged interest of the Trades Hall executive in the matter. As soon as I could get a word in edgeways, I told her that, since the death had happened in the electorate, it might be appropriate for Charlene to send her condolences to the dead bloke's workmates. Did she know anyone who could put me onto the shop steward at the meatworks?

Bernice made her snooty exasperated noise and the phone started playing a particularly frenzied arrangement of "Für Elise." While I was waiting for her to come back on, I punched the phone's hands-free button and sprayed transistorised Beethoven all over Ant, hoping art might succeed where reason had failed. Three minutes later when Bernice came back on the line, he was humming along.

"Okay," she said, "I've been talking to the Meaties. They reckon your best bet is to contact the shop steward out there. Name of Herb Gardiner. And by the way, they reckon that if there'd been any union issues involved in the death, Gardiner would have been onto them like a shot. Real stickler for the award, apparently. Hasn't said boo."

In a world of ceaseless change, I found something gratifyingly predictable about being patronised by Bernice. I scribbled the shop steward's name on a sheet of office stationery and shoved it in a manila folder along with the coroner's envelope. While I was writing, Trish came in and handed Ant a phone message slip. He glanced at it and laid it on the desk in front of me. If he made himself any more at home, he'd be on the payroll by the end of the week.

The message slip said Agnelli had rung, wanting me to call back ASAP. It was always like this. Now that I had agreed to buy into this Lollicato thing, Agnelli would be on my back every five minutes. Having to write a spurious bloody report was enough of a waste of time without ceaseless fireside chats. I stuffed the message slip into my jacket pocket and stuck my head around the partition.

Ant had ambled out into the reception area and was flashing his stomach at a pair of Coptic monks. Trish was juggling two phones, relaying something about Supporting Mothers' Benefits to a bedraggled teenage mum in a "Miami Vice" sweatshirt. A toddler in a wet disposable was pulling a Wilderness Society poster off the wall.

Without the slightest tinge of guilt, I stuck the Pacific Pastoral file under my arm and nicked out the back door. The wretched of the earth could wait, at least until tomorrow.

5

OFF SYDNEY ROAD the traffic was quieter. The streets were lined with weatherboard bungalows, single-storey terraces and, here and there, the saw-toothed roofs of small factories. This was Labor heartland, the safest seats in the country — Calwell, Batman, Lalor, Coburg, Brunswick. Electorates whose names resonated with certainty in the ears of backroom psephologists from Spring Street to Canberra. In some booths here we outpolled the Libs three to one. Made you wonder who the one was.

Red's school lay halfway between the office and home, a slate-roofed state primary. For its first hundred years it had specialised in producing football players, armed robbers and apprentices to the hairdressing trade. Now it had a library wing and ran programs in two community languages. I found Redmond in after-school care with the other dozen or so second and third graders, Matildas, Dylans and Toulas left behind when the proper parents swooped at three thirty. They were cutting the heads off models in K-Mart catalogues. Red flung his schoolbag on top of the insulation batts and we drove home.

Home was a sixty-year-old weatherboard still in its first coat of paint, one of a spec tract built cheaply in the twenties. Wendy and I had bought it soon after Red came along. The sign had read

"Promises Ample Renovation Opportunity for Imaginative First Home Buyer," meaning it was all we could afford. We were both at the Labor Resource Centre at that point, getting paid a pittance to crank out discussion papers. Workforce segmentation in the footwear sector. Industrial democracy in the electricity generation industry. Not the most lucrative of postings.

So far, Ample Renovation had consisted of Wendy planting a native garden and spending a small fortune on *House and Garden* while I did as much as a man can do using only hand tools and Y chromosomes. All up, the Opportunity had been greater than either of us was capable of rising to. The set of architect's plans pinned to the kitchen wall, token of our future there together, had long since turned yellow and begun curling at the corners.

Still, Red and I were making a pretty good fist of domesticity. Not that this was immediately apparent to the untrained eye. On the superficial indices of good housekeeping we probably rated fairly low. But we were comfortable and basic hygiene was maintained. And I doggedly persisted in addressing some of the more ongoing infrastructure issues. My objective that afternoon was to maximise our energy efficiency. First I dredged a knife out of the scrap heap in the sink and made two peanut butter sandwiches, folded not cut. "Now do your homework," I growled.

The kid rolled his eyes. "I don't have homework, Dad. I'm only in grade two."

"Then you can watch TV, as long as it's something educational."

We repeated this corny dialogue word-for-word every afternoon. It was as much a part of our routine as tinned tomato soup on Sunday nights and always being late for school. Red was the best accident I had ever had. He was clever, biddable, undemanding company, and more mature than his baby face and mop of angelic curls suggested. He had missed Wendy a lot at first and still stacked on the occasional turn, but all in all he had adapted pretty well to our bachelor-boy existence.

He took his sandwiches into the lounge room and turned on the television. I use the word lounge room in its generic sense. It might be better described as a cave with floorboards. It had long come to terms with the fact that it would never be a sunny, north-facing, energy-efficient, entertainment/kitchen area with stylish black and white checkerboard tiles.

While Red watched the Roadrunner, I changed into overalls, ran a ladder up to the ceiling trapdoor in the hall and plugged the lamp from Wendy's side of the bed into an extension lead. Then I spent half an hour hauling the bulky mattresses of fibreglass out of the car and up into the roof cavity. From outside, the roof looked sound enough. But in the confined gloom of the cavity, the sheets of corrugated iron revealed themselves to be a filigree of rust held tenuously in place by inertia and ancient cobwebs.

Squatting low on the dusty rafters, I began sidling along, cutting sections of the insulation and stuffing them into place in the irregular gaps between the timbers as I went. Working at a constant crouch was harder and slower work than I had anticipated, and I soon had a sweat up. Minute particles of fibreglass worked themselves up my sleeves and under my collar, sticking to my skin. In case they were carcinogenic I breathed through my nose. Little fragments of pink lodged in my nostril hairs.

That's the problem with working for yourself. The pay is lousy, the conditions suck, and the boss couldn't give a flying continental about safety. The job should only have taken an hour, but with all the fiddling around I must have lost track of the time. Down below the television droned on, constant and indistinct.

It was just as I was reaching over to jam the last batt into place in the tight angle beneath the eaves that something cold and hard struck me on the back of the head. A wave of nauseating giddiness roared in my ears and I toppled forwards, arms scrabbling uselessly in the air. A vice of jagged metal clamped hard around my neck, pinning me so I could neither sit nor stand. Everything went black.

The next thing I knew, a cool clamminess was washing over my face. I blinked rapidly and opened my eyes. Everything was still black. I felt panic surge, then abate as I realised what had happened.

42 • **Shane Maloney**

I had lost my balance and punched my head clear through the metal roof, jamming my neck in the hole. The darkness was the night which had fallen unnoticed around me. From the shoulders down I was locked in a painful crouch. From the chin up I was John the Baptist on a platter. By twisting my neck against my rough iron collar, I could just make out the street below, deserted but for a handful of parked cars. Far off on the horizon, the illuminated cranes and rising tower blocks of the city winked and glistened, mocking me.

"Red," I screamed, at the top of my lungs. At exactly that moment a lashing torrent of rain descended, a pitiless wintry surf. Water cascaded down the corrugations of the iron and ran down the imperfect seal formed by my neck. I crouched helpless, feeling it gushing into my overalls. Over the pounding din I could just hear the "Dr Who" theme seeping upwards, and above that a higher more insistent sound, the impatient ringing of the telephone.

The choice was between drowning and cutting my own throat. I took the second option. Screwing my eyes shut and gripping a timber cross-piece, I jerked downwards with all my might, nearly ripping my ears off and wincing as I felt my cheeks raked with sharp edges of metal.

The minor haemorrhage that resulted was nothing, however, compared with the cataract that descended onto the newly laid insulation once my head was no longer plugging the hole in the roof. I quickly stripped off my overalls, rolled them into a makeshift plug and stuffed up the hole.

Stuffed up being the operative expression.

When eventually I had staunched the flow of water I climbed down the ladder, bleeding, goose-pimpled and draped with cobwebs. Red glanced up from the idiot box for the merest second, then turned his eyes back to the screen. He had seen his father Do It Yourself before.

"Who was that on the phone?" I shouted above the rain pummelling the windows.

Red shrugged and flipped channels. "When's tea?" he said, crescent moons of sandwich crusts on his lap. "I'm starving."

The refrigerator yielded up a carton of milk, five fish fingers, two potatoes, a carrot and half a tray of ice cubes. I put the fish things in the oven, stuck the vegetables on the gas to boil and dropped the ice into a glass on top of an antiseptic dose of Jamesons.

The whiskey was more warming than the tepid trickle that issued from the antique water heater on the bathroom wall. I lathered up and listened to the whining of the pipes. The whole room joined in, crying out to be transformed into an airy atrium lined with glass bricks and filled with moisture-loving plants. I finished my drink slowly, waiting for the water to run cold and wondering where I could get hold of a cheap roofer. This was one of the few times I ever wished I had friends in the building industry unions.

At the back of the bathroom cupboard behind a lonesome rubber, its use-by date long expired, I found a bottle of mercurochrome and daubed red lines down the scratches on my ears, neck and face. As an omen of the pitfalls that were to confront me over the following three days, I can think of nothing more eloquent than the bedraggled zebra that resulted, staring back at me from my fog-misted bathroom mirror. Tetanus, cancer, involuntary celibacy, a hole in the roof. You name it, chances were I had it.

A couple of fish fingers, and Red's memory came back. "Oh yeah, Mum said to tell you she's been ringing everywhere but you're never there. She said she'll try again tomorrow. And guess what she's bought me. A Dino-Rider. The one with laser weapons."

Weapons? Apparently Canberra was doing nothing for Wendy's ideological rigour. After dinner, a little convivial family viewing and the customary buggerising around, I finally managed to badger Red into bed. The week before he'd been content to read himself to sleep, but that night he wanted to be babied. Hard day at the office, I guessed.

He dragged a big picture book out of a batch that Wendy had brought home from a sale at the Equal Opportunity Resource Centre, earnest stuff with titles like *Miranda Has Two Mummies* and *Yes, Raoul Is Different*. Fortunately, that night's choice was one of the less pedagogically strident. *Folk Wisdom of the World's Peoples* was its eagerly redundant title. Red snuggled deeper under the quilt and I opened the book at random: "Of all of the wise men of Turkey none is more famous than Nasreddin Hoca . . ."

Above the text was a pen and wash picture of a tubby old man with a bushy white beard, curly slippers and a turban the size of a load of washing. Red nodded his approval and I read on.

> One day Nasreddin Hoca was invited to give the sermon at the mosque in his village. He mounted the pulpit and asked,
>
> "O True Believers, do you know what I am going to say to you today?"
>
> The congregation looked at each other in confusion and shook their heads. "We have no idea," they said.
>
> "If you have no idea," said Nasreddin Hoca, "what is the use of my talking to you?" With that he descended from the pulpit and went home.

As I read, I glanced furtively down at the child's face, seeking out hopeful signs of sleep's imminent arrival.

> The following week he entered the mosque, mounted the pulpit and again asked the congregation, "O True Believers, do you know what I am going to talk to you about today?"
>
> "Yes," said the wily ones.
>
> "Well, if you already know," said Nasreddin Hoca, "what is the use of my telling you?" And again he descended from the pulpit and went home.
>
> The next week he mounted the pulpit and asked the very same question. "O True Believers, do you know what I am going to talk to you about today?"
>
> The people of the congregation had considered their reply. "Some of us do and some of us do not," they cried.
>
> "In that case," said Nasreddin Hoca, "let those of you who know tell those who do not."

Christ only knew what a child was supposed to make of this drivel. It sounded like a Treasury position paper. Fortunately it also produced a similar effect. A muddy glaze was settling over Red's eyes. I droned on, my tone deliberately monotonous. Halfway through the parable of the walnut and the watermelon, bye-byes arrived and slipped Red silently across the border into the Land of Nod. As I laid the book down and tiptoed out of the room, he stirred a little, scratched his head and began quietly to snore.

The deluge outside had dropped to a steady patter. I climbed the ladder and checked the roof. So far so good. My impromptu engineering was holding up remarkably well. The plug of rolled-up overalls was a sodden mass, but it had swelled to a tight fit and very little water was leaking through. Just to be on the safe side, I sat a bucket underneath, balanced on a plank running across two of the rafters.

Then I screwed the top off the Jamesons and sat down with the Pacific Pastoral file. I looked at the photos first, spilling them across the kitchen table. The corpse had a face only a mother could love, a sentimental Hittite mother with cataracts. Apart from that, all you could tell was that he could have done with a course at Weight Watchers and that he was dead. I turned to the papers.

No wonder Charlene had made a point of telling Agnelli to get them back on her desk pronto. Many strings had been jerked and much red tape scissored to get this little collection of paper together. Preliminary reports of the Department of Labour Accident Investigations Division, photocopies of internal police incident sheets, and draft summaries from the coroner's office did not spontaneously aggregate in the privacy of some filing cabinet and decide to throw themselves across the desk of the first available minister. The regrettable demise of Ekrem Bayraktar three days before had set the hidden hand of some dedicated paper chaser into motion.

But as far as I could tell, it had hardly been worth the bother. This was about as prosaic a stack of forms as death ever filled out. If there had ever been any drama here, it had quickly been reduced to a homogeneous grey soup of bureaucratese, lacking even the frisson of an interdepartmental difference of opinion. The medicos, the police, the coronial and departmental investigators were all in furious agreement.

The bare facts outlined were these. Bayraktar was Turkish. That much I had been right about. He had been in Australia three years, status permanent resident. His address was in Blyth Street, Brunswick, a flat I assumed. No next of kin was listed. He had been with Pacific Pastoral for a little over two years and as a leading-hand storeman had regular access to the plant's storage freezers. Some time during Friday afternoon he had let himself in to Number 3 chiller. He did this on his own initiative, without informing anyone and for reasons not apparent. Everyone was very clear on that point.

Some time later a refrigeration mechanic by the name of Herbert Gardiner entered the freezer to check the thermostat and found Bayraktar's body. Herbert Gardiner? Where had I heard that name before? I shuffled the papers until I found the sheet of Upper House notepaper I had used to take down the name of Bernice's shop steward. Yep, that was him.

Oh Herb, I mused out loud, whatever were your parents thinking when they planted that botanical name on you? Basil and Rosemary Gardiner and their little boy Herb. Hardly a sage choice. I shook my head in wonder and turned back to the subject at hand.

The cause of death was a heart attack, the exact time of which was subject to some speculation on account of the low temperature. Precision in this matter did not appear to be an issue, nor was any negligence or malfeasance on the company's part suggested. All in all it was pretty much an open and shut case. Bayraktar was just another of the three-hundred-odd Victorians who died in industrial incidents every year. The only unanswered question was what the deceased had been doing wandering about in a giant deep freeze full of boxes of boned beef.

No bureaucrat in his right mind would have speculated on that topic in an official document. Ever since the Freedom of Information Act had been gazetted, candour was not advisable in paperwork forming part of the permanent public record. Even the most innocuous remark made in dispatches could eventually be ferreted out by some snooping journalist or tireless special interest group, and end up splashed across the front page. Let that happen and you could kiss your preferment goodbye.

Not that there aren't ways around these things. I found what I was looking for scribbled on a yellow Post-It sticker stuck inside the back cover of the file. The handwriting matched the signature on the preliminary report of the coroner's chief investigator. "Police et al. concur most likely pilfering," it read. The boys on the scene, it appeared, had gone into a huddle, put two and two together and concluded that the deceased had been in the process of stuffing a piece of prime porterhouse up his jumper when the grim reaper tapped him on the shoulder.

Here at last was something. Not official, mark you, but potentially useful. If Lollicato and the *Sun* decided they wanted a martyr, they might try painting this Bayraktar joker as another Mother Teresa. But if I could get one of his co-workers inside the place to confirm his reputation as a pilferer, I would be morally one up on Lollicato. Relatively speaking.

Much more to the point was how much mileage Lolly & Co thought they could extract from the situation. That would depend on the attitude of the dead bloke's workmates. That, and whether there was someone inside to do their stirring for them. And I wasn't going to find that out by burying my nose in a pile of papers. I shuffled the pages together, downed the last dribble of whiskey, scratched my head, yawned, and got up for a pee.

How had Agnelli ever convinced me that the government might stand or fall on this particular piece of nonsense? Now I'd have to drive these useless papers back into town, go out and prowl around some butchery in the backblocks of Coolaroo, and waste an afternoon cooking up some bodgie report. The best part of a couple of days down the tubes. And for what? As if I didn't have better things to do with my time.

Red's feet were sticking out from underneath the covers, cold as iceblocks. As I tucked the quilt back in, he rolled suddenly, sat bolt upright, scratched his head fiercely and slumped back into unconsciousness.

By that stage bed was looking like as good a place as any. I climbed into the matrimonial cot with *Understanding Family Law, A Practical Guide to Financial Planning and Court Procedure.* Ten pages of legal prose later, I succumbed to the elemental drone of the rain on the tin roof above me and slipped into the dreamless sleep of the innocent.

Well, maybe not completely dreamless, or completely innocent. About 4 A.M. there was this cave and this sheepskin.

6

THE MINISTRY FOR INDUSTRY was fourteen floors up an octagonal guano-textured megalith a block west of Parliament. I bunged the Renault into a basement slot stencilled Strictly Deputy Director, hit the fourteenth floor at a jog, and slapped the envelope on Charlene's private secretary's desk. I was back inside the lift, standing beside an anorexic youth in orange dreadlocks and green Lycra shorts, when the half-closed doors gave a shudder and parted.

"Morning, Murray," said Agnelli, his palm flat against the call button. "What's with the face? Gone ten rounds with a cheese grater? What's Lionel Merricks going to think?"

"He can think what he likes. I've never heard of him." I made no attempt to leave the lift. The doors quivered, fighting to close.

"He's the chairman of Pacific Pastoral and we're expected in his office in three quarters of an hour. Didn't you get my message?"

I remembered the phone slip in my top pocket. "What message?"

"The one I'm giving you now. Meet me in the foyer of the Amalfi in half an hour. I'll brief you then."

"I thought company liaison was your job. I just came in to drop off the file."

Agnelli's head did a 270-degree sweep. His voice came through a clenched jaw, low and insistent. "Look, Murray . . ."

"I'd love to stand around and bat the breeze like this, fellers," said the bike messenger, "but I've got a previous at the Stock Exchange."

I wasn't going to argue the toss in front of Boy George. Reluctantly I stepped out into the corridor. Agnelli took his palm off the button. "Well piss off then, buster," he told the closing doors. He turned back to me, oozing sweet reason. "It'll only take half an hour."

"Corporate relations are your department. What do you need me for?"

Agnelli licked his lips and started talking twenty to the dozen. "The manager out at Coolaroo didn't want to know me. Typical middle management flack. So I thought I'd teach the prick a lesson. Went all the way to the top. Merricks is on the City Revitalisation Committee with Charlene. The Committee met yesterday afternoon, so I buttonholed Merricks afterwards and put him on the spot. Asked about the newspaper story and made a noise like industrial unrest. Really put the wind up him, it did. So then I told him I shared his concerns and put our little look-see proposition. He's a bit so-so about the idea, obviously doesn't want the wrong person blundering about out there treading on management's toes. Said it would all depend on the 'consultant.' 'Sure,' I said. 'I can understand that.' Told him the individual we have in mind is a real professional. 'Talk to him yourself,' I said. 'If you're not perfectly comfortable, we'll shelve the idea.' "

By this stage he had me bailed up against the wall. "Ange," I said wearily, "You're over-reacting. This whole thing is bullshit. That *Sun* story yesterday was a beat-up. There's no mention at all in today's edition. Do us both a favour, get another boundary rider."

"Nonsense, Murray. You're wasting your talents out in that electorate office. Handle this one right and you never know. Go on, clean yourself up a bit. I'll see you outside the Amalfi in half an hour." He disappeared in the direction of Charlene's office.

I pulled a tie out of my pocket and went into the men's. The fluorescent tube above the mirror wasn't pulling any punches. The cuts had stopped weeping and were beginning to scab over nicely. I'd be able to start shaving again in about a week, but it really wasn't the sort of face you'd want to go stalking corporate corridors in. I made a lump in my tie and parked it in the general vicinity of the top of my chest. This Merricks joker would have to take me as he found me. And if he didn't, so much the better. I'd be off the hook with Agnelli.

The ministry was a typical public service set up — a rabbit warren of chin-high beige partitions, half the desks unattended. I helped myself to one of the empty ones and ransacked the drawers until I found a yellow pages. There were an encouraging six pages of roofing contractors. I dialled the electorate office and ran a pen down the names while I waited for Trish to answer. When she picked up the receiver, I could hear a dog barking in the background. Every day something new.

"Any messages?"

There were plenty, but none urgent. And the guy with the tatts was back, on the doorstep at nine on the dot. Persistent bastard. I told Trish I wouldn't be in until later and to tell Mr. Tattoo that I was at the Police-Community Liaison Task Force and I'd probably be bringing some of them back with me. "And you won't forget to run off the agenda papers for Wednesday night's branch meeting?" There was a bark, but it wasn't a dog. "And, listen, if anybody rings about a roof, take the number and tell them I'll call back."

I dialled again, and again, and again, starting at AAAAce Roofing and working my way through to Versa-Tile. Twenty minutes later all I had were half a dozen engaged signals, an invitation to call back later, four answering machines, two no longer connecteds and a wife who would tell hubby when he came home.

The Amalfi was the city's newest and tallest office tower, a fifty-storey icicle of blue-tinted glass built with Kuwaiti finance and tax-free cash bonuses and designed to reflect the many moods of the sky. Its disposition that morning was decidedly unsettled.

Big corporate tenants occupied the higher floors and various government departments were housed lower down. Each had separate entrances and elevators so the business types on their way to the top could be spared the ordeal of having to rub shoulders with scruffy androgynes in polyester cardigans. The corporate entrance was a marble-clad lobby on Collins Street with imposing brass revolving doors. The government tenants entered via an open vestibule around the corner where a gaggle of furtive smokers clustered around a midden of squashed butts.

The Education Department central bureaucracy had set up shop on some lower floors and Agnelli was standing at the government entrance talking to an official from one of the teacher unions, a factional heavyweight, when I arrived. He immediately broke off the conversation and hurried over. He looked me up and down and opened his mouth as if to make some remark, thought better of it and propelled me wordlessly through the revolving doors into the open mouth of a lift.

"Let Merricks do all the talking," he said as we shot upwards into the stratosphere. "And for Christ sake, don't contradict him. These captains of industry are totally surrounded by sucks telling them how fucking brilliant they are. Makes them very sensitive." He said something else, but my ears were popping and I missed it.

We got out at the forty-ninth floor and found ourselves facing a reception desk of black lacquer, burnished to a mirror shine and bearing an arrangement of long stemmed exotic flowers shaped like the genitalia of some endangered species. Behind it sat a receptionist with a face heavily in hock to the Estée Lauder counter at David Jones and sculpted extensions so long they would have curled up and died at the mere sight of a keyboard. Agnelli she eyeballed coolly. When she got a load of me the ambient temperature dropped a good fifteen degrees.

"Mr. Merricks is expecting you." She sounded as though she could not in her wildest dreams conceive why. She led us across a carpet that murmured soft caresses as we passed, and abandoned us in a corner office with a desk you could land a Lear jet on. Two entire walls were floor-to-ceiling glass.

The view was hypnotic, vast, drawing the gaze irresistibly.

Rimmed by the green of sand-belt suburbia, the beaten pewter of the bay extended southward to an invisible horizon. Factories and freeways spread a grubby picnic rug as far west as the light would allow. Immediately below, the Spencer Street switching yards were a model train set, Hornby Double-O by the look of it. Out past the Westgate Bridge and the cubist statement of the Newport power station, oil refineries and smokestacks disappeared into a smudgy haze. But mostly it was sky, lots and lots of sky. A flock of seagulls flew past at eye level. Here and there over the bay celestial conveyor belts of sunlight pierced the clouds with radiant beams as though the Assumption of the Blessed Virgin Mary was imminent.

I sank into one of a matching pair of pale-green kid leather sofas. Agnelli strode over to the window, his hands clasped behind his back, his excitement impossible to conceal. I could feel a lecture coming on.

"Look at that." Agnelli gestured like a carnival barker. "Industry. Chemicals. Plastics. Automobiles. Foodstuffs. Biotechnology. Computers. The busiest port in Australia. Anything that gets made in this country gets made here. Compared to us the rest of the country's a fucking pineapple plantation or a gravel pit. Think, from here you can see a quarter of the country's population, the most productive quarter, too."

Far below I could just make out two figures fishing off a pier. At the periphery of my vision the word MOBIL stood out in letters four storeys high.

"Hard to imagine that most of it is already obsolete." Agnelli shook his head and frowned, barely believing how badly the place was letting him down. "Technological change, sunrise industries, value-added — they're the name of the game now. There's a hundred million fucking Japs out there." He jabbed a forefinger vigorously in the general direction of Africa. "And every one of them is trying to figure out another way to screw the rest of us. If it wasn't them it'd be the Koreans or the Taiwanese. Believe me, Murray, if we don't pull our fingers out, we'll wake up one afternoon and find ourselves sitting on the scrap heap at the end of the universe."

He picked up a silver-framed family snap from among the yachting paraphernalia on the credenza and waved it about. "And this lot, our dear old home-grown business establishment, will just sit back and let it happen if we let them. We've got to drag these inbreds into the twentieth century. Show some leadership. Get them off their well-upholstered bums. Offer them incentives to up their game. Investment incentives. Seeding funds. Venture capital. Fast-tracked planning approvals. That's why we're here today, Murray. Me to re-assure our corporate friend that the government is on the ball, you to show him we're not on some anti-business witch hunt. Main thing is, just remember your manners, old chap, and we'll be out of here in a jiffy."

Agnelli's face suddenly contorted with such patent insincerity that I thought he was bunging on a quick demonstration. "Ah, Mr. Merricks," he gushed, "So nice of you to agree to see us." His gaze was fixed on the door, the picture back in place.

Lionel Merricks was a rather short, ruddy-faced man in his mid-fifties. He progressed across the carpet with impatient vigour, preceded by his hand. The fact that he was in his shirtsleeves, coupled with his slightly flushed appearance, gave the impression that he had just been interrupted giving himself a bracing injection of capital. I realised with dismay as I took his hand that I already felt obligated to him for his time.

"Five minutes, gentlemen." The voice was fussy, half-English, disappointing. So this was the entrepreneurial class, red in tooth and claw. The shareholders of the country's seventh-largest public company might have found the tone impressive, but I couldn't see why. I stopped feeling apologetic.

"We at Pacific like to think of our workforce as one big family," Merricks began magisterially. "And believe me, nobody feels it more keenly than I when there is a bereavement in the family. A situation like this should not be made the pretext for industrial scaremonger-ing. Nor the occasion of a fishing expedition. So if you have infor-mation relevant to the conduct of our company's affairs, I would be pleased to see that it is passed on to the appropriate area. Otherwise

I see no need for outside involvement. You are not, I take it, suggesting the company is in any way responsible."

Agnelli nearly fell over himself. "I can assure you there is no question of blaming the company. It's not even that we're expecting any specific problem, sir." Sir, yet! "But it would be in nobody's interest if somebody out there went flying off the handle, would it? What harm could there be in having a quiet chat with some of the men? Test the waters, so to speak. All absolutely unofficial, of course. Avoid surprises, eh?" Chummy, now.

Merricks nodded noncommittally and turned to me. "You have a union background, I understand, Mr. Whelan." He spoke slowly as if I was a little retarded. After Agnelli's performance he could hardly be blamed.

"I was with the Municipal Employees for a while." This drew a blank. "Garbage collectors, street sweepers." Merricks' expression did not change but I knew I might as well have said "dung beetles or intestinal tapeworms."

Agnelli felt the crackle of insolence and quickly stepped back in. "There would be no disruption of day-to-day activities at the plant. Murray here could be in and out of there in a couple of hours. Isn't that right, Murray."

Merricks still wasn't having any of it. "Our corporate culture is an open book. But there are always sensitivities at the shop floor level — restrictive work practices, demarcation disputes. I'm sure you are all too familiar with these matters, Murray. Having an outsider go in asking questions, at a time like this, I'm not at all convinced it's a good idea."

I nodded absently. No skin off my nose. The sheer scale of the view out the window was mesmerising. It seemed like the whole sky was in the room with us. Out over the bay thunderheads were marching in from the west in mile high battalions. I wondered how helpful the plug of overalls would be once that lot broke. Not the sort of problem Mr. Lionel Merricks would ever have to deal with. None of his roofs was ever likely to have a pair of soggy King Gees stuffing its inadvertent apertures. Not the gabled mansard one in Lansell

Road, Toorak, or the cantilevered art deco one on the cliff top at Portsea or the mossy slate one on the homestead at Macedon.

"It's entirely your decision, of course, Mr. Merricks," I said softly, "but do keep in mind that I have already discussed this matter with one of the industrial officers at the Trades Hall. You know what the unions can be like. If they were to form the opinion that your company is being obstructive . . ."

It was Merricks' turn to examine the meteorological panorama. Conditions looked more and more unsettled by the moment. Across the room Agnelli's eyes had gone wide with caution. The clouds moved closer. The moment continued. Merricks' attention seemed to linger on a tanker idling in the bay, waiting for a berth.

"Very well," he said at last. "I'll instruct our on-site management to cooperate. But I must insist that liaison be directly with me. Your findings are to be communicated directly and confidentially to me, and to me alone. I trust I am understood?"

There was a knock on the door and the ice queen opened it all the way. Merricks rose, nodded tersely. "Understood?" he squeaked.

"I'm sure Charlene will appreciate your accessibility, Mr. Merricks," Agnelli cooed, but Merricks had already disappeared.

I looked at my watch. It was just on eleven-fifteen. Merricks had been in the room precisely five minutes.

I shook my head. "Not a word, Agnelli," I said. "Not a fucking syllable."

7

COOLAROO LAY on the furthermost northern edge of the electorate, out where the fringes of the city finally frayed into paddocks of shoulder-high scotch thistle and the rusting hulks of cannibalised car bodies. Any further out and the voters chewed their cuds. I drove there straight from the city, the highway slick with drizzle, wanting only to get it over and done with.

Half a kilometre past the Ford factory I turned off into an industrial estate of warehouses and small factories. The road narrowed to a single lane of asphalt and I hugged the margins, wary of the lumbering sixteen-wheelers that were the only other traffic. The Renault threw up a slurry of mud and gravel as it went, the suspension feeling its age in the potholes. If I could have afforded anything else I'd have got rid of the shitheap years before. It was the French, not me, who deserved to be punished. I wasn't the one turning Micronesia into a croque monsieur.

The Pacific Pastoral meatworks was a block long and half as wide, three storeys high, ringed by a chain mesh fence and fronted by a wide asphalt apron. I pulled into the employees' carpark opposite and eased into the gap between a panel van with chrome exhausts and a lime-green Kingswood with a luminous Cedars of Lebanon bumper sticker. Through the swish of the wipers I had a clear view of the faceless brick behemoth across the road.

Nothing said trouble. No cluster of pickets at the gatehouse, no windbreakers and beanies, no hands being warmed at smoking ten-gallon drums. But there wouldn't be, would there? It was all bullshit, a figment of Agnelli's overactive imagination. There was nothing but a brick wall punctured at regular intervals by huge doorways, great yawning maws opening into impenetrable darkness. The shit holes at the end of the universe.

The drizzle stopped. A tip-truck came out of one of the doorways and a maintenance crew in navy overalls started shovelling steaming bitumen into pot holes in the apron. I turned off the wipers. As I stepped out into the carpark, my right shoe sank to the ankle in a puddle of oil-slicked ditchwater. I'd make Agnelli pay for this crap one day, I vowed.

The gatehouse attendant directed me towards one of the cavernous doors, apertures big enough for even the largest refrigerated truck. As I passed the first of the great portals I slowed my pace to squint from the silvery glare of the daylight into the interior, but could pierce the Dickensian gloom for only a few metres. From deep inside I could hear the mash and rev of forklifts and a voice shouting instructions, but the only human life I glimpsed was two spectral figures in white hosing down a floor.

As I neared the far door I felt my scalp crawl. I'm no vegetarian, so I knew it wasn't revulsion at the proximity of so much slaughtered flesh I was feeling. I shrugged off the creepy sensation and stepped into the enveloping darkness.

The place seemed even bigger inside, a maze of alleys and sub-buildings. It was older, less high-tech than I had expected, smelling of stale diesel fumes and wet concrete. Just inside the great door was a steel companionway with a sign pointing upwards, marked Office. I went up the stairs and followed the peck of a typewriter along an open deck running along the top edge of a deserted canteen.

The pecker was a well-upholstered woman of middle years, her sausagey fingers threaded with rings. She finished pecking a sentence and looked up without curiosity. "Yes, love?" I asked if I was in the right place to see the manager. The sausages wrapped themselves around a telephone handpiece. "Someone to see you, Mr. Apps." There was something about the way she said the mister part that made me smile.

Deep gullies of tedium had etched themselves into the woman's face as though she had spent reluctant decades trapped behind that big metal desk. Next to her typewriter a dusty monstera was taking a long time dying. On the wall behind, a sign said Thank You For Not Smoking. I wished I still smoked so I could start one up, just to see what would happen. Next to it a corporate mission statement in a moulded plastic frame began: "We at Pacific Pastoral think of our workforce as one big family."

Apps exploded out of an inner office. He had a beeper on his belt, a long thin face with twerp written all over it, and hands that dangled somewhere around his knees. One of them snaked up to tug at his collar. His Adam's apple came out for a look, didn't like what it saw, and ducked back in.

"Look here," he started in, his mouth a pinched slot. "This is tantamount to harassment. You lot at Export Certification seem to think you can ride roughshod over people. Once, just once, the US Department of Agriculture slaps a rejection sticker on a container of our product. Suddenly half the Australian quarantine service is crawling all over us, demanding right of inspection every five minutes. I thought you lot were supposed to be on our side. Just how many times do we have to go over this?"

I wondered just how anyone might mistake me for an officer of the Primary Industry Department. Had I grown a hat? Did I have a piece of straw sticking out the corner of my mouth?

The big vein in Apps' neck was ticking like a metronome. Without pausing to draw breath he stuck his scrawny wrist in my face and tapped his watch. "Two o'clock, I was told. And what is it now? Twelve-thirty. Ever heard of courtesy?"

I had but I wasn't going to waste any on this prick. "Lionel Merricks' office will have rung," I said. "Whelan's the name."

Apps arched his neck irritably like the mistake was mine and shot the woman behind the desk a filthy look. The woman ignored him and resumed torturing the typewriter. "Why didn't you say so?" he snapped. "Head office said you probably wouldn't be here for a day or so."

"If this isn't a convenient time . . ." I shrugged.

Apps writhed halfway between rage and obsequiousness. "Full cooperation they said. So full cooperation it is. Our corporate culture is an open book."

But a repetitive one. And I didn't like the tone he was reading it in. "So I understand," I said. "They explained I'm here to talk to some of the men?"

Apps fished. "Something about workforce attitudes to this death thing, they said. Bit hazy on the detail."

I made a vaguely affirmative noise in the back of my throat.

"Everyone seems to think I've got nothing better to do with my time than conduct guided tours. I suppose you want to see where it happened then?"

The place was cold and dispiriting enough without a guided tour of some bloody freezer. "Er, not really," I started, nowhere near forcefully enough. My words drowned in the clang of Apps' footsteps on the steel plate of the deck. Cooperation, even of the grudging variety, could be so disarming. I tailed Apps deep into the bowels of the great shed, struggling into researcher mode. "What's your contingent here?"

Apps bounded ahead, making no effort to conceal his irritation. "Pretty quiet at the moment, as you can see. Best time for what you want is five o'clock in the morning. That's when the trucks come in from the abattoirs up the bush."

"You couldn't put a number to it?"

He wasn't giving anything away. "Varies. It's a seasonal industry. Core establishment — storemen, maintenance, cleaners, clerical — between twenty-five and thirty. But on top of that there's anything up to fifty casuals at a time in the place."

We passed a safety slogan in English, Greek and Italian. "Lot of Italians?" I asked.

"Don't take any notice of that, it's twenty years old. First it was Italians and Greeks, then Yugoslavs. Now its all Lebanese, Turks. Vietnamese even. Try to keep up and we'd be changing the signs every five minutes."

We turned into a sort of truck-width street lined with cool rooms the size of houses. "You'll be wanting to interview the first on the scene, I daresay. He'll be about here some place."

"Gardiner?" I looked about, hurrying to keep up.

"You seem very well informed." It sounded like a reprimand. "One of the cleaners, actually. Gardiner's on leave for a few days. They kept him here till nearly eight on Friday night, getting his statement and so on. Bloody red tape. I told him to take a few days off to get over it. He's no spring chicken, as you no doubt already know. He's due to retire next month."

Here was a fly in the ointment. Gardiner was the only contact name I had. This little excursion onto the shop floor was already enough of an exercise in futility. Without Gardiner to interview, it would be even more so. It struck me that if old Herb was that close to retirement then Apps had probably insisted he use up a bit of his accrued sick leave, save the company a couple of bob in termination pay.

"This is it."

A heavily padded parka was thrust into my hands. A key rattled, a white-clad wall slid away and the interior of Number 3 chiller yawned before me, sucking warmth.

"This really isn't necessary," I protested, a wave of cold air wrapping itself around me.

The words "No trouble at all" formed in the mist now coming out of Apps' mealy mouth. The door slid back into place behind us and Apps disappeared into the gap between towering pallet loads of waxed white cartons.

The chiller was large enough to get lost in. One man had died there already. I stuffed my exposed extremities into the jacket, pulled the hood cord tight and followed Apps. Talk about a snow job. This was the original Antarctic runaround. And not a single dead cow in sight to enliven the view, just row upon row of boxes. The whole place was nothing but a very cold storeroom.

"The men," I insisted through teeth already beginning to chatter. "I'll only need to talk to two or three of them today." My wet sock had begun icing up.

Apps led me down a narrow canyon of roof-high boxes and stopped at a hatch about a metre square set into the wall. "Emergency exit," he fumed. "Working perfectly it was. No question of culpability."

He shoved a spring-loaded handle with his elbow and the little door swung silently outwards. He gestured for me to take a gander. There didn't seem to be much choice. I stuck my head through the hole.

The hatch opened into a narrow access alley running along behind the row of chillers. A man was standing in the alley, smoking a cigarette. He wore white overalls, white rubber boots and a white showercap. The sudden opening of the hatch caught him by surprise and he half-turned towards me, peering out from under his shower cap with dark marsupial eyes. He was about fifty, stocky in a pounded-down sort of way, Mediterranean, with skin the colour of old parchment. For the shortest of moments a flare of defiance lit his melancholy eyes. Then a curtain of indifference descended. He took a final drag, crushed the butt under the toe of a white rubber boot, turned away abruptly and was gone.

I pulled my head back in and rubbed my hands together. "Very interesting, I'm sure," I said. "Now can we get the fuck out of here before I freeze my arse off." Apps smirked like there was something obvious I'd missed and led me back out.

The man in the white overalls was passing the chiller door, slowly propelling a trolley of buckets and mops ahead of him. Apps put a hand on the trolley and squinted at the ID tag pinned to his chest. "Ah, yes, Memo. Go with this man, Memo. He's from the government."

Memo's round mournful face turned green. "Poliss?"

Apps was taking the piss, palming me off on the mop jockey. Bugger him, I thought. He didn't know I was just going through the motions. And the sooner I divested myself of management the better.

"Not police," I said emphatically. "Government." Probably a fine technical distinction wherever it was that this poor downtrodden Memo prick came from. Cyprus possibly. I turned back to Apps. "Anywhere private I can do this? And any chance of a couple of cups of tea?"

Apps' elastic larynx rushed from its hiding place and assumed several curious shapes in rapid succession, but the jerk himself said nothing. He led me and the cleaner into the empty lunch room and pointed to a hot water urn and a pile of polystyrene cups on the counter.

"I'll need to talk to the safety officer next," I said. "You do have a safety officer, don't you?"

Apps looked huffy and disappeared. I motioned for Memo to sit and went over to the lukewarm urn. One of the disposable cups was half-full of plain-label tea bags. There was no milk. I made two cups of black tea and pushed one across the table. The cleaner accepted with a dip of his head. His eyes remained fixed on the chipped formica tabletop. Conversation was not forthcoming.

I suppose I must have looked about as gruelling as a Polish film festival at that point, what with the scarified dial and being as stroppy as buggery at having let myself in for this utter waste of time. Memo, on the other hand, gave no indication of what was going on behind those impassive eyes of his.

"Memo, eh?" I said. "What's that, Greek? Short for Agamemnon, is it?"

The guy sat there like a stuffed mongoose, not touching his tea, his hands jammed between his knees. He gave the question ample consideration and eventually shook his head.

"Not Grik," he said. "Memo same like Mehmet. Mehmet Gezen is my name." The words were extruded tentatively like this maybe wasn't the answer I wanted. "From Turkey."

One of the deceased's compatriots. Good. Aside from a minor detour into the minefield of the Greek-Turkish border region we were headed in the right direction. "Like the man who died here last week?"

Mehmet seemed to search for the right word. "Similar," he admitted at last. But not too similar from the sound of it.

Honestly, I could have got more information out of the tea urn. "Was he your friend?"

Memo took his time. He took so much that I was beginning to wonder if he had understood the question. At last he spoke. "Friend?"

"Yeah," I said. "Friend. Mate. Pal. Cobber. Buddy. Bosom companion." Memo shook his head.

So much for the small talk. "You like it here, Mehmet? Good place?" This was safer ground. Memo cheered up.

"No worries," he said. "No fucking worries."

MACWAM would be pleased to know that a representative cross-section of the cleansing department had no immediate grievances. There was a tap at the door and a pair of blue overalls and a horseshoe moustache rolled in. "I'm McGuire, the safety officer."

"Thank you, Memo," I said, relieved. "That's all for now." The cleaner looked confused then scuttled out of the room, as relieved as Stalin's barber.

McGuire pulled a chair out and straddled it backwards. I got straight to the point. "What's the attitude of the blokes to this death on Friday?"

"They couldn't give a stuff. Bit of a prick from what I could tell. Not to speak ill of the dead."

"Have any particular mates, did he?"

"Wouldn't know."

"What about the health and safety aspects? Anyone upset about them?"

He sniggered. "What is there to be upset about? It was a heart attack from what I hear. He wasn't exactly Twiggy, you know. No-one to blame but himself if you want my opinion."

"What about safety around the place generally? Any gripes?"

"If you can get this lot interested in their own safety you're a better man than I am, Gunga Din. This joint has more turnover than a rotisserie chicken. New set of faces every time you look around. Ethnics mainly. In for a spot of ready cash, then Arrivederci Roma. I do what I can — put posters up in the canteen, make them wear the right gear if I catch them, but what else can you do? We've had the odd accident, but you could count them on one hand."

He held up his right hand. Most of the ring finger and the top half of the middle finger were missing. He leered through the gap. "Got three grand for these babies."

And this was the safety officer. What a dump. "Union active in the workplace, is it?"

"Well, it's a closed shop, if that's what you mean. They make sure they collect their dues and the pie warmer gets fixed when it breaks down. Beyond that, you'd have to ask the shop steward, Herb Gardiner. He deals with that lot." He jerked his thumb upstairs towards the office.

One thing was for sure. This place might have been a shit hole, but it was no powder keg. Agnelli could not have been barking up a wronger tree. Unfortunately for me, he was barking hard and trying to get me to join the chorus. He really had his dick in the wringer over Lollicato and no amount of persuasion was going to convince him to pull it out. My only way out of this wild goose chase would be to find a way to keep Agnelli chasing his tail until the next fleeting enthusiasm came along and he found someone else to buggerise around.

As I shook McGuire's stumps goodbye, I heard the tramp of feet on the walkway above me. I looked up and saw Apps scuttle past, bobbing deferentially to a woman two steps ahead of him. She wore a dark pants suit, her greying hair pinned back with a gold clasp, and she carried a briefcase. When they got to the bottom of the stairs, their backs still turned to me, Apps held the case while the woman slipped her arms into a white dust coat. Then they vanished between two rows of freezers.

Upstairs, the lady with all the rings was sifting through a stack of time sheets. "If you're looking for Mr. Apps," she said, "he's down on the floor." She held up a fleshy wrist and flashed a diamante watch. "With his two o'clock appointment. The inspector." Her eyes twinkled like rhinestones. "Something in particular was it, love?"

"I'm supposed to see last Friday's roster. And milk, you don't know where I can find some milk, do you?"

"Personnel records are confidential, love." But she got a carton of milk out of the private bar-fridge in Apps' inner sanctum. "You'll have to see his nibs. And I'm not sure how long he'll be."

The longer the better as far as I was concerned. "A cross-section of names, that's all I need," I said. "No personal particulars or anything."

She fiddled with an electric kettle at a sink in a small alcove. "Sugar too, love? Or just milk?" My novelty value was slight, but at least I was better than nothing. "What happened to your face?"

"Possum," I said, pulling a chair up beside the desk. "I've got an on-site van up the river. The thing must have got in through the air vent and been stuck there all week. Soon as I opened the door it went for me. Half-starved probably."

Not bad at short notice, I thought. She clucked sympathetically, whether for me or the possum I couldn't tell, and put a cup of something brown in front of me. Then she opened her top drawer, took out a glass ashtray and put it on the desk next to my elbow. She dredged a packet of Alpine out of her bag and extracted a cigarette. "If His Highness comes in, this is yours. Okay?"

I grinned and sipped the weak oversweet instant coffee like it was pure ambrosia. "No worries," I said. "No worries at all."

She held the end of the cigarette to the glowing element of an electric radiator tucked under the desk near her feet. When it caught she put it to her lips and puffed it into action.

I gave her my most hapless look and nodded towards the time sheets. "I'm running a bit late," I said. "I don't suppose I could . . ."

She shrugged. "Long as you're quick," she said. "I don't imagine it'd do any great harm."

I flipped through the sheets. They were dated for the previous week. The employee's name was handwritten in the left-hand column, the daily hours in boxes in the middle, the confirming signature of the shift supervisor on the right. It was perfect.

I began copying the left-hand columns. A couple of dozen names would do, I figured. Enough to keep Agnelli running around Trades Hall like a blue-arsed fly for weeks, trying to figure out if any of them had Lollicato connections. As I wrote I began to whistle under my breath.

The names were a real ethnic grab-bag, heavy on Yugoslavs if anything. Zoltans, Zorans and Dragons, lots of -ic surnames. Some were real puzzlers — Amol Ratna, Zeki Muren. But Italians, if anything, were underrepresented. If Agnelli was looking for an Italian connection he would be disappointed.

I was well into the third page before I glanced over at the signature running down the right-hand margin. It was an almost childish scrawl, half block letters, the mark of a hand that rarely held a pen. E. Bayraktar it read. I rapidly flipped through all the sheets on the desk. The signature appeared on three of them, against more than thirty names.

Agnelli is going to love this, I thought. If he must have his seedbed of simmering discontent, what better place for it than among the deceased's most intimate working companions? I scribbled furiously. The names on Bayraktar's first sheet were the usual cosmopolitan mishmash, but about halfway down the third page they became more decidedly Turkish. Well, they seemed Turkish. Dursun and Orhan and Oguz were Turkish names, I felt almost sure. Kartal Tibet, that was harder to pick, sounded Himalayan. Ahmet Ayik, now surely that was Turkish. And Nasreddin Hoca, that rang a bell.

Ding dong, it went. Jingle jangle. Clang, clang, clang. It rang loud and it kept ringing. Nasreddin. That was a name I'd seen somewhere before. But where?

"These permanents?"

"No, love. That's the casuals. Permanents get paid direct into their bank accounts. Only casuals get weekly cash. Filling out that many different bank transfers every week would be a bloody nightmare, pardon my French. Look at those names. Honestly, you couldn't spell half of them if you tried."

"That must be a lot of fiddling around for you, making up the pay packets."

She snorted smoke out her nose. "I've got enough to do as it is, love. The packets get made up by Armaguard. All part of the service. I send them the forms and they deliver the pays on Friday, all ready for the shift supervisors to take round after lunch. Speaking of which, you'd better hurry up with that lot. I've got to get them finished this afternoon."

"All finished," I said, quickly noting down the last half-dozen names on Bayraktar's page. I took the cup to the sink and rinsed it. "Tell Himself thanks for the welcome and that I'm not sure when I'll be back," I said. "Could be any time." She liked that.

The ashtray had disappeared back into the drawer, butt and all.

"Oh, one last thing before I go. You wouldn't happen to have Herb Gardiner's address on file here somewhere, would you?"

8

GARDINER'S PLACE WAS in Coburg, back towards the electorate office, a fifteen-minute drive. On the way through Broadmeadows I looked for lunch. Out that far, Sydney Road was already the Hume Highway and all I found were fast-food franchises and used-truck yards. Behind them, tract houses spread across the plain where once the Woiworung had hunted and gathered. Presumably with more success than me. I passed the Colonel and kept going.

By comparison Coburg was almost picturesque, a two-time Tidy Town runner-up. It was a world of fifties cream brick-veneer, ruler-straight lawn edges, garden gnomes, roll-down garage doors, low fences, oleanders and lemon trees. None of your unruly natives were tolerated here, dropping their leaf business on the paths and clogging up the guttering. Herb Gardiner's house was the neatest in his street. A big For Sale sign was planted on the front lawn.

I stepped over the wrought-iron gate and rang the doorbell. As a four-note chime sounded distantly, a white silky terrier hurtled around the corner in a frenzy of yapping. I braced to defend myself, and a female voice screamed in my ear. "Garn. Git."

The fanged snowball skidded to a halt, turned and limped away. A woman of about Charlene's age, respectably made up, was standing behind the heavy grille of the screen door wiping her hands on an apron.

"Mrs. Gardiner?"

"Vera passed away six months ago."

"But this is the Gardiner house?"

She didn't want anybody getting the wrong idea. "I'm The Nextdoors. I pop in now and then to give Mr. Gardiner a hand with the housework. If it's about the house, he's up the street I'm afraid."

I was suddenly acutely conscious of my appearance. I straightened my back, ran my fingers through my hair and tried to look as prospective as possible. If I'd been wearing a hat I'd have taken it off and fiddled with the brim. "Been on the market long, has it?" I enquired politely.

"The sign has only just gone up."

"Well, another time, I suppose."

The screen swung open. "Herb won't be a moment, I'm sure."

I wiped my feet vigorously and stepped onto the salmon pink carpet of the entrance hall. The wallpaper was pink, too. A pink on pink fleur-de-lis motif, with a row of miniatures, ballerinas in candy tutus. The telephone table was white though, Queen Anne, to match the antique ivory and brass telephone. I followed the wall-to-wall through to the lounge.

Mrs. Nextdoor went into an impromptu pitch. "As you can see it's too big for one person. Herb's been here on his own ever since . . ." She tactfully left the sentence unfinished. "It was the same when my husband went. Herb, I said, you can't live forever surrounded by memories."

"I can understand that," I said. And I could.

Herb's memories were pure oestrogen. The lounge was the hall writ large. The sofa was done in pink floral with matching throw cushions. The pelmets above the windows were upholstered in the same pattern, with little valances matching the gathered lace of the drapes. Rows of porcelain dolls with painted blushes stared out of a blondwood crystal cabinet towards a print of a sad-eyed clown with a ruffled collar hanging on the rambling-rose patterned wallpaper. There was so much pink I thought my eyes must be hemorrhaging.

On the mantelpiece in front of a bevelled mirror etched with lilies was a big oversized brandy balloon half-filled with rose petal potpourri, but the smell was that of thickly laid-on air freshener. The only visible evidence of human habitation was a scattering of brochures and documents on the pink-tinted glass top of a brass-rimmed coffee table. Beside them sat a copy of *Best Bets*, tell-tale male spoor.

The helpful widow offered me the sofa. "I'd best leave the formalities to Herb. I'd feel a bit strange showing someone around someone else's house, if you know what I mean." That was a relief. I perched gingerly on the edge of the crepe de chine.

I decided I'd give Gardiner five minutes. If he hadn't shown by then, I'd take the phone number and call him from the office. To tell you the truth, I wasn't even sure why I was there. Covering my arse, I suppose. Dotting the t's and crossing the i's.

She of the Nextdoor hovered, uncertain of the protocol. "Nice big place," she improvised. "Ideal family home. Too much cleaning for one. Herb's new place is fully serviced. Hot though, Queensland."

"Queensland?" I improvised back. "Nice weather."

"Can't say I blame him, day like today. But I don't know how he'll get on by himself. A man needs someone to look after him."

Indeed, he did, I admitted. Make that three minutes.

"Anyhow, you might as well have a cuppa while you wait. Fully equipped kitchen." That about exhausted the conversational possibilities. She opened the door through to the kitchen. Baking smells, good ones, came in and fought with the evil air freshener.

A white cuckoo clock ticked loudly in the silence. My stomach growled back at it. Past two-thirty and I still hadn't eaten. I picked up the form guide, put it down, flicked through one of the brochures. Ocean Towers, Broadbeach. Absolute beachfront. Two and three bedroom apartments from two hundred and fifty thousand dollars, plus on-road costs.

I tossed the glossy folder back down onto what could have been a title deed and looked around. Not a bad swap, a quarter of a mill's worth of sea views and a spa for a crocheted tissue box worth maybe half that, absolute maximum, drizzle running down its windows. Old Herb must certainly have been stacking it away all these years. And why not? A lifetime on your back on the concrete with your mouth full of self-tappers, staring up into the innards of a bung compressor. Make a nice change, Broadbeach would.

My own old man had done something similar when they bought the pub out from under him for a drive-in bottle shop. But instead of the high-rise condo in Surfers he'd gone for the fibro shack on Bribie Island and the aluminium runabout. Horses for courses. Plus it looked like Gardiner had a bit more nous in the financial planning department. That wouldn't be hard. Whelan senior had been through six pubs in twenty years, each smaller than the one before it.

I was thinking about making a break for it when a little tan Toyota Corolla scooted into the driveway and disappeared down the side. The dog yapped a bit, then the front door opened. For a man in his sixties, Herb Gardiner was very well preserved, a bit of a gent in a Fletcher Jones tweed jacket, corduroy trousers and a rollneck navy-blue jumper. He had the nuggetty face of an ex-pug and the lightness on his feet of a man who'd just taken out the box trifecta at Eagle Farm. He wore the crooked grin of a short man on good terms with the whole world. If he was suffering from post-fatality trauma, he was bearing up well.

"And who are you, then?" he demanded with exactly the inflection you'd use yourself if you walked into your lounge room and found a total stranger with a scabby face dawdling on the divan.

As I stood up to tell him, the widow came out of the kitchen. "He's come about the house," she said. The apron had disappeared and she'd plumped up her hair. Gardiner shrugged off his tweed jacket, brushed the raindrops away with the meticulousness of a bloke who took good care of his tools, and draped it over the back of one of the pink armchairs.

"Actually," I said guiltily, "the union suggested I get in touch."
"Did they just?"

Fair enough. This one called for a very straight bat. "It's a courtesy call really, Mr. Gardiner. My name is Murray Whelan. It's about the, uh, incident last week at work."

Gardiner gave me the stop sign. "Those scones of yours smell scrumptious." He sprayed charm all over the widow, splashing some on me in the process. He scooped the brochures up off the coffee table and slotted them into a gap in a blondwood shelf of whitebound encyclopedias. "I'll make a bit of space. Sit down, Mr. Whelan."

"Murray, please."

The scones appeared before my bum had even hit the cushion, straight out of the oven. A good three inches tall, they were, on a tray with jam and whipped cream and little linen serviettes. As Mrs. Nextdoor bent to lower the tray, Gardiner, master again in his own house, patted her rump. She all but purred. He looked at me across her backside and winked. Here was a man who had it made, and didn't he know it. For the first time all day, I was beginning to enjoy myself.

"Leave you boys to it, will I then?" she said.

"Rightio, pet. Thanks a lot." Gardiner pulled up his sleeves daintily and reached for the teapot. Under the grizzled hair of his forearm was an ancient tattoo — a faded, languorous mermaid. "I'll be mother," he said.

Entertaining Herb's uninvited callers was clearly not what the good widow had in mind when she'd come round to play house, but she copped it sweet. Gardiner would be around for a little while yet. She went out through the kitchen and I heard the back door close.

"So, what's this all about, son?" Gardiner said amiably.

It was long past the point where there was any mileage in playing funny buggers. I put my cards on the table, face up between the apricot conserve and the turf tips. "I work for Charlene Wills," I said. Gardiner accepted my credentials with a nod. The local member was well known.

"Dunno if you saw it," I went on, "but there was bit of speculation in the *Sun* yesterday to the effect that this business out at Pacific

Pastoral on Friday might lead to some kind of industrial problems. The government would prefer that didn't happen. A committee in the Industry Department has called for a report. Since I work in this area they decided I was just the bunny to write it for them. And because you're the union rep and also happened to be on the spot when the body turned up, I thought I'd come straight to the horse's mouth."

Gardiner took all this in, nodded again and broke open a scone. "I went through all of this pretty thoroughly with the police and so forth on Friday."

I hastened to reassure him. "Oh, I'm not interested in the death *per se*, just any possible industrial implications."

Gardiner applied butter. "Who else you talked to?"

"No one much, yet. Lionel Merricks." This was nothing but craven big-noting. I wasn't even sure he'd recognise the name.

He raised his eyebrows. "You don't muck about, do you, son?"

I brushed it aside, modestly. "Just protocol really. It's the situation on the ground at Coolaroo that interests me. And you'd know more about that than any chairman of the board."

"What about Apps?"

"Correct me if I'm wrong," I said. "But I got the definite impression Mr. Apps wouldn't recognise an industrial situation if it bit him on the bum."

That got a chuckle. Gardiner relaxed back into his armchair, cup and saucer on his lap. "Bit tense, was he?"

"Yeah," I said. "Is he always so stroppy?"

I must've been making a good impression. Gardiner touched the side of his nose and proceeded to slip me the inside oil. "Couple of months ago a mix-up happened in one of our shipments to America, sub-standard meat or something. There was hell to pay. Threat to the credibility of the export industry, all of that. Apps copped a bit of flack from the higher-ups and he's been like a bear with a sore head ever since. You talk to anyone else?"

"Not really. Some bloke named McGuire, the safety officer. A cleaner called Memo. My impression is that I'm on a fool's errand."

So far I was doing too much talking. At this rate those scones would get away from me. I smeared one and bit down hungrily. "What do you reckon?" I mumbled through the crumbs and cream. My mouth filled with heaven, all melting and warm.

Gardiner picked up his cup and settled deeper into his seat. "Well it's all news to me, son. I've been there sixteen years, ever since I left the service, and in all that time we've had fewer than half a dozen strikes and stoppages. And they were all at the behest of the union, backing up the log of claims and so forth. The slaughtermen, up to their knees in guts and shit all day, now they go out at the drop of a hat, and who can blame them? But our lot, industrial action isn't their style. Most of them would rather have the day's pay and solidarity be buggered. I just can't see it, myself. I certainly haven't heard anything, son. And I would, believe me, I would."

This was music to my ears. I tackled another scone and moved on. "So what do you reckon he was up to in that chiller? Bayraktar, the bloke you found?"

"Well, he wasn't working on his tan, I can tell you that much."

"Fair bit of that sort of thing goes on out there, does it?"

"As much as anywhere else, I suppose."

"So it's pretty widespread?"

"Stands to reason that a man who works in a meat warehouse would be a mug to buy his own chops. But not everybody's walking out the front door with a side of lamb under their arm, if that's what you mean."

I'd walked into that one with my eyes wide open, practically called the man a thief to his face. I backed off at a million miles an hour. "Bit stiff, though. Freezing to death for a couple of kilos of free sirloin."

"Maybe he was greedy. Had quite an appetite by the look of him."

"Ever had much to do with him?"

Gardiner wiped his fingers on one of the little floral serviettes. "Knew him to look at. The ethnics keep pretty much to themselves."

"Speaking of which." I pulled the time sheet list out of my pocket and folded it down to the bottom half. "Know any of this lot?"

Gardiner took a spectacle case out of his pocket, slipped on a pair of half-glasses and tilted the sheet of paper to the light.

"What's this, the Cairo phone book?"

"They were all on Bayraktar's shift last week."

Gardiner shook his head. "I'm not much good with ethnic names, I'm afraid."

I drained my tea and began to get up. "Well, thanks a lot."

"Anytime, son. Happy to help. Need anything else, just let me know. But you'd better be quick. I'm due to be demobbed any day now. Only a couple more weeks of 5 A.M. starts and I'm my own man."

"So I hear." I took the list back. Not an entirely unproductive half-hour all in all. A free feed, plus old Herb had driven yet another stake through the heart of Agnelli's conspiracy theory, at least the Pacific Pastoral part of it. I changed the subject. "What do you think you'll get for this place?"

"The agent thinks ninety-five, ninety-five and a half. I wouldn't know these days. It needs a lot of work."

Apart from the decor I couldn't see where, but then Gardiner probably changed the tap washers once a week. "That'd make my place worth about fifty bucks. You should see it. Talk about needing work! I was up in the ceiling putting in some insulation last night and the roof fell in on me. That's how I got these."

"Nasty," said Gardiner.

"They're the least of my worries." I fingered my scabs. "Think I can get a roofer to come and give me a quote? Been on the phone half the day I have." Well I would be, as soon as I got back to the office.

Gardiner got up and started wrapping the remaining scones in a serviette. "Here, take these, son," he said. "She'll get shirty on me if she thinks we didn't eat them all. And while you're here, give me your details. I've got a mate in the building trade who might be able to help you out."

"You sure?" I hesitated only long enough to be polite before stuffing the bundle into my pocket.

"Sure I'm sure," he said. He wrote my address and phone number on a pad by the phone and opened the front door. "I'm getting as much as I need." Faint kitchen noises came from back in the house. "Believe me, son. Believe me."

Out on the street, the rain had let up. All that remained of the puddles was an iridescent glaze. By the look of it, things were on the improve. When I glanced back, Gardiner was still standing at the open door, the little white terrier nuzzling his hand. I gave a nod and climbed into the Renault, one hand already dipping into the package in my pocket. A quick half-hour drafting up the MACWAM report and I'd have this thing knocked on the head.

9

Context, I THOUGHT. Make that *Background.* Double underline. The words in my head began to shape themselves into a preamble.

<u>Background</u>
     A situation has recently arisen in the context of the ongoing legislative process relating to the Industrial Insurance Act such as to suggest it advisable that specific consultations be undertaken in relation to addressing uncertainties which may have been perceived to have arisen as a consequence of press speculation concerning a recent workplace fatality in the Melbourne metropolitan area.

Not bad for openers, I thought, mentally moving on to <u>Implementation</u>. But my concentration was slipping. An image kept surfacing in my mind, a tubby little man in harem pants.

Nasreddin Hoca, he of the hefty turban and curly slippers. He of the bushy beard and pithy parable. Fancy him working at Pacific Pastoral. It was a bit hard to imagine that wry old wiseacre in a pair of white overalls and a shower cap, hefting a side of beef out of a refrigerated semi. Not his style at all. Not unless the arse had fallen out of the obscure epigram business.

If Red's bedtime story book was right and this Nasreddin Hoca guy was a famous Turkish legend, up there in the Mother Goose category, then wouldn't Bayraktar have known he was signing off against a false name? Interesting.

Since I was out and about, I decided on the spur of the moment to roll past Bayraktar's address. From what I could remember of the coroner's file, it was either 363 or 636 Blyth Street. Either way, the detour would not take me far out of my way. A few extra minutes of solitude in the car would help me finish mentally drafting the report.

Blyth Street is a broad avenue running east-west from the Merri Creek to Sydney Road. I started at the Merri end and cruised past respectable homes with barley sugar columns holding up their porches. Three-sixty-three was a Shell self-serve, so I followed the numbers up towards Sydney Road.

Once upon a boom the local gentry had lived up this end, in polychrome brick villas and imposing terraces fretted with iron lacework. Things had taken several downturns since then and all that remained to hint at the vanished grandeur was the occasional one-winged terracotta gargoyle or the peeling curve of a bay window. Mostly it was blocks of flats, crummy, identical strata-titles, pockmarking the streetscape. Six feet of red scoria and a dead cabbage palm out the front, letterboxes exploding with junk mail down the side. Bayraktar's joint was bound to be in one of those.

But closer to Sydney Road, things were on the up and up. Skips full of builders' rubble sat by the curb outside big Victorian terraces, evidence of renovations in progress. Brass plates and Mercedes hinted at solicitors and pathologists. And 636 was no dingy block of flats, flung up in the sixties.

It was a classic two-storey boom-era Italianate mansion, modestly substantial and trying its best to look inconspicuous behind a cast-iron fence, the original by the look of it. A dinky little square tower sat on top, and jutting out above the front door was a coach-porch sort of arrangement. Everything had been painted a matt white with fetching gloss highlights in olive green on the woodwork and the little iron balconies wrapped around the first floor windows.

The overall charm was complemented by little security cameras mounted under the eaves at each corner. Taken together with the gunmetal grey BMW parked under the portico they gave the place the discreet and impenetrable air of a private casino on the Côte d'Azur.

Far too fancy a set of digs for a meat lumper, even if he was a foreman. By the look of it, somewhere along the line someone had screwed up the paperwork. I slowed to a crawl and peered out the passenger window at the brass plate on the gatepost. Etched in black were the words Anadolu Klubu, then underneath in smaller letters Anatolia Club.

An irate toot sounded behind me, a glazier's truck in a hurry. Up ahead, the lights at the corner had just gone orange. I hit the accelerator and raced them, turning up the hill into Sydney Road. Past the Patras Emporium and Appliance Discounters I went. Past the Court House Hotel and the Edinburgh Castle, past Barnacle Bill's, past the black walls of Pentridge. Two blocks past the electorate office I pulled into the curb outside the Turkish Welfare League.

The League was another shopfront opening directly onto Sydney Road. The only other businesses this far up were in the motor trade. Direct-to-the-public retread wholesalers, windscreen replacements while-u-wait, Midas Mufflers. And up here, the road was an industrial-strength drag strip.

Apart from the rent being cheap, there was a certain logic in this choice of location for the League's office. Most of Melbourne's Turks were factory workers, imported by the jumbo load to fill the assembly line at Ford or Repco. So if any Australian-made car less than fifteen years old ever missed the turn and ploughed through the League's plate glass window, it had a better than even chance of connecting with the very bloke who had spot-welded its front assembly into place.

I locked the Renault, a purely symbolic gesture in this neighbourhood, and walked inside. The League's front office consisted of two dented filing cabinets, an ancient Gestetner mimeograph machine, probably the last in captivity, and three battered desks.

Paperwork trays overflowed with forms and documents and handbooks from various government departments and philanthropic organisations. Posters from the local screen print co-op covered the walls, creating an atmosphere of embattled engagement that not even the damp seeping upwards from the threadbare linoleum could dispel.

A cluster of men was hunkered down around one of the desks, men with faces that were maps of a wide brown land. But not this wide brown land. Not yet anyway. At their centre was Sivan the Kurd.

I didn't know then, and still don't, if you can tell a Kurd from a Turk by looking at him. But for my money Sivan was everything you could have wanted in a manifestation of that proud and embattled race. He had the beak of an eagle, shoulders built for bandoliers, a torso the size of Asia Minor and a crop of grizzled stubble that had me reaching self-consciously for my own lame thirty-hour growth.

He made a rumbling noise, a thick geological growl that began deep inside and came erupting out his toothy grin. "Murray, my friend." His arm swept wide. "Meet Sayfeddin, Gokhan, Bulent."

A good head for names was indispensable in my line of work, standing at a politician's shoulder refreshing her memory. But to my unending dismay, Turkish names could rarely find purchase on my mnemonics. Greeks I could do — they were all Jim or Con or Nick. Italians, no problem, even since the Johnnies and Joes had taken to reverting to Giovanni and Giuseppe. And no one ever got fired for calling an Arab Mohammed. It was bound to be in there somewhere. Unless he was a Christian, in which case George or Tony was usually a safe bet. But Gokhan? Bull ant? Sayfeddin? Say what?

"Merhaba," I mumbled. Yassou. Ciao. Howdy doody. This I could do in a full range of community languages, including Maltese, but I'm a great believer in the unifying influence of English, so that was as fluent as I was going to get.

"Merhaba," they all replied, looking at me expectantly.

I cocked my head towards the back of the building. "Ayisha in?" I wanted a quiet chat, not to go live-to-air on Radio Istanbul.

Sivan indicated a narrow corridor opening in the back wall of the room. "Girl mechanic today."

The corridor was lined with tourist posters of the Bosphorus and newspaper photographs of heads that looked like they belonged on the banknotes of some very foreign currency indeed. I found Ayisha kneeling on the floor of an office that was a smaller, pokier version of the one out front, her head buried in the innards of an antique photocopier. Bits of machinery were spread in an arc on the floor around her backside. She had her back to the door and didn't see me arrive.

Her hair was wrapped in a scarf, and as she reached purposefully behind her for some part or other, her hands black with toner powder, she looked for all the world like a Heroine of Labour resolutely overfulfilling her norm for Xerox repair under the first Five Year Plan. My heart clenched itself into a fist. Forward to the World October, it silently shouted.

I had been leaning against the door frame, silently admiring her industry, for nearly a minute when she pulled her head out of the machine's interior and sprung me. "Jeeze, Murray," she said. "What are you perving at?"

A question very much to the point. I felt heat spread across my cheeks. "That name I mentioned yesterday," I countered quickly. "Find anything out?"

"Nearly scared the shit out of me," she said. "Sneaking about like that." Clearly, she had forgotten to ask. She stood up, demonstratively kneed the photocopier door shut, and palmed the print button. The machine whirred and began ejaculating copies. "You all right?" She came right up to me and stared at my face, deliberately much too close for comfort.

I tried to hold her gaze. "Just a few scratches, that's all. It's not contagious or anything."

"Those faction fights can get pretty rough, I hear." She patted a sooty palm against my cheek. I felt myself flush under the smear of graphite. It was a wonder she didn't get third-degree burns.

I stepped back abashed, and cracked the back of my head on the door frame. "You should have seen the other guy."

Suddenly a hand clamped down on my shoulder from behind and spun me round. "Trying to seduce Ayisha, eh?"

It was Sivan. He must have been reading my mail. "It is useless," he said. "Many have tried, all have failed."

"Get stuffed," said Ayisha. She plonked herself down behind her desk and started rolling a grubby cigarette. "Murray here wants to know about some guy he thought we might know. Name of . . ."

"Ekrem Bayraktar."

Sivan repeated the name, rolling it around in his mouth like he was making concrete out of it. "Bayraktar means he who carries the flag, the standard bearer." Sivan had been a schoolteacher before the army tore up his diploma and poked matches under his fingernails. What he was saying was all very interesting, but I wanted lowdown, not etymology.

"You heard of him?"

Sivan shook his head.

"What about any of these guys?" I handed him the payroll list.

He ran a hairy finger down the names, turned to Ayisha and broke into a broad grin. "He wants to know if we have heard of Nasreddin Hoca."

A sly twinkle crossed Ayisha's face. She caught me watching and dipped her head to light her sooty fag. I didn't want her thinking I was a complete drongo. "The parable of the walnut," I said, quick as a flash. I pointed to the name underneath. "What about this guy, Gazanfer Bilge?" Rhymed with pilfer.

Him, Sivan knew. "Wrestler," he rumbled. "Very famous in the nineteen fifties. You know Turkish wrestling? First they put oil on their bodies and . . ." He advanced, arms spread, intent on demonstrating a key grip. I fended him off with the next name. "Orhan Gencebay. That Turkish?"

Sivan froze in mid-stride. He rolled the list into a tube and waved it about in front of his mouth. *"Bir tesselli ver,"* he wailed, his voice weirdly high and strangulated. *"Yaradanin askina."* He swayed from side to side and with his free hand pounded a beat on the edge of the desk.

I rolled my eyes towards Ayisha. She didn't know what was going on either. Sivan threw his arms wide and changed languages, holding the same tune. *"Everybody make mistakes,"* he sang.

I got it now. "Singer?"

"Bingo," he said. "Tom Jones. Molly Meldrum." He ironed the paper microphone flat on the surface of the desk and dropped back into pedagogic mode. "You know Turkish music? The saz is similar to the bazouki, the drum is called darbooka, the . . ."

"Kartal Tibet." I snatched up the list and read the next name. "Let me guess, husband of the famous Donna Kebab."

"Close," said Ayisha. "Movie actor, I think. Before my time. More Sivan's vintage." Sivan was all of thirty-five.

"Commercial crap," said Sivan. "Do you know the films of Yilmaz Guney? For example, *The Herd*?"

A mythical sage, an oily athlete, a pop singer, a film star. The early shift at Pacific Pastoral was beginning to look a little top-heavy with talent. I interrupted Sivan's discourse on modern Turkish cinema. "Ever heard of a place called the Anatolia Club."

Sivan stopped talking and gave Ayisha a very strange look. "Oh, very bad place, my friend," he growled. "You should not go there."

"Why? What is it?"

Before he could answer, Gokhan — or was it Sayfeddin — burst through the door. He said something terse in Turkish, a harsh sounding phrase, then abruptly turned and disappeared.

"Shit." Ayisha was on her feet, slinging her bag across her shoulder.

"What?"

She came round the desk, chewing her bottom lip, and took off out the door. My entrails turned to iced water and I took off after her. She shot out the front door like a rocket, turned left and sped up the footpath.

A burly, hard-faced man in a military-style jacket was standing beside the Renault, resting a jack-booted foot provocatively on the front bumper. He was levering up the blade of my windscreen wiper. "Hey," I demanded. "What do you think you're doing?"

He turned and lazily raked me with cold contemptuous eyes, sure of his own power. Then he slowly raised his arm and pointed back over my shoulder. Without looking, I knew what he was pointing at. CLEARWAY, the sign beside me read, 4:30-6:00 P.M.

"Fair go, mate," I pleaded, staring in disbelief at my watch. 4:32, it said. He thrust a pink piece of paper into my hand. Pay the City of Coburg forty dollars, it said. Or else. Further up the street Ayisha opened the door of a newish metallic-blue Laser. She waved gaily and drove off, scot free.

A line of trams was backed up along the centre of the road, leaving the Renault blocking the only other northbound lane. As far back as I could see, traffic sat stalled, horns blazing. For the briefest moment I considered leaving the car where it was and going back inside to ask Sivan what he had been about to say about the Anatolia Club. The Grey Ghost tapped his behaviour modification pad against his thigh. "I'd shift it," he said nastily. "If I was you."

I took my time, rolling the parking ticket into a ball as I went. I slammed the door, gunned the engine, pulled out around the nose of the tram, threw an illegal u-turn in the face of the oncoming traffic, stuck my arm out the window, gave the by-laws Nazi the finger, hit the gas, and burned rubber. It wasn't forty dollars worth, but it was consolation of sorts.

Up to that point, you'd have to admit, I had been doing pretty well in the amateur sleuth stakes. In barely four hours not only had I confirmed that industrial action was unlikely at Pacific Pastoral, but I had established that something dodgy was going on in the vicinity of their payroll, and that there was more to this dead bloke Bayraktar than met the eye.

So as I parked behind the electorate office and slipped in the back door, I must confess to feeling as pleased with myself as a man might with a squashed-up forty dollar parking fine in his pocket. I even had enough unanswered questions to justify paying another visit to Ayisha's office fairly soon.

Back in my cubicle, I found things exactly as I had left them. The same overflowing in-tray, the inevitable yellow pile of phone message slips, the same tattooed oaf sitting in my visitor's chair with his size twelves parked on the walnut veneer.

Our more troublesome sort of customers usually got bored after a couple of hours of the cold shoulder and took their grievances elsewhere. Two full days was a new record. Not that I told Mr. Adam F. Ant that. He might have taken it for encouragement. Instead I pretended he wasn't there, sat down and dug out the Pacific Pastoral file. Without the coroner's envelope all it held was a single sheet of paper with Herb Gardiner's name written on it. I added the payroll list and ticked off the four names I knew for sure were phonies.

There were any number of reasons why someone might work under a false name. Minimising tax on a second job was one. Holding down a paying job while pulling the dole was another. Illegal immigrants did it. All you had to do, after all, was fill in a false tax-declaration form and put some bogus details no-one would ever check on the personnel department sheet. Half the uni students in the country were doing it, including some majoring in Ethics. Shit, I'd done it myself a dozen years before, signed on for bar work as F. Engels. It was a bad undergraduate joke, made worse by the fact that I kept forgetting to answer to the name Fred. Not that the boss gave a toss, long as the job got done.

But this was different. One fictitious name was unremarkable. Two would have been a coincidence. Four or more, all of the same ethnic persuasion as the foreman, suggested an altogether different kettle of calamari. Either Bayraktar was turning a blind eye to the legal niceties on behalf of a clutch of his compatriots, or stuffing the odd bit of stray beef up his overalls was not the only means he had found to diddle Pacific Pastoral.

Of course, neither the internal financial administration of Pacific Pastoral nor the affairs of the deceased Bayraktar were any of my business. But things were now developing a momentum of their own at a level well below the threshold of rational thought. An idle mind, as the Brothers used famously to say. Curiosity had me by the short and curlies.

I picked up the phone and dialled Wageline, a telephone service operated by the Labour Ministry to provide information on award wages and conditions. The going rate for a part-time casual labourer in the meat industry was nine dollars eighty an hour. I did some rapid arithmetic on the inside cover of the file. Nine dollars eighty times forty hours equalled close to four hundred dollars. Less tax, I figured on a take-home pay of three twenty-five. About thirty dollars a week less than me. Not brilliant money in anyone's language.

After that, the figures were pure hypothesis. Any company operating a hand-delivered pay-packet procedure was crying out to be ripped off. Bayraktar had keys. He'd been in a position of trust. Suppose, just for argument's sake, that he'd also been in a position to add dummy names to his work team, then confirm their attendance and hours?

The four fake names were due a total of thirteen hundred dollars. Multiply that by, say, twenty-five weeks a year and the figure totalled somewhere in the neighbourhood of thirty-two thousand dollars, a very attractive part of the world. Even if the fiddle was only being worked one week in four, it was still a nice little earner. All in cash, in handy buff envelopes.

What gave this conjecture enormous appeal was not only the possibility that a barely literate migrant was sticking it up snotty-nosed Lionel Merricks to the tune of many thousands of dollars, but that he was doing it using names equivalent to Friar Tuck, Brute Bernard, Frank Sinatra and Robert Redford. If it was true, this Bayraktar deserved a posthumous industry award for having more front than a well-known city emporium.

Diverting as I found all this conjecture, it wasn't plugging the hole in my roof. I closed the file, tossed it on top of the ever-increasing mound that was my in-tray, shot Adam Ant a filthy look, and turned my attention to the swatch of phone messages that had accumulated on my blotter since the previous morning.

Most of the little yellow slips logged calls from missed appointments. Three were from Agnelli. These I threw in the bin. Two were call-backs from roofing companies. The first was engaged. The second, A-OK Allweather, couldn't have been more obliging. A very chatty woman made sympathetic noises, took my particulars and offered to send a man round to assess the situation at my earliest convenience. I suggested seven that evening, asked Ant to switch the light off before he left, and was out the back door before Trish even noticed I'd been there.

As I settled into the traffic flow I began to hum a tune that had lodged in my brain and wouldn't go away. *"Bir tesselli ver,"* I crooned. I was sure I had the pronunciation right. But I couldn't for the life of me remember what it meant.

10

TUESDAY NIGHTS meant something special for us Whelan boys. To be precise, it meant the Manager's Special at the Bell Street Pizza Hut. Hawaiian Slice with extra pineapple plus the All-You-Can-Eat Dessert Bar for only $5.95. Lucky me, eh?

The cocktail hour crowd was thin, a handful of birthday revellers in paper hats with balloons tied to the backs of their chairs. "Grade Ones," Red sneered dismissively as we slid into our usual booth with its panoramic view of the car park. The party table were tourists all right, lowering the tone of the joint. But to give them their due they had brought their mothers along, some of whom were a bit more interesting to look at than the artificial stag fern that constituted Mr. Hut's idea of decor.

The mumsie crowd, faces half-familiar from the schoolyard gate, were jammed into a booth against the far wall, smoking, drinking white wine, and laughing too loud. When Red and I came in they looked up and watched us cross the floor and I nodded a tentative hello in their general direction. They nodded back and returned to their conversation.

One of them, a red-headed looker in the early Bette Midler mould with satellite dish earrings, held my gaze for several seconds longer than was absolutely necessary. A fellow single parent, no doubt about it. The idea that she was probably wondering who had attacked my face with a Whipper Snipper failed to occur to me.

Anyway, just as I slid my backside in next to Red and my eyes motherhoodward, my line of sight was obstructed by an adolescent waitress in a red and white pants suit that made her look like a piece of boiled confectionery. She thrust a laminated menu into my hand and in a single breath intoned that if our order did not arrive within five minutes we would not have to pay.

"Starting when?" said Red.

My heart went out to the poor girl. Some hormonal eruption had given her face the texture of a coconut macaroon. Being forced to dress up in a ludicrous corporate costume was humiliating enough without having to cop lip from every smartarse seven-year-old that walked through the door.

I elbowed Red in the ribs and ordered our usual. The instant the words departed my lips, Red whipped his sleeve back and locked in on the dial of his precision-engineered four-dollar digital timepiece. I left him to it and sauntered over to the pay phone near the door, taking the long way around, as close as plausibly possible to the group of women. The redhead looked up and gave me the eye. True, I swear it.

I fed the phone and dialled Greg Coates at Immigration and Ethnic Affairs. It was just on six, past office hours, but Coates hadn't got to be a Dep. Dir. by flexing off at 4:52. He answered on the second ring. I threw him a speedy pleasantry and cut to the chase. "Do us a favour," I said. "Punch up a name for me on that computer of yours."

Coates must have been on his way out the door. "Can't it wait until tomorrow?"

Sure it could. But that wasn't the point. It wasn't as though I was asking for the world. All he had to do was tap a few keys and he'd be through to the departmental database in a nanosecond. If some anonymous global corporation that didn't know me from Adam could commit itself to delivering my pizza in less than five minutes, surely Greggy-boy could bend over his desk and press a couple of buttons for me. Aside from which, standing at the phone gave me a much clearer view of you know who. I gave Coates a gentle reminder about the nature of mateship. "You still running for the state admin. committee?" I asked.

Party rules stipulated that a member attend at least three branch meetings a year to remain current. Thus far Coates' total for the year was exactly zero. Not that there was anything unusual about that. If the attendance rules were enforced, half the office bearers in the party would have been out of a job. The reason they weren't was because they had mates like me, branch secretaries who made sure their names went down on the roll, show or no. It was the sort of thing mates did for each other. Like looking up the odd file.

"No need to get stroppy," Coates said. "What's the name?"

"Bayraktar," I said. "Ekrem." I gave him what little detail I had from the coroner's file and listened while he made some keyboard noises.

"While you're here," he said. "What's your little pal Agnelli up to? He's been working the phones in a major way, I hear, but I can't get a word out of anyone he's been talking to."

Typical Agnelli. Having sworn me to secrecy on his hot election tip, here he was blabbing it to half the town. And since when had he been my little pal? I started telling Coates what Agnelli had said about the early election, and a blaze of sparklers hurtled past my shoulder. The waitress plonked a spluttering cake in the middle of the Grade Ones and a ragged chorus of "Happy Birthday" twittered across the restaurant. The redhead, bending misty-eyed over the birthday girl, glanced upwards. Our gazes locked. No doubt about it, I was in with a chance.

"Access denied," Coates said.

"What?"

"Access denied, that's what it says on screen. I got a folio number, so this bloke's in the system, but I can't call the file up."

This was interesting. "Why not?"

"Dunno. Probably just a software stuff-up."

Computer talk was all double-dutch to me. More likely Coates was sticking it up me for getting shirty on him. Fair enough. "I'll try again in the morning," he offered. "If that's soon enough for you."

By the time I got back to the table Red had all but demolished the pizza. "Four minutes and thirty-two seconds," he said dismally. You'd have thought it was him who was paying.

The last of the birthday crowd was straggling out into the rapidly gathering dark with their lolly bags and balloons. I sent Red over to the dairy-whip dispenser and ambled nonchalantly over to where the birthday girl and her mother were packing presents into a shopping bag. Mumsie was about thirty, obviously a child bride. Close up, the red of her hair was shot with henna, an affectation from which I took strange encouragement.

"Hi," I started in. "I've seen you at the school, haven't I? I'm Red's dad." I indicated the fruit of my loins, who was engrossed in constructing a half-scale model of Mount Kilimanjaro out of aerated dairy fat.

Henna-head smiled and nodded. So far, so good. "This is Alice," she said. Alice looked like a proper little miss. Her mother had a squeaky little voice that sounded like a cheap fountain pen signing a bad cheque. Still, conversation wasn't the only thing I had in mind. I gave the brat a courtly bow. "Happy birthday, Alice." A few short years out of circulation, I thought, and I'm reduced to this.

Alice took one look and bolted. "Daddy, Daddy," she screamed. Daddy was coming through the door in a camel-hair overcoat and striped scarf, a tenured sociologist or a freelance travel journalist by the look of it. He gave torch-head the kind of self-deprecating look that women seem to go for. "Darling," she trembled.

I scuttled over to the dessert bar and fiddled with the sno-cone dispenser. From the icy mirror of its stainless steel my face stared back at me, bathed in sweaty condensation. A face like a freshly ploughed field. The face of a man who had just made an inept play for a married woman in a Pizza Hut at six-thirty on a Tuesday evening, stone cold sober. "Phew," I told it. "That was close."

"Sure was," it replied and watched me pull myself a comforting big bowl of sugared gloop.

Red sidled up beside me. "Nuts," he said. "No nuts." So that was the problem. We took All We Could Eat back to our booth and I watched Red eat one-handed while he did the puzzles printed on his place mat. Join the Dots. Spot the Mistake. Between scoops of ice-cream he gnawed the end of his pencil and furiously scratched his head. "Want to hear a riddle?" he asked. "What's white and bites and lives in your head?"

I made like it took some figuring out. "Teeth?" I hazarded.

Red crowed. "Ha, ha. Wrong. Guess again."

I guessed all right, amazed I hadn't thought of it before. That crawling in my scalp earlier in the day at the meatworks definitely hadn't been unconscious revulsion. Grabbing Red's head I shoved him cheek-down onto the laminex. He fought for a second, then went limp, resigned to humiliation. I pinned his head in place and ferreted through his hair. Within seconds I found the first of the tiny white specks. "Nits," I hissed.

Jesus wept, how had I not noticed them before? All that scratching in the night. And if Red had them, I had them too. We'd been sleeping in the same bed all winter. We paid the bill, went out into the drizzle and headlights, spent thirty minutes finding an all-hours pharmacy where we could buy flea shampoo for double the recommended retail price, and drove home to our dark and damp house. As we turned into the street, the seven o'clock news came on the radio and a flat-bed truck with A-OK Allweather painted on the door passed us going in the opposite direction.

I put Red in the bath with a foaming halo of toxic dioxins, stuffed the washing machine full of bedsheets and tipped in half a bottle of Pine-O-Cleen. Then I changed into a pair of old jeans and a moth-eaten jumper and braced myself to climb the ladder into the roof. Rain had been falling off and on for most of the preceding twenty-four hours and I guessed at least some of it had found its way past my makeshift plug.

That's when I noticed that the lounge room ceiling had changed colour. It used to be an off-white. Now it was a pale tan, the exact shade a milk arrowroot biscuit turns when you dunk it into a cup of steaming hot tea. Worse, it had developed a slight but distinct droop. Wrestling the kitchen table into the centre of the room, I put a chair on top, climbed aboard, reached up and pressed the palm of my hand against the surface of the plaster at the point where it sagged lowest. It felt clammy, but firm. I pushed gently upwards. The plaster strained back against my hand. Right then, Red started screaming from the bathroom at the top of his lungs that he had shampoo in his eyes and unless I rushed in and removed it instantly he would go permanently blind.

Judging by the weight, my ceiling now housed an undercover aquatic recreation facility deep enough to drown a small mammal. But not for long. The exploratory pressure of my palm, slight as it felt, was sufficient to produce an immediate effect on the precarious hydraulic dynamics of the situation. The exact amount of water and sodden plaster that fell on top of my head at that point may never be known. It felt like a lot. And it hit me hard enough to tilt me off balance. I flailed out, looking for my equilibrium, and found the cable holding the ceiling light pendant.

It was handy, but I don't think it had been designed to be swung from. A blue spark jumped, a pop and a fizzle sounded, and the entire house was plunged into darkness. By then I was flat on my back on the floor, the light fixture in shattered pieces beside me, gungy water dripping into my open, stunned-mullet mouth.

The very moment this happened, Red's sight was miraculously restored. Being a clever kid, he immediately noticed that the lights had gone out and, lest this fact escape his rather dim father, decided to bring it to my attention. "Dad, Dad," he called. "Dad. The lights have gone out. Dad, Dad."

At that point the phone began to ring. General de Gaulle, it is said, permitted no telephone within earshot of his office in the Elysée Palace. Not for him the presumptuous summons of some anonymous jangling bell. I wished I had his singlemindedness. I stumbled through the blackness, dripping and twitching like a half-drowned Labrador, following the siren wail of Red's voice.

"Dad, Dad," he was chanting. "Dad. The phone's ringing. Dad, Dad."

"Shut the fuck up," I screamed reassuringly in the general direction of my only child as I grabbed the phone. Long distance pips sounded. Either it was the prime minister calling to offer me a place in Cabinet or Wendy calling from Canberra.

"Oh, it's you," said Wendy.

I took a deep breath, shook a couple of litres of filthy water out of my sleeve and counted to five. "Red's in the bath," I wheezed, calmness itself. "I'll get him to call you when he gets out, if you'll still be there." Meaning the office, the flat, wherever she was calling from. A busy woman is always on the hop.

"What do you mean, if I'm here? You're the one who's never there."

"What do you mean, never here? Never where?" It was all going swimmingly, so far.

"Don't worry about it," she said in a tone that meant I should do precisely that. "I know how much he enjoys his bath." Unlike his cruel father who would drag him out at a moment's notice to come to the phone. "Tell him I'll see him on Thursday. I'll be down for a few days for the Construction of Gender Reference Group. And maybe you and I should have a bit of a talk then, too."

"We're talking now, aren't we?"

"You know what I mean."

I guessed I did.

"You've got to think about Red," she added, gratuitously. Was I right in imagining the Methodist Ladies College was resurfacing in her voice, that censorious interrogative at the end of sentences? "And don't worry, I'll be staying at Mum's."

So, it was out in the open at last. "Okay," I said meekly. Let her think I was ready to throw in the towel even before the fight began, that was my strategy. Then when the bell rang, come out fighting.

Wendy was booked on a two o'clock flight and told me she'd go straight to Red's school to pick him up. That's what she thought. Let Red out of my sight and the next time I'd see him would be on a monthly access visit.

I lit a candle and inspected the damage. As well as the roof problem, I now had a gaping hole in my lounge room ceiling and a severely shorted-out lighting circuit. Nothing that several thousand dollars I didn't have couldn't fix. I took the candle into the bathroom, stripped off my clothes, climbed into the tub and sank my fingers into Red's scalp, rubbing until their tips were numb and both of us were limp with hysterical exhaustion. "Mum will be here the day after tomorrow," I said.

"I know."

"She wants you to stay in Canberra with her."

"I know."

Knowledgeable little bugger. I wondered what else he knew, but decided to leave well enough alone, for the time being at least.

We sat on the edge of the big bed wrapped in towels and he let me comb the dead nits out of his hair by the light of a lamp plugged into the power circuit. Half an hour of nit-picking produced a dozen white pinheads, a couple of dead insects and a child as limber as a rag doll. I engineered Red into his pyjamas, slipped him into the freshly made bed and waited quietly until he was abducted by the sandman. His locks, drying around his drowsy face in corkscrew ringlets, gave him the aspect of a Botticelli cherub.

I took my own scarified dial out into the black hole that was the laundry, rubbed some of the creosote-smelling flea wash into my scalp, pulled on some clean-dirty clothes and went to work.

Navigating by the light coming in the window from old Mrs. Bagio's sleepout next door, I rolled the lounge room rug into a squelching cylinder. It was a tribal kilim, a little something Wendy had picked up in India, way before my time. I dragged it to the back door and pitched it into the yard, managing to snap off her *Grevillea robusta* at ground level into the bargain. Then I used newspapers to mop up the grimy dribble trickling down from above. I did this somewhat reluctantly as the only papers I could find were several dozen back copies of the *National Times* and the *Guardian Weekly* I had been warehousing against the day I got a federal grant to catch up on my reading.

Take my tip. Never use the *Guardian* for this sort of work. The flimsy airmail paper has practically no absorbency. The *National Times,* on the other hand, would soak up practically anything. It was a pity to waste them and I worked slowly, giving the copy the quick once-over in the candlelight as I reluctantly discarded the pages, catching up on a couple of Royal Commissions as I went.

The worst of the wet was just soaking into a ten-page piece on the roots of monogamy when a feature in the finance section from the previous July caught my eye. The article was headed "Darlings of the Market." It was a safe bet that this did not refer to the Trash 'n' Treasure conducted at the Coburg Drive-In every third Sunday. Below the headline was a row of photographs of well-barbered male faces sporting expressions that suggested butter might safely be stored in their mouths. Among them was a head I recognised from earlier that morning when I had seen it attached to the body of Lionel Merricks. I took the paper over to the window and held it up to the light.

Lionel Merricks, according to the introductory blurb, was one of the new breed of knock-'em-down drag-'em-out financiers who were cutting a dash through the currency desks with their bold visions of an untrammelled tomorrow. Spread across two pages were illustrated profiles of Lionel and his fellow high rollers, the text even more gushing than the crap coming out of my ceiling. I don't know what these guys were doing for the economy, but they excited the hell out of the media. Normally I gave this sort of thing a wide berth. But, now that I knew one of these objects of veneration personally, I read on, fascinated.

Young Lionel, it said, had displayed early promise, making book for the upper sixth at Grammar before doing his patriotic stint as a naval supply officer. A blurry photo illustrated this moment, Lionel all white socks and knobbly knees. Barely out of uniform and here he was, the up-and-coming executive, a divisional GM at Ayers Land and Livestock, back before they merged with ICU Resources to form Pacific Pastoral. Here was the mature Lionel coming aboard the board, here Lucky Lionel in the chair. Finally here were Lionel's visionary plans to haul the ladder up after him and flog off those components of the company currently encumbered by the tiresome necessity of actually growing, making or trading things. The time had come, he declared, to concentrate on the basics. What, I wondered, was more basic than killing animals and cutting them up for food?

Only towards the end of the page did a sour note intrude. The speed of Pacific Pastoral's asset rationalisation, warned the last paragraph, might be hampered by market concerns at the threat to the value of its meat export operations posed by . . . continued on page 47.

Page forty-seven was a sodden mass, somewhere underfoot, lost in the dark. I searched for it briefly and gave up. Finance was beyond me, and the increasing frequency with which we were bombarded with updates on Dow Jones and the All-Ordinaries had done nothing to enlighten me. Three billion, six billion, nine point eight billion. The press was full of these incomprehensible figures. All it appeared to take to be hailed as a major player was to pick a digit, stick a dollar sign in front of it, add a long row of zeros and wait for the applause.

Some financial wizard, this Merricks. An Anatolian fatso who could barely sign his own name had, in all probability, been tickling his till to the tune of two grand a week and hadn't even been noticed. But that was the point though, wasn't it? Not noticing. All the puny fiddles of all the world's Ekrem Bayraktars would never amount to more than a drop in the vast ocean of moolah that Captain Merricks and his crew of Old Grammarians blithely sailed upon.

And if the Premier, Agnelli, Charlene or anyone else thought they could quietly slip aboard the good ship Big Bucks and run their social agenda up the mast when nobody was looking, they were flattering themselves. Merricks and the rest of his class were no fools. They'd been repelling boarders since back before their great-grandfathers had sailed through the Heads with an axe in one hand

and a blank title deed in the other. From high in their glass towers, they could see us coming a mile away.

I dropped Lionel Merricks face first into a damp patch and climbed up into the roof for a spot of damage control. The overalls, heavy with rainwater, had fallen out and knocked over the bucket, possibly as far back as the night before. Using rags and plastic bags I made the best of a bad job, trusting in luck, a change in the weather and the speedy return of A-OK Allweather. Afterwards, I stood in the dark with my head in the laundry tub and washed the parasites out of my hair. Then I went to bed and read *Understanding Family Law* until the words began to blur together, blew out the candle, rolled over and parked my lustful dromedary in the caravanserai of dreams.

11

TWO UNIFORMED COPPERS, one male, one female, with the faces of twelve-year-olds and big revolvers jammed next to their kidneys, were standing at Trish's desk when I pushed the office door open the next morning. During the night someone had prised the bars off the outside of the bathroom window, smashed the glass, climbed in and ransacked the joint. Why they bothered to do this beggared the imagination. The most valuable items in the place were the photo-copier and a four-drawer filing cabinet, both of which were still sit-ting against the wall beside Trish's desk.

The only thing missing was the petty cash tin, containing a dozen thirty-seven cent stamps and an IOU from the week before when I'd raided it for lunch money. Total value twelve dollars.

"Anything else?" said the girl cop, doodling details onto a trip-licate incident sheet. I went up the back to count my paperclips. Everything on my desk had been bulldozed into a heap on the floor, the drawers rifled and my wastepaper basket upended. By the look of it, nothing was missing. Worse luck.

"You think it's politically motivated?" the boy cop said.

"It's got Baader-Meinhof written all over it," I said.

"Kids, most likely, then," he agreed.

Well it wasn't the gang from Mensa, that was for sure. It took me a full minute to work out that the thing drawn on the toilet mirror was a dick. While I was still standing there in a pile of broken glass, who should walk in but Adam Fucking Ant. He put a toolbox on the toilet seat and began slipping new panes of reinforced glass into the louvre slots.

"What's he still doing here?" I went out and asked Trish.

"Making himself a damned sight more useful than you," she said and stuffed a fresh batch of phone messages into my paw. Declining to rise to this bait, I went back to my cubicle and rummaged through the mess on the floor until I found the yellow slip from the day before with A-OK Allweather's number. I dialled, hoping that last night's little timing glitch had not put me in bad odour with them. They were engaged. So was the other mob. No sooner had I hung up than the phone rang. Guess who?

"Well?" said Agnelli.

By that stage, considering the more pressing domestic disasters I was battling, any lingering curiosity about Ekrem Bayraktar and the goings-on at Pacific Pastoral had well and truly evaporated.

"Just like I said it would be," I told Agnelli. "Nothing to connect Lollicato to anyone at the Coolaroo plant. And even if there was, industrially the place is as dead as a dodo. On top of which nobody out there has a good word for the dead bloke, who by the way was probably on the fiddle in at least two different directions at once. In short, a total fucking waste of time. All of which will be in an appropriately worded report on your desk at the close of play today, as promised. End of story. Full stop."

Predictably, Agnelli had to put up a fight. "Half a day, Murray, is not what you might call an exhaustive approach to the issue."

I got down on my hands and knees on the floor and began searching the desk debris for the Pacific Pastoral file. If I could find that list of bogus names — Gherkin Marzipan, Cartoon Niblet and the rest of them — I could send Agnelli off chasing his own tail around the Trades Hall while I got on with the more urgent task of repairing my near-derelict hacienda.

"And what about the funeral?" Agnelli was saying.

"What?" I was buggered if I could find the bloody folder.

"Dead bloke's funeral. Mood of the crowd and so forth, always a good indicator in this sort of case." Agnelli sounded like he'd been watching too much television. The idea was bizarre.

I had six months worth of paperwork spread out across the carpet tiles by this stage. Still I couldn't find the fucking file. Worse, I was starting to listen to Agnelli. And that, believe you me, is never a good idea. "Who did they release the body to?"

"Stuffed if I know," said Agnelli. "Family, I suppose."

As far as I knew from the coroner's documents there wasn't one. "Who's doing the honours?"

"Martinelli."

"I thought Martinelli only did Italians."

"Martinelli will bury anyone. Believe me, mate," he said. As if he'd know. "It's listed for ten at Fawkner. Call me back afterwards and we can discuss the report then."

That's what he thought. Personally speaking, I had better things to do with my time than go tramping about a cemetery in the rain looking for a scene out of a social realist movie. Things like getting my desk back into some sort of order and finding a roofer and an electrician. I was thumbing through the phone book with exactly that in mind when there was a knock at the partition and Xenophon Xypnitos from the community health centre came in and opened his briefcase.

This appointment had been in my diary for a month, so there was no getting out of it. On top of which Trish's crack about my recent absence had been quite correct. It was about time I got back to doing what I was being paid for. In this case it meant reviewing the terms of reference for a survey of projected needs in the provision of health services to the aged. Charlene had swung the funding and the consultants were being paid a small fortune, the sort of money you don't fork over unless you know the results in advance. I got up off the floor, apologised for the mess and started talking service delivery.

By the time Xenophon closed his briefcase it was just about to go ten. Fawkner Cemetery was only a kilometre or two up the road.

I rang Martinelli's funeral home and commemorative chapel and got directions to the plot. The interment, as they called it, was imminent. Questions about who was paying for it were politely deflected.

Before I left I quickly drafted the final version of my report to MACWAM, concluding that there was no evidence of incipient industrial action at the Pacific Pastoral plant. I gave it to Trish to type and put in the internal courier. If Agnelli thought I was going to spend any more time on this crap than absolutely necessary, he was mistaken.

The outlook that Wednesday was for showers, with fresh to strong westerly winds ahead of a change, a gale warning for the bays, and a sheep weather alert in southern and mountain districts. I didn't have any sheep worth alerting. I took my collapsible umbrella instead. Three blocks up the highway a sign read Mulqueen and Sons, Funeral Directors. Underneath it said *Provinciale Servizio Italiano*. Weren't the Irish dying fast enough? Or were they all dead already? They might as well be. Once upon a time party and union rolls in this town read like the Ballymalarkey baptismal register and the sons of Erin cut some ice. But those days were long gone, thanks to the Church and the Left and about a thousand boatloads of Thracians and Piedmontese.

An arrow said Necropolis Next Left. A nice democratic town, Necroburg. Catholics, Orthodox, Muslims, Christadelphians, all bedded down together in the sprawling suburbs of the dead. Along Box Forest Road, the forest of yellow boxes long replaced by the tin sheds of cut-price monumental masons, I found what I was looking for. In a muddy paddock backing onto the railway line a silver-grey Martinelli hearse was drawn up beside the customary dark rectangle. Two pallbearers sat in the cabin catching a quick puff before the mourners arrived.

A singularly dismal sight it would have been, too, if not for an incongruous splash of colour against the yellow clay of the earth. Draped over the coffin was a piece of scarlet fabric. A flag. A red flag. The people's flag of deepest red. That which shrouded oft our martyred dead. On top of the flag was a modest wreath of white carnations. It looked like Agnelli was right, the union would be bunging it on in no uncertain terms.

I cruised once more around the little ring-road and fell in with a cortege just arriving at the grassy area opposite. I parked unnoticed in clear view of the Bayraktar plot. A light drizzle began falling and the pallbearers got into the cabin of the hearse. I turned off my engine and waited.

Teardrops of vapour emerged out of the mist forming on the inside of the windscreen, swelled, and tumbled slowly downwards. I wound down my window and the sound of weeping women came softly across the lawn beside me. Short vertical lengths of pipe had been sunk into the grass to make recessed vases. Here and there, little posies of mixed flowers sprouted straight up out of the turf, cellophane and all. Gradually it came to me that this was where they buried the children. I quickly looked away.

A car had pulled up over near the hearse and two men were getting out. I knew immediately they were not union officials. For a start their clothes fitted them properly, expensive-looking overcoats protecting well-cut suits. Also, the car was a recent model BMW, sleek in the rain. The two were heavy set, and crossed the field of mud with a business-like sense of purpose. There was no doubt that they were compatriots of the deceased. Rather well-heeled ones by the look of the togs and the wheels.

The Martinelli crew had dumped their fags and settled into postures of respectful solicitude by the time the pair reached the graveside. Muted words were exchanged and heads bobbed all round. I bent forward and wiped a hole in the condensation. The pallbearers withdrew a little and the two dark-haired men stood together and faced the coffin, their backs to me. Then, and this part really made me sit up and take notice, they snapped to attention and executed a couple of brisk, well-practised military salutes. They stood like that, elbows rigid, immobile in the soft rain, for perhaps fifteen seconds.

Then, as if at an invisible signal, the arms descended and the shorter one bent and picked the white carnation wreath up off the casket. He handed it up to his companion, who read the card then tossed the whole thing like a frisbee onto the green carpet covering the mound of dirt beside the grave. Meanwhile the first guy had grabbed a handful of the flag and was hauling it towards him like a waiter changing a dirty tablecloth. As he swept the fabric into his arms, I caught a flash of white, a crescent moon and a star. Bayraktar was being laid to rest not under the ruby standard of the workers of the world, but beneath the banner of Ataturk.

The flag was swiftly folded and the coffin disappeared into the earth. The mystery men put their erect carriages into the BMW and drove away. It was all over in less than two minutes. Not exactly a state funeral, but honours of some sort, honours I was prepared to bet were not for services to humanity.

Mustapha closer look at this, I told myself. As soon as the BMW was out of sight and the Martinelli hearse had driven off, I put up my umbrella and squelched across to the hole. The box stared up at me silently, not the budget model either, by the look of the silver handles. The card on the wreath read "RIP — Management and Staff, Pacific Pastoral."

So much for family feeling. The pricks hadn't even sent someone to the funeral. The union hadn't showed either, but that was arguably grounds for relief. The first sight of that red flag had me worried, if only that Agnelli was about to be proven right. But a union like the Meaties, with probably twenty thousand blokes on the books, could hardly be expected to turn out every time a member fell off his perch. They'd never get any work done. Not that you'd notice. On the other hand, a company the size of Pacific Pastoral sending fifteen bucks worth of carnations to the interment of a man who died on the job, that was just plain lousy. It wasn't as though they knew he was ripping them off, after all. It was just plain contempt, pure and simple.

Bayraktar might have been a fat pig with sticky fingers and some pretty dodgy-looking militaristic friends, but so what? The same could be said of the federal Minister for Defence Procurements. A principle was at stake here. A man carks it *in situ*, the least the management can do is send a representative to stand at the graveside and pay the widow the courtesy of some hypocrisy, should she happen to be there. It didn't have to be the chairman of the board, that would be too much to expect. But they could have sent along the third assistant deputy under-boss. Where was Apps, that gangling streak of officiousness?

Merricks had insisted that I keep him appraised. Well, appraised he would be. Appraised of incompetence in the administration of his Coolaroo plant's payroll. Call me bloody-minded, but one member of Pacific Pastoral's management at least would be made to rue the day he hadn't taken half an hour off to whip down the highway and shed some crocodile tears over the coffin of a recently defunct employee. A quick phone call to the CEO's office describing the discrepancies I had discovered in the administration of the payroll, and the company auditors would be running their fingers through Apps' books before you could say "performance indicators."

"Headstones from $395," yelled a sandwich board at the exit. There were more pressing demands on my finances. An electrician, I figured, would set me back about sixty dollars to get the light working, which would be a lot to pay to have a fuse replaced and listen to a sales pitch about how the whole place needed rewiring. Still, if anyone was going to get electrocuted, I preferred it to be an accredited and fully insured tradesman. The cost of a new roof I didn't even want to think about, let alone the prospect of wringing half of it out of Wendy, present circumstances considered.

Rather than dwell on the ugly subject of money I did not have, I turned my thoughts to the strange obeisances I had just witnessed at Bayraktar's graveside. Some of Labor's all-but-forgotten heroes and heroines were buried here and I could imagine what they might have said if they knew foreign military types were goose-stepping among their headstones. Was that grey BMW, I wondered, the same one I had seen parked under the carport at the Anatolia Club, a place Sivan described enigmatically as somewhere to be avoided?

Since I had to pass the Turkish Welfare League anyway, it would only take a couple of extra minutes to pop in and see what light the encyclopaedic Kurd could shed on the subject. And with a bit of luck Ayisha would be there, too.

I found Sivan pinned down behind his desk, his palms spread defensively in front of his chest. "Ah, Murray, my friend." He leapt to his feet, like I was the foreign legion come to relieve the fort. "Meet Muyesser, Hatice, Huriet."

Muyesser was a classic crone in a shapeless floor-length skirt and head-scarf who looked like she'd come straight from offering Snow White a poisoned apple. Her two offsiders were younger and not as conspicuously folkloric. They were busy giving Sivan a hard time and had no intention of being taken in by his transparent diversionary ploy. They stopped their hectoring only long enough to nod in my general direction, then resumed talking over each other and waving pieces of official-looking correspondence. Somewhere in the incomprehensible torrent I clearly heard the phrase "Taxation Department."

Parked next to one of the women was a stroller out of which a toddler was attempting to writhe his way to freedom. His hair was cropped to the bone, his burning little cheeks varnished to a high gloss with fresh snot. Poor Sivan slumped back into his seat, resigned.

Better you than me, mate, I thought. This situation was a perfect example of why I was such a keen supporter of funding for the League. If Sivan hadn't been here, available to have the shit annoyed out of him in an appropriate community language, these three wicked stepsisters would have been half a mile down the road annoying the shit out of me in broken English. More better this way.

I cocked my head in the general direction of Ayisha's office and raised my eyebrows.

"With a client," Sivan semaphored over the din.

While I was waiting, I helped myself to the spare desk, dialled directory assistance and got the number for Pacific Pastoral's head office. The call bounced upwards off a series of buffers until it reached the forty-ninth floor. I could hear the well-coiffured hair of the ice queen turn at the sound of my voice, but she put me through without argument. Merricks came on briskly, the great man's time still too valuable to squander on courtesy. "Well?"

The jabber of Turkish across the room increased in volume. I stuck a finger in one ear. "Something a little outside my terms of reference has come up," I said. "But since you asked to be kept informed, I thought I should share it with you."

"Yes." Spit it out, man. Time is money.

"It concerns irregularities that have come to my attention concerning your operations at Coolaroo."

Merricks took this on board and walked it around the deck a couple of times. "Irregularities? What sort of irregularities?" His peevishness register had dropped a notch.

"I'm not an accountant, Mr. Merricks," I said blandly.

"But you are implying some sort of dishonesty?"

"As I said, I'm merely keeping you appraised of my observations," I said. And having a jolly good time of it, too.

"Look here, Whelan." The strangulated English squeak was back in Merricks' voice. "I'm beginning to have very serious reservations about this whole exercise. Is your minister aware that you have taken it upon yourself to start tossing about these sort of vague inferences?"

I'd expected the darling of the markets to greet the news that he was being diddled with some degree of scepticism, perhaps even to question my motives. But at least he could have shown a little more curiosity about what exactly it was I was alleging before issuing a barely veiled threat to dob me in to Charlene. I should have known that managerial caste loyalties always took priority. What a pompous arsehole, I thought. Stuff you, Charley.

"Listen, Lionel," I said, dropping all pretence at deference. "If you prefer I could always bring this matter directly to the attention of the appropriate authorities. Frankly I don't give a fuck either way."

Just as I was beginning to think Merricks had hung up on me, he spoke. "I understand," he said, his words measured and full of meaning.

The toddler in the stroller had given up trying to escape and was navigating his way around the room by dragging himself along the furniture. He advanced steadily towards me, hand over hand along any object within reach, blowing elastic bubbles of mucus ahead of him as he came. I fended him off with a tissue.

"Do you have a figure in mind?" Merricks was saying.

All I had was a list of Turkish celebrities, and I wasn't even sure where that was anymore. But I certainly wasn't going to tell Lionel Merricks that. I realised I should have taken the trouble to think the whole thing out before I placed the call. It was beginning to feel like a lot of trouble to go to just for the sake of getting a rocket fired up some crappy plant manager I'd only met for five minutes.

But since I was in this deep, I thought I might as well lay it on with a trowel. "Fifty thousand," I said. "Maybe more, depending on what else turns up."

"Now wait a minute." Merricks seemed to be struggling with his emotions.

It was then that the kid dragged the telephone cord out of its socket. Ripped it right off the wall, plug and all. The phone went dead in my hand. By the time I had extracted the cord from one sticky little fist and plugged it back in, all that remained of Lionel Merricks was a dial tone. Which was just as well, because one of the women had taken it upon herself to whack the wretched mite so firmly across the knuckles that the only thing Merricks would have been able to hear was a high-pitched wail. Fuck him, I thought. Merricks, not the kid.

Despite the decibels being emitted by the child, Sivan's conference with the harpies was continuing unabated. The expression "Supporting Mother's Benefit" was now cropping up with some frequency. I decided on a tactical withdrawal in the direction of Ayisha's office. The door was shut. I tapped lightly and poked my head inside. Ayisha was in professional mode, leaning intently forward on her elbows, giving her full attention to something being said in Turkish by a man in a sports coat sitting with his back to the door. "Sorry to barge in," I began.

The man stopped talking and swung around, irritated at the intrusion. He had thick curly hair and a self-important, intellectual air. I almost didn't recognise him without his shower cap and white overalls. Away from the harsh artificial light of the meat works, his face had lost its ghastly jaundice. Like this, a cheap tie knotted at his neck and a grace note of grey at his high temples, he could have been a professor of history. But no doubt about it, it was Whatsisname, the cleaner from Pacific Pastoral.

He recognised me immediately, too. And our little chat the day before had clearly made a deep impression on him. Either that or he wasn't quite the full felafel. In rapid succession, he uncrossed his knees, lurched to his feet, and stumbled backwards, knocking over his chair. His eyes filled with betrayed disbelief and began furiously darting about the room.

"Hi," I said.

The cleaner looked daggers at Ayisha. If she had any better idea than I did what was going on, she wasn't showing it. Getting no response, he came to a rapid decision. He extracted his legs from the tangle of fallen furniture, marshalled his dignity, drew himself upright and advanced towards the doorway. When he was almost on top of me, he clenched his fists and thrust his arms forward, wrists pressed together. "Yes. It was me," he cried. "I killed Bayraktar."

12

I DIDN'T KNOW whether to spit, shit, or go blind. This was a joke, right? How could this broom pusher have killed Bayraktar? He hadn't even rated a mention in the documentation. Christ, I couldn't even remember his name. "Huh?" I heard myself say.

I looked across at Ayisha, but she wasn't laughing. If anything, she had gone a little grey around the gills. I looked back at the guy in the sports coat and searched his face for some clue, some skerrick of explanation as to the meaning of these theatrics. The bland, self-effacing look that had sat so naturally across his features the day before had been replaced with an intensity that was almost incandescent. He pumped his fists forward again, insisting on being hand-cuffed.

Up the corridor behind me came the wailing of the snotty tot and the background jabber of Sivan's case work. I stepped around the door to enter the office properly, and the cleaner reeled back before me as though expecting a blow.

"Go on," he challenged. "Arrest me, Mr. Policeman."

Well, that got a laugh, thank Christ. I was beginning to think all the oxygen had been hoovered out of the room.

The laugh came from Ayisha, a high nervy snigger. Then she said something in Turkish, a curt little sentence, the immediate upshot of which was that her client suddenly looked like a horse had kicked him. The ominous glow disappeared from his eyes, replaced by a rather touching look of bewilderment. His gaze dropped to his hands, as though he now had serious doubts about their ownership. His fingers were long and fine, the skin that covered them shiny with scar tissue. He stuck them rapidly into his pockets and a single eloquent word that needed no translation escaped his lips. "Shit," he said.

Too late, pal. "You killed Bayraktar?" I said. "How?"

But the fire was dying. The man turned, hauled his chair back upright, sat down with an audible oomph, and covered his face with his hands. Ayisha came out from behind her desk, firing me a questioning look. When I shrugged she went down on one knee at the man's elbow and began whispering in Turkish. First he just sat there with his shoulders hunched, slowly shaking his head. Eventually she extracted a couple of reluctant monosyllables. She persisted, persuading him to lower his hands. Then began a hushed and insistent tide of explanation.

From the man's sideways glances I could tell that at least part of the time he was talking about me. Why they were whispering, I didn't know. I couldn't understand a word they were saying, after all. After a while I began to feel like a bit of a geek, standing there with my back to the door, so I went across and sat down behind Ayisha's desk. Whatever it was she was saying, it seemed to be doing the trick. The guy looked across at me a couple of times in a half-apologetic sort of way, like we were strangers in a pub and he'd just knocked over my beer and we were waiting for the barman to bring me another.

I still hadn't been able to shave, and my whiskers were at that stage where they itch like nobody's business. I sat there trying not to scratch, wondering what the hell was going on. Ayisha's tobacco was sitting on the desk. I opened the packet and rolled myself a cigarette to keep my hands busy. Out of solidarity with Wendy I'd given up smoking when Red was on the way, and my rolling technique was now a bit rusty. The best I could manage was a lumpy little greyhound with lots of brown threads sticking out the end.

By the time I'd finished carefully prodding the loose fibres of tobacco into place, Ayisha and the cleaner — his name was Memo, I remembered, Memo Gezen — had been whispering away in front of me forever. I was beginning to feel a little excluded. So I leaned forward on my elbows and struck a match. It flared dramatically, erupting into the tide of Turkish and bringing it to a halt. "Don't mind me," I said.

For want of an equally spectacular follow-up, I put the flame to the end of the fag and sucked in. The smoke hit deep — a dirty, forbidden, anarchic, exhilarating taste. My head spun and the tips of my fingers tingled. "Feel free to chat among yourselves," I exhaled.

Ayisha got up and sat on the edge of the desk. "It's all a misunderstanding, Murray," she said. "Memo here thought you were a cop. I've straightened him out. I told him you're okay, and you wouldn't dob him in. You won't, will you?"

If anyone else had asked I might have taken offence. Memo had perked up somewhat by this stage. He was positively cheerful, in fact. Obviously Ayisha had convinced him that she could put the genie back in the bottle. "So you didn't kill Bayraktar at all?" I asked him.

Convinced that he was safe from immediate arrest, Gezen obviously felt some need to explain his weird behaviour. He fished a packet of Winfield out his jacket pocket, lit one, and gave me a what-the-hell look. "I locked him in the freezer and he perished," he blurted, half in remorse, half in defiance.

Perished? I wasn't sure whether to laugh or congratulate him on the improvement in his vocabulary over the preceding twenty-four hours. Terrific word, perished. So apposite. Very Scott of the Antarctic. Gezen's accent was much lighter, too.

Ayisha was off the mark like a bush lawyer. "It was an accident," she snapped. "Besides, the guy was a thug. He deserved to die."

I held up one hand. "You don't have to tell me anything, you know that, Memo."

He nodded, looked to Ayisha for confirmation and nodded again, almost eagerly. He didn't have to, but he wanted to. Something was bothering his conscience and he wanted to clear the air. He had a dose of the Raskolnikovs real bad, and he wasn't going to let either me or Ayisha stand in his way. "I was angry," he said. "Bayraktar, he called me a mountain Turk."

Hardly grounds for homicide, one would think. I raised my eyebrows. "Are we losing something in the translation here?"

"It's what right-wingers call the Kurds," Ayisha explained. "Memo here's a Kurd."

Naturally. Any more Kurds weighed in around here and you could start a cheese factory.

"The money," she said irritably, as though Gezen was a slow child. "Tell him about the money."

Now that he had stopped hyperventilating, Gezen was practically garrulous. "Forty dollars a week. He said I must give him forty dollars a week or he will say I am stealing. I get sack. Jail maybe." He hastened to add, "I am not a thief."

At Pacific Pastoral? Heaven forbid.

"He should have told us here at the League," Ayisha butted in. "We'da fixed the prick." I waved her into silence, lest she break the spell. This was all just too fascinating. "So you locked him in the freezer and he perished?"

"No," said Gezen. "I paid. More than two thousand dollars he took from me. Then, last week, he wants more. Fifty dollars a week. Inflation, he says. And all the time he calls me these insults." He dragged his chair closer to the desk, going into a kind of confidential huddle as he got to the good part.

"That is when I think I will lock him in the freezer. But not to kill him. That was not my . . ."

At last his English faltered. He searched for the right word, vibrating with frustration. He used a Turkish word, glancing again at Ayisha.

"Intention," she said. She'd obviously heard this bit before.

"I meant only to frighten him. Then I would rescue him. Understand?"

Not really, I didn't. Well, sort of. It seemed a rather fraught way to win friends and influence people, but I could see a sort of desperate logic at work. "But something went wrong?" I said. The roll-your-own was a greasy brown stub in my fingers. As I butted it out Gezen hurried to offer me a fresh tailor-made. Out of courtesy and not wanting to interrupt his momentum I accepted, but didn't light it. It's not like I was really a smoker.

I could see what Gezen was doing. He was enlisting an ally. The Australian, the government official, on the other side of the desk must be made to understand exactly what had happened, must be won over.

"What I do is this. From the beginning I watch him. He does not see me, but always I watch. I see everything. What I see is this. Every Friday, just before knock-off time, he goes to Number 3 freezer. He looks to see that nobody watches, then he goes inside, two maybe three minutes. It is very cold inside, you understand. Ten minutes and a man will die."

Yes, I recalled. A more than unusually nippy spot.

"So last Friday, after lunch, I move a forklift truck so it is parked against the emergency exit. This is not allowed, but it happens all the time. Nobody notices. Then when Bayraktar goes inside." He mimed the snapping of a padlock. "I lock the door."

Gezen's speech had taken on a vivid present-tense intensity. I remembered the cigarette in my hand and lit it. It was insipid, but I drew deep anyway.

Gezen went on. "I wait one minute, two, three. Bayraktar will be very frightened. Soon I will open the door. Then the other one comes."

"Other one?"

"The mechanic, Gardening."

It was hard not to laugh. He was trying so hard. "Gardiner?"

"Yes. I do not think he will come so soon. He unlocks the door and goes inside. Quickly I move the forklift away. Still Gardiner is inside, long time, six or seven minutes. Then he leaves and I look in-side. Bayraktar is there, perished. Then Gardiner comes back with the boss. Ambulance comes. Police. They ask if I saw something. I say nothing."

Gezen shrugged, laying his offering at my feet. Take it or leave it. Smoke rose from the cigarette folded into the cup of his hand, the filter squeezed between forefinger and thumb. His fingers were fragile, a pianist's or a surgeon's. He followed my gaze downwards and rolled his wrist, the better to display the translucent veneer of hardened scar. Was this an appeal for sympathy, I wondered, or somehow part of the story?

Ayisha broke the silence. "People's justice. Self defence. Whadda ya reckon, Murray?"

What I reckoned was that the sooner I got myself out of there the better. Gezen's yarn had less internal logic than a Democrat campaign promise. Trying to follow the who did what to whom part had been hard enough, let alone the other questions that sprang to mind. And Gezen himself, hysterical one moment, sucking calmly on a fag the next. Was he telling the truth or weaving some bizarre, self-justifying fable?

Not only was this impromptu little confession unintelligible, it was unwelcome. My plans for a strategic withdrawal from all this Pacific Pastoral bullshit were rapidly coming undone. I was already regretting my little chat on the phone with Merricks. He had probably immediately called Agnelli, or even Charlene, to bitch about me. If giving cheek to a captain of industry wasn't bad enough, here I was involving the office of a minister of the crown in some sort of ethnic criminal extortion revenge murder mystery caper. Shit, the *Sun* would have a field day.

On the other hand, there was Ayisha. She was sitting on the edge of the desk, her eyes blazing conspiratorially. Excited. Impatient. Come on, they seemed to say. Impress me with your masterly command of the situation. Let's fix this together, the two of us.

Come across as some sort of pen-pushing apparatchik and I could cancel forever my hopes of forging a bedroom alliance here. "What else do you know about this?" I asked her.

"Nothing. Dead set," she swore, looking to Gezen to back her up. "This is the first time I've seen Memo in months." Gezen nodded confirmation. "He came in out of the blue about twenty minutes ago. Said the cops were after him. Wouldn't say what for. Said he wanted to give himself up. Then you stuck your head through the door and he chucked a mental and started talking about killing someone. Reckoned you were a cop." Gezen was trying his best to look chastened, not entirely succeeding. "You gotta help sort this thing out, Murray," Ayisha pleaded. "Memo can't go to prison. It'd kill him."

I helped myself to one of Gezen's cigarettes and turned the situation over in my mind. For a start, a confession of murder would be welcomed by nobody. The official coronial enquiry was still months away, but if the documents Agnelli had slipped me were accurate, a finding of natural causes was a foregone conclusion. The cops and the Labour Department investigators were unanimous. They'd look like a proper pack of idiots if it turned out to have been murder. The Department of Labour was probably already busy drafting amendments to the legislation on mandatory aisle widths. Pacific Pastoral had just said good riddance, said it with flowers. In short, unless some new evidence turned up, nobody would want Bayraktar's death to be anything other than it appeared to be.

Maybe Bayraktar deserved what he got, maybe not. The idea that he was conducting a bit of extortion in the workplace wasn't at all inconsistent with what I already knew about him. Maybe Memo Gezen had meant to kill him, maybe not. He didn't seem the homicidal type, if there was any such thing. And if he could live with the consequences of his actions, I certainly could, at least until someone better qualified to judge came along. What the guy needed was a bit of decent legal advice. "Know any lawyers?" I asked Ayisha.

"There's a firm we refer our compo cases to," she said, moving around the desk. "You want the number?"

A workers' compensation specialist wouldn't be an ideal first choice in a case like this, but she had given me an idea. A lawyer was a lawyer, after all. Client confidentiality and all that. "I know someone," I said. "Top gun. He'll be keen to help." He'd better be, I thought. It was him who got me into this shit in the first place. "But first, I need some assurances. For a start, this conversation never took place. Not a word to anyone until you hear back from me. Understood?" Their heads bobbed, corks on a rising tide. Ayisha was having the time of her life. "No more confessing, okay Memo?" Gezen bowed his head sheepishly. "Act normal. Go to work as usual. Do nothing to attract attention to yourself. Sit pat. Do not contact me. Ayisha will be in touch. Understand?"

"But the poliss."

"Don't worry about the police," I said. "Right now, I don't think they suspect anything. Even if they change their minds, they still have to make a case against you. You'll be okay as long as you keep your mouth shut. Presumption of innocence and all that."

"Presumption?" said Gezen. "What means 'presumption'?"

"It means you got away with it, Memo," said Ayisha, cheerfully defying me to contradict her.

But Gezen still had a problem. "Why do the police watch me, then?" he said.

The guy's bad conscience was certainly working overtime. I must have done a poor job concealing this thought. Gezen's eyes flared again, the weirdness back in evidence. Then he was up, heading out the door. We found him staring down the passage. "There," he gestured.

The three women and their yowling child had gone. Sivan was deep in a phone conversation, bent low, taking careful notes. Gezen jerked his head again. I stepped in front of him, following the line indicated through the plate-glass window, out into the street. Across the road in front of my Renault two dark-suited men were sitting in a parked car, the one in the driver's seat making an elaborate show of reading a street directory.

"That's not the jacks," I said. For a start the Victoria Police didn't go tooling about in sporty European coupes. Also, I recognised the men. It was the goons from the cemetery.

Ayisha jostled in beside me, the two of us squeezed together in the narrow passageway. I bent closer, feeling her hair graze my cheek. "Not ours, anyway," I whispered. "More like the Turkish secret police, wouldn't you say?" She swivelled her eyes around, knowing it wasn't the cops out there, letting me have my lame little joke.

"What's the Anatolia Club?" I said quietly, a secret conversation, just ours, my mouth accidentally against her ear, in danger of electrocution. She creased her brow into a silent question, her two perfect eyebrows arching like downy black caterpillars. "I think Bayraktar was a member," I whispered.

Her jaw hardened and a flare of alarm shot across her face. She repeated the short, sibilant, deeply expressive word that Gezen had uttered earlier. "Wait," she snapped. She turned and closed on Gezen, making reassuring sounds in Turkish, propelling him backwards down the narrow passageway until he disappeared into the obscurity of its far end. Then she wheeled and advanced on me. "Stop pissing about, Murray," she hissed, not in the least bit playfully. "This is serious."

Her face was so close I could taste the mixture of spearmint and tobacco on her breath. Any closer and I would do something I'd regret. "Take it easy," I said, backing off. "I'm on your side, remember."

Sivan looked up from his phone call, registered our presence, and returned to scribbling notes.

Quickly I described how I had driven past the address in Blyth Street the day before and seen a BMW like the one parked across the road. For good measure I threw in the goings-on I had just witnessed at Fawkner Cemetery. As she listened, Ayisha gnawed her bottom lip and glanced anxiously out the window. "It's a gambling club," she said. "Run by right-wing thugs. Maybe more, even."

"More? Like what?"

"Rumour is they keep an eye on things in the local community for the consulate." She shrugged meaningfully. "You think they're really after Memo?"

She said something else, but I didn't hear it. I was already out the door, feeling the wind cut like a knife. Streams of traffic hummed past in both directions, as I dodged and skipped towards the twin yellow stripes at the centre of the road.

As a rule of thumb, I kept my nose out of ethnic matters, for all the obvious reasons. When it came to complex, bitter and intractable conflict, the Labor party more than met my needs. Tolerance, however, had its limits. Obscure foreign toughs could not be allowed to go cruising around my patch, staking out the offices of a perfectly respectable welfare organisation, without having their activities at least remarked upon. You have to draw the line somewhere.

I was standing on that line now, waiting for a wall of semi-trailers to pass, their tires raising a slurry off the wet asphalt. Through the flashing gaps between each successive truck I saw the faces in the BMW turn impassively to observe my approach. Blue-shaven faces, hard-featured, don't-fuck-with-me, no-speaka-da-English, see-this-knife faces. I closed on them, ten metres, five, two, suddenly regretting my bravado. A less confrontational, more oblique, more measured approach might be appropriate. Hi there, I could say. Looking for something? Can I help? Behind me Ayisha was on the footpath, gnawing that lip again.

The BMW trembled gently, flashed an indicator and inserted itself into the latest wave of steel and rubber hurtling down the southbound lane.

"Piss off, you mongrels," I yelled at its departing bumper bar, fist in the air. "You're in Australia now." An ancient Greek in a tram shelter looked up impassively from his cane. "Not you, mate," I hastened to reassure him. "Not you,"

Ayisha stood shaking her head in amazement, clapping and grinning, and I realised where my urge for heroics had come from. In like Flynn, I told myself. Up the Revolution.

Back inside, Sivan was still engrossed in his phone conversation. The inner office was empty. I walked through to the backyard. Gezen wasn't in the outhouse either. Ayisha had slung her coat, a huge quilted thing, over her arm and was back on the footpath, looking up and down the street. "We've got to talk," I said.

"Later." She climbed into a taxi and wound down the window. Her arm came out and I felt her palm, cool on my cheek, brushing past with the forward momentum of the cab. "You were fantastic. You won't say anything, will you?"

Shit no. Leastways not until I got to a phone.

13

"HERE," SAID ANT. "Hold this."

Two days before, this Pacific Pastoral caper had been a minor chance to earn a few brownie points with the powers. Now it was a major can of worms. If only I had come straight back to the electorate office after the funeral, I would have been sitting at my desk finishing off Charlene's correspondence while arranging for some super-efficient roofing firm to drop around and seal my drips. Instead, it was already noon and, not only were my drips still dripping, I was standing around with a fluorescent tube under my arm watching Ant balance on an upended milk crate on the top of my desk.

Fixing the flickering overhead light was item four on a list of odd jobs Trish had given the tattooed complainant that morning. The first was replacing the toilet window the burglars had broken. Then came adjusting the automatic closing gizmo on the front door, and eliminating the rattle in the gas wall-furnace. Trish was never one to let a chance go by. "He's got nowhere else to go," she told me when I returned from the League and found him hoisting the milk crate onto my desk. "Apparently his girlfriend, Gail . . ."

"G.A.I.L."

"She really has kicked him out. This morning I found him

asleep in his car out the front. If you're going to hang around like a bad smell all day, I told him, at least make yourself useful."

So there he was, making himself so fucking useful I couldn't get at my desk. How a man was supposed to get anything done in that lunatic asylum, let alone have a discreet telephone conversation about manslaughter, was anyone's guess.

I passed the fluoro tube up with one hand and dialled the ministry with the other. Agnelli was such a smart lawyer, he was bound to know some similarly talented criminal lawyer. Between the two of them they could take Gezen off my hands, along with any uncomfortable legal consequences his impromptu confession might have thrown up. Presuming he ever surfaced again. More likely he'd had second thoughts about unburdening himself so freely and was currently sitting with his luggage in the international departure lounge at Tullamarine waiting for the next direct flight to Ankara.

I tried Agnelli's direct line again. It was still engaged. Somehow Ayisha's tobacco and matches had found their way into my jacket pocket. I rolled myself a calming smoke and called A-OK Allweather.

"Yeah?" This time it was a younger woman, bored and snappish.

"Is that A-OK Allweather?"

"Hold, please." Inane repetitive music blared.

"Rip-off merchants," said a voice from above. Ant was slipping the diffuser panel back into place. "I done a job with them once. The specs said four gauge but they used two point six. Said no-one would notice. Twenty years time the brackets'll be completely stuffed. Shit work, mate, take my word for it."

A deejay screeched in my ear like an enraged mouse trapped in an empty margarine container. "You telling me you know something about roofing?" Number plates I could imagine, mail bags, a bit of hot wiring. Trish might have been impressed with this odd-job stuff around the office, but as far as I was concerned all it amounted to so far was oiling a sticky hinge and changing a few light bulbs.

"Gas fitter by trade," said Ant. "But I've been around. Metal fabrication. Plumbing. Concrete. Roofs. You name it."

The mouse went heavy metal. "What about domestic? Ordinary houses?"

Ant dropped something solid into his tool box and stepped down. "I might not be Bertram Russell, sport, but I know what domestic means."

A-OK was still somewhere on the other side of a dozen howling chartbusters. I was sure that I would live to regret what I was about to say, but I was desperate enough to say it anyway. "Listen," I said. "I might be able to put a bit of work your way, round my place. We could nip across now if you like, have a quick look, tell me if you're interested."

"Get fucked," said Ant amiably. "You're just trying to get rid of me."

"By showing you where I live? You want some paid work or not?"

"What sort of work?"

Fifteen minutes later we were standing on the footpath outside my front gate. The rain had stopped for the time being, but the sky pressed low and menacing. Drips hung from the rust-frayed gashes in the guttering and my ball of rags protruded above the line of the roof like a goitre. Ant clicked his tongue ominously. "I'll need a ladder," he said, and headed down the side path, peering upwards and shaking his head. Winding me up for a big slug, I assumed.

As the front door key snicked into place, a sound erupted inside the house. Heavy footsteps pounded in the bedroom. A shadow flashed across the leadlight panel, retreating towards the other end of the house. I twisted the key, cursing the stiffness of the lock. As the door finally flew open, a crash came echoing up the hall, followed by a muffled oath. I flew through the house and shot out the back door.

Ant was sprawled on his back, blood and broken teeth spewing out his mouth. The side fence rocked. I vaulted the rickety timber slats and landed amid the Vesuvius cups of Mrs. Bagio's foundation garments flapping on a rotary hoist. Footsteps sounded down the side of the sleepout. A second fence loomed, an obstacle course of old water pipes, Mr. Bagio's bean trellis. Up and over I went, rubbish bins breaking my drop. Down a driveway towards the street a car door slammed. I hit the nature strip just in time to see the tail-end of an early model Falcon 500, a flash of aqua blue, go fishtailing around the corner. But not before I got the last three digits of the rego number.

When I got back inside, Ant was sitting at the kitchen table. A damp towel tinged with pink was pressed to his mouth and he was poking around in a saucer filled with fragments of denture — a palaeontological exhibit, the upper jaw of homo pictorial. He peeled away the cloth to display a mush of split lips and swelling nose. "Fuck was that?" he lisped. "Cunt hit me in the face with the screen door."

It didn't seem like an appropriate time to instruct him on non-sexist language. "Some junkie low-life, I guess." I panted. "Driving some piece of shit."

"Get anything?"

I doubted it. Whoever it was — not that I'd actually seen them — had not been moving like someone with a television set under their arm. I took a look around. There was no sign of forced entry, no broken window or splinter marks around the locks. Everything seemed pretty much as I had left it when I'd gone to work. I had to laugh, imagining the look of dismay on the face of any housebreaker unlucky or dumb enough to target this place. Across the mouldy-smelling carpet of damp newspapers covering the lounge room floor the stereo was untouched.

A couple of years before, Wendy had come home and found the front door open, the place clumsily ransacked, the portable tape deck missing. It was a nuisance and an intrusion, but the occasional break-in by bored kids or junkie desperados was only to be expected. It was all part of the inexorable process that begins with heritage colours and native gardens and culminates in some Liberal-voting busybody ringing your bell one night while you're eating dinner to ask if you'd be interested in helping set up a local chapter of Neighbourhood Watch. If you found the odd burglary impossible to live with you might as well sell up and lock yourself away in some high-security terrace in Fitzroy or a flat in St Kilda. If you were going to be pillaged like a member of the gentry, you might as well live like one. All it took was about fifty grand, which I didn't have.

The bedroom was a mess, but no more than usual. By the look of it, we'd disturbed the intruder early in the piece. I lingered, shutting drawers and smoothing down the bed covers, slight gestures to re-assert my presence. Discarded socks, mine and Red's, lay scattered on the floor. I began scooping them up. It was like I'd been caught in a car accident wearing dirty underpants.

Having some joker sneaking about the house didn't worry me much — I'd just sent the creep packing, after all. But this was the sort of thing that could easily upset a little kid. It wasn't as though I'd found a steaming turd in Wendy's knickers drawer or anything, but a couple of hours either way and it could have been Red's face being smashed in with the screen door. Better not to mention it. I paired off the socks and tossed them into the laundry basket until I was down to a solitary old black thing with a hole in the heel. "Just the one sock missing, then, sir?" I could hear the police asking.

I knelt beside the bed and stuck my hand under. What I found wasn't a sock. It was a zip-lock plastic bag containing more marijuana than I had ever seen in my life. There must have been a good two ounces of it, packed down hard. Either Red was more precocious than I gave him credit for, or our unknown intruder had fled with considerably less than he came with. I sat on the edge of the bed and stared at the grass, wondering what to do with it.

Ant stomped up the hall, his ballooning lip curling back to reveal an obscene flash of tongue and gum. "Where's that ladder, then?"

I quickly stuffed the package into my pocket. The presence in my home of illegal substances was not something I wished to reveal to this tattooed yoik. "I suppose I'd better call the cops, report the break-in."

"Waste of time," Ant grunted. It was clear he preferred as little contact as possible with the sherlocks.

I figured he was probably right. We'd have been sitting around for a good hour waiting for the uniforms to arrive with their clipboards so they could fill in a triplicate incident report for the non-existent insurance claim. I'd give them the dope and the digits I'd memorised from the Falcon number plate. Six months later, assuming the car wasn't stolen, they'd ring me up and want me to take a day off work and hang around the magistrate's court so some whacker with pin-prick eyes could spend six months having his criminal skills honed at the taxpayers' expense. No thanks. I got the ladder.

Ant disappeared into the ceiling, bloody towel in one hand, torch in the other. I rolled one of Ayisha's smokes and stood in the gloom of the hallway, staring up at the trapdoor and hoping to Christ I was doing the right thing, thinking I should have got references.

When he came down his lip was curled back in a sneer, whether from the swelling or with contempt I couldn't tell. "Rooted," he snorted. "Totally fucked. Battens are stuffed. Iron had the dick years ago. You need rewiring too."

"How much?"

"Just the roof? Sixteen hundred."

I had no idea if it was high, low, or off the register. I thought long and hard for about ten seconds. Unless I acted soon the place would be down around my ears by the time I got a proper quote. Aside from which, it seemed a bit churlish to quibble with a man who had a notch down the middle of his face in the shape of my back door. "How soon can you start?"

Ant shoved a fuse into place and the lights came on. "Soon as this weather stops."

"Discount for cash?"

"Sixteen hundred is cash. Two men for two days plus materials."

"Insurance? What if you fall off and break your neck?"

"Drag me onto the street and leave me to die."

"My pleasure." We shook on it and drove to a materials yard. Ant told them what he needed and we organised delivery for the next morning. They even accepted my cheque. I was overdrawn, but they weren't to know that. Things seemed finally to be moving in the right direction.

On the way back to the office it occurred to me that the intruder might return to look for his drugs, maybe when Red was in the house. I didn't want that happening, but I could hardly sit around the house waiting for him to turn up. A better idea would be to get to him first, give him back his dope and tell him to fuck off in no uncertain terms. Of course I couldn't do something like that myself. But the man who could was sitting right beside me.

First things first, though. Ant needed new teeth and I needed to figure out who owned that lairy blue Falcon. I dropped Ant at a tram stop in Sydney Road with twenty dollars and instructions on how to find the dental college. You could get free dentures there if you didn't mind being used for practice by the students. I didn't mention the students.

A year or so before, Trish had a boyfriend who worked at motor registration. He'd come to our Christmas party, got legless and barfed taramasalata all over my desk. The two of them had a big break up soon after, not related. When I got back to the office Trish was at lunch. Lover boy's number was still in her teledex.

"I'm calling from the minister's office," I said. It was half true. "Trish suggested I call." It was he who had done the dirty, so I figured mention of Trish might trigger some sense of obligation. "I don't know if this is your department, but she said that if anyone could head me in the right direction you could. The thing is, Mrs. Wills was doing some shopping over the weekend and somebody dinged her car. Stove the tail-light right in, snapped off part of the trim. Pissed off without as much as a howdy-do. Luckily somebody witnessed the whole thing, took down the offender's make and model and half the rego number and stuck it under the windscreen. Naturally Charlene doesn't want to make a federal case out of it, but I was wondering if there's any way to track down the owner?"

"You need the Search Section." Lothario had better things to do than favours for half-forgotten workmates of old girlfriends. "Bring in some ID, fill in an application and pay a search fee. You'll be notified in about a week."

"Oh," I said. Not the powerless "oh" of a individual faced with a remote and uncaring bureaucracy. The "oh" of a mover and shaker realising he is talking to a turkey. There was an almost imperceptible change in attitude, a minuscule drop in barometric pressure. "It was a Falcon 500," I said. "Aqua blue, mid-seventies model. Something, something, something, eight six five."

"I'll have to go downstairs," he said, just so I'd know how much trouble was involved. "I'll call you back."

I hung up, then dialled again, the Turkish Welfare League.

"No, Ayisha has not come back." Sivan didn't sound particularly concerned. "I thought maybe she was with you," he added slyly.

"The client she was with, any sign of him?"

"Client?"

"The curly-haired guy in Ayisha's office about two hours ago."

"Memo Gezen?" Sivan hadn't seen him, but he knew who he was. "Leading anti-fascist fighter. Tireless worker for the PKK."

PKK? I'd seen those initials before on posters along Sydney Road. Clenched fists, upraised Kalashnikovs, armed revolution, Kurdish nationalist guerillas. The full kit and caboodle. "No, this guy's a cleaner."

"Very clever disguise, eh? Did you know that since the coup d'état more than eighty thousand people have been imprisoned? It is the policy of the regime that . . ."

Many migrants remained politically active in the affairs of their native land. There was nothing unusual in that. Lots of Italians were members, office bearers even, in the Italian Communist Party. The El Salvadorean who repaired our office photocopier was reputed to be on the central committee of the Farabundo Marti Liberation Front. And now that I knew of Memo Gezen's political dimension a whole lot of pieces fell into place.

I cut into Sivan's flow of baleful statistics. "Look, get Ayisha to call me as soon as she gets back in, will you? And one other thing. Look out the window and tell me if there's a BMW parked across the street."

"I can't see one. Why?"

"Nothing. Get Ayisha to call me, okay."

"Sure, Murray. I think you like her, huh?"

I'd liked her a lot more before I'd begun to feel like I was having my string jerked. According to one of the yellow slips on my desk Greg Coates had called while I was out. There was a tick in the Urgent box. Ayisha's tobacco was down to powdery dregs. I rolled as I dialled, one-handed, back to the old form.

"You prick," Coates said. "Dropped me right into it, you did." He was as pissed off as I'd ever heard him.

"What are you talking about?"

"That Turk of yours, Bayraktar. He's hot property. I did like I promised and called up his file this morning. Access was still denied and five minutes later two of our security blokes lobbed on my doorstep wanting to know what my interest was. Took quite a bit of tap dancing before I managed to convince them it was a clerical error. Very keen to interview the man, they were. I think you'd better tell me why you're so interested."

Coates would have to wait until the waters cleared. Anything I told him would be around the traps like a dose of the crabs before the day was done. Which was only fair enough. I'd do the same for him. "Nothing to tell. The bloke's name appeared in a story in Monday's *Sun* linking Charlene to a potential industrial conflict. I was just following up."

"You know where to find him?"

"I've got a fair idea. What do they want him for?"

"Everything short of buggering his dog, from what I could tell. He's got a record as long as your arm in West Germany. Grievous bodily harm, drugs, you name it. The krauts were compelled to show him the door. Then he slipped in under our net. Came in as a temporary resident, supposedly working for some cultural exchange mob called the Anatolia Club. Stated occupation, ceramic artist, believe it or not. He throws things all right, but they're not pots. So, if you know where he is . . ."

"Try Fawkner Cemetery," I said.

"He's dead?"

"I understand they're very reluctant to bury you there otherwise. Tell your security blokes they can read all about it in Monday's edition of the *Sun*. Cause of death was reported as a heart attack."

This put Coates back in good humour. He'd be getting mileage out of this one for years. Nothing like a bit of mutual pocket-pissing to keep the fences mended. "Look," I said, while he was so cheery, "There's this other Turkish bloke I was wondering about."

"No way," he said. "Not until things quieten down. I've got security clearance to maintain here, pal. And what about a bit of quid pro quo. You never finished telling me about Agnelli's big scoop on the election date."

"Agnelli's sworn me to secrecy," I said. It always pays to over-emphasise the value of your information, I find. "Word from the Cabinet room is it'll be a snap job. Pre-Christmas. Second week in December probably."

"Shit, that's barely ten weeks away. Sounds like crap to me."

"I'm just telling you what he said. And from what you told me about the punishing he's giving the phones, I'm not the only one he's telling."

"He could be making a fool of himself on this one. I know for a fact that the state admin committee is up to its neck in a substantial rejig of campaign structures. It wouldn't be too smart going to the polls with half the party machine in dry-dock. Still, there might be something in it. Worth putting in a couple of calls to check out."

"Let me know how you go."

"Don't forget to apologise for me tonight at the branch meeting."

The idea that Agnelli might be wrong about the imminence of an election wasn't surprising. Everything I had learned since yesterday afternoon about the alleged Lollicato–Pacific Pastoral connection cast serious doubt on his credibility.

Jesus, though, this stuff about Bayraktar was interesting. It certainly backed up Gezen's tale of extortion, as well as the police suspicion of thievery in Number 3 chiller. This connection with the Anatolia Club was a major worry. An organised group of paramilitary right-wingers, possibly connected to a foreign government, running a political and criminal standover operation out of a well-secured building in the middle of a Melbourne suburb. And I'd just blown them a very public raspberry.

The phone rang. It was Loverboy at Motor Rego. "Got a pen?" he said. "It's a bit of a mouthful. I'll spell it for you. Car's registered to an Ekrem Bayraktar. B-A-Y-R-A-K-T-A-R. Get that?"

No I didn't. I didn't get it at all.

14

BAYRAKTAR WAS DEAD. I'd seen the photographs and stared down a pit at the silver handles on his Martinelli rosewood deluxe. So who the hell had been thumping down my hallway leaving a trail of cannabis behind in their wake? Was there some essential internal logic at work here that I was failing to notice?

The disordered mass of files and paperwork the previous night's intruder had dumped on the office floor lay in an untidy sprawl across my desk, half hidden under a yellow confetti of phone message slips. On top of everything else that was happening, half the known universe seemed to want to talk to me. I began systematically sorting through the mess, hoping that some superficial restoration of order might help me make sense of what was going through my mind.

Some of the calls were from local party branch members. No doubt they would be wanting to know if there was anything interesting enough on the agenda of that night's meeting to tempt them out for the evening. Others would want their apologies noted. Gavin Mullane, the son of the local Lower House MP, had rung to confirm a four o'clock appointment I had made with him the previous week. Roofing companies were now returning my calls, proving the axiom that it never rains. Old Maestro Picone had left word that he wanted to talk about Charlene's celebrity appearance at the Carboni Club dinner dance. Mundane as it was, this housekeeping was beginning to look pretty alluring compared with the dramas on offer elsewhere in the electorate.

By the time I had finished working my way through the jumble of paperwork, I knew for sure I no longer had the Pacific Pastoral file. The previous afternoon it had been sitting on top of my in-tray. Trish hadn't seen it either, or so she signalled as she sat chatting on the phone with her mother.

I called Agnelli. He was at lunch, so I flashed Trish five fingers and walked down to the shops, figuring a bite to eat and the taste of smoke in my mouth might help the mental processes along. On a bench in the market arcade I ate a bucket of chips and broached a new packet of Winfield, trying to figure out the connection between a dead man's car, the botched burglary of my home and a missing file. Nothing fitted. It simply didn't make sense.

Apart from the question of why anyone interested in Pacific Pastoral would also steal a petty-cash tin and draw a penis on the bathroom mirror in felt-tipped pen, the file itself was useless. All it contained was the list of names from Bayraktar's shift — names on record out at the Coolaroo plant, a few random jottings, and a handwritten draft of the introductory paragraph of my report for MACWAM. Stealing that made no sense at all. The file, I decided, had to be back at the office somewhere staring me in the face.

The Falcon presented two possibilities. One was unconvincing and the other downright scary. Either it had been stolen and its use in the attempted burglary was sheer coincidence. Or Bayraktar's mates at the Anatolia Club had it and I'd got myself stuck in the middle of some kind of internecine Turkish-Kurdish thing.

According to Coates, the Anatolia Club was down on the file as Bayraktar's sponsor, which meant the Immigration Department security boys must have already checked it out. So either the spooks were satisfied it had no connection with Bayraktar's criminal activities or they were running their own agenda. Shit, what was I thinking? They hadn't even known Bayraktar was dead. They were probably too busy framing little old Greek ladies on phoney pension fraud charges to be any help to me.

That left the cops, either the locals or the big boys downtown. And I couldn't see them getting interested unless I turned on a pretty convincing production number. Dropping Charlene's name might help crank up some muted enthusiasm. It might also result in a headline reading "Labor MP Aide in Ethnic Feud Death Probe." And talking to the cops wouldn't be much point without spilling the beans on Memo Gezen, which would be a breach of faith. Worse, it would be a surefire guarantee that I could kiss my prospects with Ayisha Celik goodbye forever.

And where did Memo Gezen fit into the picture anyway? This story of his about being stood over by Bayraktar tallied okay, but thereafter the tale had got decidedly unconvincing. The man himself was impossible to read, one minute impassive and compliant, the next wild-eyed, sparks erupting out the top of his head. And to top it all off, there was his connection with militant Kurdish politics.

The problem was I had no tangible intelligence to work with. What I had to do was persuade Greg Coates to change his mind and sling me Gezen's immigration file. Maybe then I'd have some hope of working out what was going on. Another thought occurred to me. Maybe Gezen hadn't disappeared of his own volition. With Sivan on the phone and Ayisha out in the street watching my mock heroics, could someone have slipped in the back way and spirited him out the back door? Take it easy, I told myself, there are enough far-fetched ideas flying around here already.

Halfway back to the office a steady shower began. I tucked my head under my jacket and took the short-cut up the back lane. I was only a few paces into the narrow bluestone-paved canyon of back fences when I heard the throaty rev of a souped-up engine somewhere behind me. In this area, a lowered chassis, fat tires, and a basso profundo engine timbre is virtually mandatory among large sections of the male population. If I'd looked around every time someone dropped a notch and spread rubber, I'd have had a twisted vertebrae before you could say fuel-injected overhead cam.

But when I heard the crunch of a sump hitting the curb immediately behind me, I swung around automatically. A turquoise flash of chrome and paintwork was roaring towards me, its windscreen a rain-streaked blur. I turned on my heels and took off as fast as my legs would carry me.

The lane opened into a side street a hundred metres away, an impossible distance. On either side were the back gates of shops and houses, all of them closed. Leading with my shoulder I threw myself against the first I came to, a teetering outhouse door of a thing. It was more solid than it looked. Bouncing off, I felt my feet slither out from beneath me and came down hard on the weathered bluestone cobbles. I scrambled to my knees and found myself staring between my legs at the oncoming grille, reading off the digits of Bayraktar's number plate, the numbers closing fast.

Across the lane I could see Ciccio's pile of empty Bisleri bottles through the gap where the sheet-metal halves of his back gate were held together by a sagging coil of heavy-duty chain. Catapulting across the Falcon's path, I smashed my head into the gap, hoping to Christ I could force it wider. I felt the whip of steel links against my neck and heard the hinges scream.

Bottles rose to meet me, an avalanche of empties skidding across the wet concrete of the yard. A smear of blue streaked past at the edge of my vision. Then one of the bottles was in my hand and I was back in the lane watching it tumbling end over end, its slow-motion trajectory ending in a milky wash of white as it shattered the Falcon's rear window. The sound of breaking glass came back down the lane towards me, mingled with the rapidly fading screech of tires as the car disappeared.

My heart pumped hard and fast, fed by the jitter of adrenaline coursing through my veins. This was getting beyond a joke. Back down the lane my flattened pack of Winfields was demonstration of the driver's murderous intent. Don't you just hate it when somebody tries to kill you and you don't know who or why?

Ciccio had come to his back door, wiping his hands, the old card players behind him, craning for a view. I brushed past them, my voice rasping in my ears. "Corretto." I needed a drink and pronto.

Ciccio fished around under the bar and came up with a bottle of grappa. He tipped a hefty measure into a strong black coffee and watched me down it in one. It was nearly enough to stop my hand shaking. But not quite. I took the second and third slugs neat.

"Fucka idiots," he said. "Orta be a law."

That was it. Things were getting far too hairy to be tolerated any longer. This sort of thing was well beyond the requirements of my job description. If you wanted a meeting stacked or a booth-by-booth breakdown of voting trends with emphasis on the flow of preferences, I was your man. Needed your how-to-vote cards printed cheap? See me. But being a homicide victim? I didn't have the training.

I took a last shot of grappa, punched a fresh packet of fags out of Ciccio's vending machine and ordered my rubbery legs out the door and around the corner to the cop shop. By the time I got there, my hands had stopped shaking enough to prise the cellophane off the cigarettes. "Someone just tried to kill me," I said.

The uniformed walloper behind the counter was an athletic-looking lug in his late twenties with the full-page crossword in *People* open in front of him. He looked up like he resented the intrusion. "That so, sir?" he said, his eyes taking a long slow cruise over my three-day growth, past my skewiff tie to the damp patches the puddles in Ciccio's yard had left on my pants.

"Yeah," I said. "First they broke into my house, then they tried to run me over." The grappa seemed to have finally settled my nerves. I managed one of the smokes out of the pack and inserted it between my lips.

"And who would this be you are referring to, sir?" Next he'd be saying " 'ello, 'ello, 'ello."

"That's what I want you to find out," I said.

He took a pen out of his shirt pocket and clicked it emphatically. "Your name?"

I was thinking about the rego number of the Falcon. The image kept fluctuating in and out of focus. Something, something, eight six five. I must have moved my lips. The cigarette fell to the floor. As I straightened from picking it up, the copper leaned right across the counter, following my progress, wrinkling his nose.

"Have you had a drink at all today, sir?" he said.

"No," I said. "Well yes, but . . ." I couldn't quite find the matches. "You wouldn't have a light, would you?"

The copper gave me a facetious look and squared off the edges of a little pop-up card on the counter that read Thank You for Not Smoking. Why don't they ever just say No Smoking? I patted myself down and felt a lump in my inside jacket pocket, a trafficable quantity of a prohibited substance. The idea of this visit, I concluded, had been a deeply flawed conception.

Talk about making a bad impression. I had got myself so far behind the eight ball that the only way I'd ever convince this guy of anything would be to tell him the whole story. Even then I couldn't see him believing me, let alone taking any useful action. An unknown assailant, no apparent motive, no injuries, no witnesses, the complainant some half-pissed bozo with a pocket load of wacky weed. I turned on my heels and strode out the door. From now on I would rely on my own ingenuity. It wasn't much to be going on with. I started by botting a light from a passer-by.

Trish had locked the office and stuck a Back in Five Minutes card inside the door. I locked the door behind me, left the card in place and dialled Greg Coates' number. "Couldn't you stretch a point?" I wheedled. "Just one little file. Another Turk, name of Memo Gezen."

"Jesus, not again?" he said. "Unless it's official, I can't help, at least for the time being. I've stuck my neck out for you far enough for one day. Beside which, if I was you I'd be more interested in what a certain Italian of our mutual acquaintance is up to."

"Agnelli? What's he got to do with it?"

"Get off the grass, mate. I've been applying the blowtorch to some friends of mine at the state office, and very tight-lipped they were too. All this ringing around Agnelli's doing, he's not peddling gossip. He's lining up support for a career move."

Somehow this did not surprise me. A lot of lawyers fancy themselves as legislators and Agnelli had all the required qualities — vanity, ambition and untrustworthiness. It had only been a matter of time before his parliamentary aspirations surfaced. "Yeah? So whose seat is he after?" I couldn't see Agnelli contesting anything marginal.

"This was where my sources got very circumspect. But if I were you I'd try imagining him in a frock and sensible shoes."

This had to be bullshit. No way was Agnelli dumb enough to make a play for Charlene's seat. No way would the faction allow a popular member to get dumped in favour of a sleazebag like Agnelli. I pleaded for the names of Coates' sources at state headquarters, but got no more out of him. I accused him of having me on, sticking it up me for the business with the Bayraktar file. By the time he hung up I was convinced he was serious.

And the truth or otherwise of what he was saying was not the only issue. Speculation of this sort had a tendency to take on a life of its own. And as Agnelli himself pointed out, some sections of the press would only be too happy to jump on the bandwagon. Let alone the idea that one of her most senior staff members was stabbing her in the back. If I didn't nip this little furphy in the bud toot sweet, it would be all over town before you could say knife in the back.

It took me half an hour, but I finally got through to Agnelli. All it would take for him to put Coates' gossip to bed was a simple denial. That, and an oath on his mother's soul. "Something urgent has come up. We need to talk."

"I'm in a meeting right now." Other voices eddied around in the background. Agnelli put his hand over the receiver and said something. When he took it away the noise had stopped.

"I'll come in," I said. "Ten minutes is all I'll need." I wanted to be looking at Agnelli's face when he talked to me. After we'd cleared the air on his plans for the future, we could move on to the legal issues thrown up by Memo Gezen's confession. "I can be there in half an hour."

"No." Agnelli all but jumped down the phone. He immediately back-pedalled, softening his tone. "I'll call you back, okay?" Click. The prick hung up in my ear.

Well, fuck you, pal, I thought. I dialled the House again, asked for Charlene and got put through to the party room. She was in the chamber, someone told me, the final reading of the Insurance Bill. The information came as a relief. The impulse to call Charlene had been ill-considered, a knee-jerk reaction. Bothering Charlene with uncorroborated gossip that one of her most trusted lieutenants was planning to do a Macbeth smacked of lack of judgement. Sitting in front of me on the desk was Ennio Picone's phone message slip. I decided to activate the nonna network.

"Maestro," I cried. "Many apologies for not calling earlier." I took my time, confirmed Charlene's appearance at the Carboni Club dinner dance, and made the right noises as the old man went on and on about the catering arrangements. Finally I popped the question.

"Angelo Agnelli," I said. "He's got terrible manners, I know, but Charlene finds him useful. Only I think he might be looking around for a new job. Have you heard anything?"

Maestro Picone shrugged audibly.

"Old Mrs. Agnelli senior, you wouldn't consider having a quiet word with her for me, would you? See what you can find out."

If Agnelli's grandmother didn't know what he was up to, Picone would work his way through the family tree until he found someone who did. Right up his autostrada, this sort of thing, keep him happy for days. Naturally he'd want something in return. I'd deal with that when the need arose. He promised to call back as soon as he had news.

While I'd been talking to Picone, Trish had come back, bringing with her a pile of photocopies, the agenda papers for that night's branch meeting. Most of the time chairing branch meetings was a tedious chore, a quasi-official part of my job. But it was also a way of maintaining close links with the local rank and file. And any candidate for pre-selection would need substantial local support. So if

Agnelli was planning a challenge, he would sooner or later have to make his intentions known among the natives. Which was something he could hardly do without me finding out.

Trish dumped the papers across my desk in a row of neat but still uncollated piles. An agenda, minutes of the previous meeting, a sheet of draft resolutions, a discussion paper on federal resource development policy. Such was the ammunition with which the membership waged its eternal war against the pragmatism of those it sent to parliament. A ceaseless and often hopeless battle perhaps, but a politics of persuasion, not of muscle-flexing and murder attempts. Not like some places I could think of. Sydney, for example. Or a lane off Sydney Road.

My thoughts must have shown on my face. I looked up to find Trish squinting across the desk at me. "You look a bit like a bloke who used to work here," she said. "He was in more often than you, and wasn't as much of a derelict." She was right. I was beginning to resemble one of our more unwanted customers. I guiltily stubbed out my cigarette on the inside of the wastepaper basket. "He didn't try to burn the place down, either," she jibed. "Better smarten up, Murray. Your four o'clock appointment's here."

Gavin Mullane was something indescribably minor in the Miscellaneous Workers. His father had been the area's Lower House MP for longer than anyone could remember, and it had long been agreed within the faction that when he eventually fell back on his parliamentary superannuation Sonny Jim would succeed him. I made myself respectable and went out to greet him. "Great to see you, Gavin," I said and took the poor bastard next door for a coffee. Behind his back as we passed Trish made a repetitive stroking gesture, thumb and forefinger touching at the tips.

Young Gavin had grown up in the shadow of his father, an experience that had left him damp. The family tendency was to thin lips, Presbyterian noses, and the kind of unflinching worthiness that could put a doorknob into a coma. The fact that Junior still lived with his parents, though well into his thirties, was perfectly understandable. I could see them sitting around together, reading Hansard and listening to the wireless. Gavin let me buy the coffees without offering to pay.

The idea of dynastic succession among the Labor aristocracy was an affront to my democratic sensibilities, but in Mullane's case I could see its merits. To pass the time until his inheritance arrived, the heir apparent was serving his political apprenticeship as councillor for the north ward of Coburg. Even within the sorry milieu of local government he displayed such a conspicuous lack of talent that it was universally agreed that the sooner he went elsewhere the better. All the way to the back benches of the state legislature if necessary.

Eventually nature would take its course. Mullane senior and his ageing cronies would die off, and the young dauphin would be despatched to the tumbrels. But right now there was no point in rubbing Daddy the wrong way. Besides which, the old man kept his ear pretty close to the ground in the party room. And who knows what juicy snippets had been dropped at the Mullane family dinner table? On more than one occasion Junior had inadvertently let the cat out of the bag. Mullane waited until Ciccio brought the coffees, then bent gravely across the table. "Somebody's going to be killed," he said. "Soon."

I froze in mid-sip.

"The way they come down that hill, it's only a matter of time before there's blood on the street."

With relief I realised Mullane was merely peddling his current pet project, a personal campaign for the installation of a pedestrian crossing at Edwardes Lake, a splotch of recreational water bang in the middle of his council ward.

"You reckon you could hassle Charlene to hassle the Minister for Transport to hassle his department to hassle the Road Traffic Authority, ASAP?"

"No hassle," I said. "At least not from Charlene's point of view. She's behind you 150 per cent on this."

In fact Charlene wouldn't go near the Minister for Transport with a twelve-foot Croatian. And she and the Treasurer had already privately agreed that in an area already so adequately resourced infrastructure-wise, road funding would be better directed to pressing community development and social justice issues — such as the capital construction costs of the Carboni Club.

"The problem will be getting it past those pen-pushing pricks in Transport," I warned, conjuring an elaborate map of the decision-making process. "But give her the bullets," I said, "and Charlene will fire them."

Mullane proceeded to crap on about traffic density ratios, while I waited for a chance to change the subject. "Heard this talk about an early election?"

"I'm sure the leadership has the matter well in hand," Mullane said primly. A tendency to mouth platitudes was another family trait he had inherited early.

"Angelo Agnelli reckons early December."

Mullane opened his mouth to say something, thought better of it and snapped his teeth shut. His was a face not well suited to deception. His jaw worked overtime. Something was trying hard not to burst out. "I'm not big on idle speculation." He pushed his chair back and stood up. "Practical issues, that's what concerns me. Things that are important in people's daily lives, traffic safety for one."

I headed him off before he started in again. "Couldn't agree more, Gavin."

When we shook hands and Mullane turned away, he had the look of a man whose team is six goals up at three-quarter time, a man more pleased with himself than any paltry assurances about some stupid fucking zebra crossing warranted.

By now it was four-thirty, more than five hours since Ayisha and Gezen had disappeared on me. I rang the League. A heavily-accented male answered, one of their volunteer workers, I guessed. Ayisha was not there, he told me. Nor was Sivan. I left my home address and phone number with a message for either of them to call me urgently. It was a painful process of careful enunciation, slow spelling and double checking. Even then I wasn't entirely sure I'd been understood.

The agenda papers still needed collating, and in barely ten minutes I would need to leave to pick Red up. I sweet-talked Trish into helping me, a gesture towards restoring workplace harmony. She locked the front door and I laid the piles of pages out across the reception area floor, passing the finished sets to Trish to staple together. We were just getting up a head of steam when there was a tap on the front window.

Herb Gardiner was outside on the footpath, a spry leprechaun, as cheerful as ever. I unlocked the door, but didn't ask him in. "Just happened to be in the vicinity, son." He glanced knowingly towards Trish and gave me a wink.

You get some of these retired or near-retired guys with too much time on their hands. They start looking for an interest. The last thing I needed was the old goat taking me under his wing. "I'm pretty busy right now, Herb," I told him.

He eyed the pages on the floor and dropped his voice. "That your report?"

I shook my head warily, not in the mood for any more confidential revelations of shenanigans at Pacific Pastoral. Gardiner lingered, looking for something to say. He seemed to be expecting me to speak first. It occurred to me that he'd had second thoughts about his comments on the prevalence of pilfering at Coolaroo. Nobody wants to go down in the books as a dobber. He checked out Trish to see if she could hear us. She was noisily punching staples into completed agenda sets. "What you said," he started.

I got there ahead of him. "My report only covers the industrial situation," I said. "Anything else, I can be relied on to keep to myself."

This confirmed what Gardiner was waiting to hear. "Right you are, then, son," he said. "You're calling the shots." Then he paused pregnantly, expecting me to continue.

What else was there to say? I was tempted to ask if he knew Memo Gezen. From what he'd said before about the ethnics keeping to themselves, I thought it unlikely. And even if he did, what useful information could he possibly have?

Gardiner kept glancing towards Trish, then taking little steps backwards, as if to draw me outside. I didn't have the time for this kind of chit-chat. If I didn't get away soon, Red would be standing in the schoolyard all alone, frightened he'd be left there all night. "Back at work yet?" I said, clearly a concluding remark.

"Crack of dawn tomorrow," he said. An idea seemed suddenly to occur to him. "The reason I dropped in, that roof of yours. That builder mate of mine says he can nip around tonight, take a look. You going to be home?" He said this quite loudly so Trish could hear.

Some inexorable law of mechanical determinism was at work here. Buy something, five minutes later you see a better one at a fraction of the price. If this builder mate was anything like old Herb himself, he was probably a top tradesman. "You wouldn't read about it," I said, "I've just lined someone up."

Gardiner sounded a bit cheesed, like he was being pissed around. "Don't be hasty," he said, forcefully. "You might regret it." Boy, was he toey all of a sudden.

No point in having him think I was ungrateful. "Thanks anyway," I said. "But tonight would have been impossible anyway. Monthly branch meeting. I'll be freezing my arse off in a back room at the Lakeview Hotel until well after ten."

Poor old Herb shook his head like he couldn't believe what he was hearing. Like he couldn't see why I was passing up an offer this good. "You sure you know what you're doing?" he said.

I told him that I did, and that I had work to do, edging him out the door. He backed off, looking puzzled, his palms spread. "Have it your own way," he seemed to be saying. As I bent back down to the agenda papers Trish cleared her throat noisily and rolled her eyes sideways. Gardiner was still standing outside the window, watching. He jerked his thumb over his shoulder, beckoning me outside.

I didn't have time for this. I turned away, ignoring him. When I sneaked a furtive look a minute later, he was gone.

15

RED PULLED AN ENVELOPE out of his schoolbag. It had a Health Department logo.

Your child has been examined today and found to be infested with headlice. Until appropriate treatment is commenced, he/she cannot attend school.

With the note came a glossy brochure. "Headlice," it read, "live equally happily on the rich, the poor, the clean and the dirty, regardless of age, occupation and status." Genially egalitarian as this made our little visitors sound, if Wendy turned up and found Red off school with a lice infestation, I would never hear the end of it. The high moral ground would rise beneath her feet and become an unscaleable mountain. But what constituted appropriate treatment?

A haircut, we decided, and a second shampoo. The place Wendy usually took him was in High Street, Northcote. Snipz Unisex Salon, children a speciality. Only now it was Voula Modes. It smelled of singed cats and was full of bottle-blond matrons in animal print leotards and cashmere sweaters with shoulder pads and appliqued sequins.

We walked up the hill, me on the outside, half an eye cocked at the slow crawl of outward-bound traffic in the far lane. A window displayed badger-bristle shaving brushes, briar pipes, and a black and white print of Tony Curtis. "No way, Jose." Red shook his head and we kept walking, past a newsagency with a good price on Winfields.

The shops changed. Bed'n'Bath and Seconds'n'Samples gave way to an Indian restaurant, a hip record store, boutiques. The next hairdresser was called Hair-o-Inn, a retro horror full of lava-lamps and cone-chairs and other knick-knacks of the sort anyone over thirty had spent their adolescence trying to escape. We stepped inside and a tweenie in black came smirking out from behind somebody's father's kidney-shaped rumpus-room bar. Red gazed about like he was in a museum, flipped open an English fashion magazine, a catalogue of tribes.

"Give him a trim," I told the coiffeur and nicked back up the street to the newsagent. Midweek Lotto had jackpotted to five million that week and the counter staff were flat chat handling a late rush of systems entries and syndicates. It hardly seemed worth the wait considering that I didn't really smoke. I waited anyway.

Back at the hairdressers, Red's Botticelli locks were a trampled heap on the floor. A sheet flapped like a conjurer's prop and the boy himself emerged from the chair transformed. His upward-tilted moon of a face, his babyhood, was gone. The new face was keenly alert, a face sufficient-unto-itself, a proper boy's face. My son the apprentice jockey, in a flat-top several sizes too small.

"You're going to die," this stranger accused, glaring at the cigarette in my mouth.

"I'll be dead when your mother sees you," I told him, grinding the cigarette into the linoleum. Furtively I scooped up one of Red's discarded ringlets, a relic of my baby's vanished infancy. "For the mother," I murmured, catching sight of a live louse in the debris.

We shopped, loading the car with groceries. I was jittery, jumping at the clatter of supermarket trolleys, nervously pacing the half-deserted aisles. After the dramas earlier in the day, these rituals of normality should have brought relief. Instead they made me all the more apprehensive. Red's presence only made it worse. The package of grass was burning a hole in my pocket.

A military funeral, Gezen's confession and subsequent disappearance, an intruder in the house, a wild chase over backyard fences, the business with Bayraktar's car. Collectively, they were adding up to a mystery I felt powerless to unravel, but whose lingering menace I felt everywhere around me. In the cereal aisle at Safeway I put my arm on Red's shoulder at the approach of a swarthy stranger. He was looking for the Coco Pops. When no one was looking I tucked the marijuana deep down behind a rack of muesli. A little bonus for the late-night shelf-stackers.

There I'd been, Mr. Clever Dick, bunging on a white knight act, trying to impress Ayisha in front of Bayraktar's heavy-duty crim mates, when all along she'd been hiding the fact that Gezen was not telling the whole story. Then she'd gone and disappeared, leaving me a sitting duck in a game whose rules I couldn't even guess at. What a bitch she was turning out to be.

As the Renault reversed out of its slot in the supermarket car park, a flash of dusty colour caught the corner of my eye. I pulled the steering wheel in an arm-wrenching arc and craned backwards over my shoulder. You're chasing ghosts in the twilight, I told myself. Two blocks from home, I glanced up at a stop sign and found a cube of lurid blue framed in the rectangle of the rear-vision mirror, an aqua Falcon, its windows impenetrable in the halogen wash of the newly lit street lights. I barked at Red to stay where he was and stepped out onto the road.

The Falcon had the same wide-mouthed grimace as before, but in other ways was subtly different. The paintwork shone with a higher polish, an air-intake duct sprouted from the bonnet, the tires were comically fat. The plates were personalised. VROOM, they read. The driver's window came down and Van Halen came out, loud. Then a head, Adonis with acne. "What's eating you, squirrel dick?" it shouted.

It was a good question. Before I could think of a pithy retort, the head disappeared and the Falcon peeled past, its horn blaring the first two bars of Dixie. "Dickhead," said Red. I didn't dare ask him who he meant.

Two men in suits were sitting in a parked car at the end of our street, a white Commodore. It was the two CIB dicks from Ciccio's. I parked outside the house and they got out, hoisting their belts up as they came. When they were two houses away I took out a two dollar note. "Go get some milk," I told Red. By the will of Wendy he was still too young to go to the corner shop alone. "You can spend the change." He grinned wildly and trotted off. With that sort of money he'd be standing at the lolly counter for half an hour.

I hoisted the bag of groceries and held the gate open for the coppers. "Murray Whelan?" asked the older one. He had a low centre of gravity and a bulbous aggressive nose but his tone was polite. "I'm detective sergeant Dalziel. This is detective constable York." York had been working out. He nodded, real friendly like.

"Acting on information, gentlemen?"

York ambled down the side of the house. I put my key in the front door and jiggled it about. "Do you have a warrant?"

"Do we need one?" said Dalziel pleasantly. I held the door open and let him in ahead of me. I hoped to hell nothing else had been planted around the house while I was away. We went through to the kitchen. Out the window I could see Mr. Muscle step across Wendy's rug and stick his head in the toolshed. Dalziel looked around like what he saw confirmed his worst suspicions. "You don't seem surprised to see us," he said.

"In my line of work you learn not to be surprised," I said, dumping the groceries on the bench.

He was walking around with his hands in his pockets, freely scrutinising everything in sight. "And exactly what is your line of work?"

When I told him, he showed no reaction, but I could hear the gears whirring as he tried to place me in the wider scheme of things. "People think their local member can wave a magic wand, fix their problems," I said. "If they don't get what they want, they blame me.

Some of them start throwing threats around. Anonymous tip, was it?" I had the groceries out of the bag and started loading the fridge.

"We're required to follow these things up," he said. "I'm sure you understand."

"What was it?" I said wearily. I prised the top off a stubby and waved it in his general direction. "Child pornography? Wife beating? Drugs?"

The copper ignored the beer. He tapped the window and waved York back out front. "Do you have any idea who might make such allegations?"

"No," I said. "But when you find out I'd certainly like to fucking well know."

Dalziel handed me his card. "I don't think we need disturb you further," he said. At least he didn't shoot me, which is more than some people can say about the Victorian police.

Being a functionary of the party in power arguably put me on the same side as the police. But as far as I was concerned, no quirk of political circumstance could alter the fact that, by disposition and training, all coppers were bastards until proven otherwise. I had suspected as much as a child, watching my father unlock the saloon bar in the lull after the six o'clock swill. No point in getting on the wrong side of the law, he'd whisper, reaching for the top shelf. My ambivalence was violently reinforced one afternoon in my first year at university.

There was a march. I can't even remember what it was about. It was a demo a minute in those days. This one was nothing major, no Springbok tour or US Consulate job. Just a few banners and Eureka flags. A couple of hundred chanting long-hairs. I'd just tagged along for a look. The hard left were a pack of wankers, as far as I was concerned, middle-class kids trying to pass themselves off as otherwise with bad manners and a lot of beer. But there was this girl, Georgina something, that I was thinking of making a play for. She was right up the front, holding the lead banner.

We were almost back on campus when the ambush happened. Hundreds of blue uniforms appeared at the top of a rise, more of them than us. An inspector with white epaulettes bellowed something unintelligible through a megaphone. An order to disperse, I guess. There was nowhere to disperse to. Then they charged. They went through us like a dose of the salts. Batons, horses, you name it. They'd taken off their numbers, so they could get energetic without fear of being identified. And they really knew how to enjoy themselves.

A big sergeant got me in a headlock while two of his mates took turns giving me the old one-two. I'd lost two teeth and nearly choked on my own blood before their interest flagged and they moved on. Georgina's boyfriend had his collar-bone broken, so from my point of view it all turned out to be for nothing. The next time I saw the sergeant was a decade later. Deputy Commissioner/ Operations I think his title was. He was sharing an official dais with Charlene.

But we get nowhere dwelling on past grievances. The dicks were gone and Red was back with a musk cigar and a packet of gum. Big bubbles. No troubles. I stuck him in front of the telly with the chicken pie we had picked up priced-to-clear at the supermarket bakery counter, rolled up my sleeves, and waded into a frenzy of housework. Wendy would be arriving tomorrow. Things needed to be done. The nit scare had been bad enough; having her find the house looking like a half-demolished rat-trap would have been tantamount to self-destruction.

I drained the lounge room swamp, washed dishes, vacuumed floors and hung damp laundry over the clothes horse to dry. While it felt somewhat ludicrous to be window-dressing the house I had shared with Wendy for seven years, it was also imperative that she find no evidence of inability to cope, no pretext for complaint that the child's welfare and comfort were at jeopardy in his father's hands. I did a particularly fine job on the toilet. In my experience, the link between bathroom cleanliness and female psychology cannot be overemphasised.

All this mindless activity gave me time to think. Someone breaks into my house, plants drugs, then calls the cops. The same somebody tries to run me over. It was impossible not to believe it was all connected to Memo Gezen and the toughs in the grey BMW. But how did they know where I lived? And what was all this supposed to achieve? And what if they came back? Was Red safe? Maybe a few days with Wendy might not be a bad idea, after all. Just until I got this business sorted out.

I was on my knees with a brush up the S-bend when the phone rang. Expecting it would be Wendy, I braced myself. It was old man Picone. Agnelli's uncle's brother-in-law, a market gardener from Werribee, had been at a family lunch on Sunday. Over the vitello tonnato he had been told that Agnelli would definitely be in parliament as of the next election.

I called the House straight away. Charlene wasn't in either her office or the chamber. I asked to be put through to the members' dining room. The head steward came on the line, recognised my voice and informed me that Mrs. Wills had just had some kind of collapse and a colleague had taken her to hospital. He didn't know which one. I rang the Royal Melbourne, the Women's, the Queen Victoria and St Andrews, which was closest to the House. She hadn't been admitted to any of them. All I got on her home number was the answering machine.

The rain had let up, so I took a Vegemite jar of Jamesons out into the backyard and we incinerated a couple of tobacco bushes together. When I thought about it, Charlene had been burning the candle pretty brightly over the previous two years. The election, the euphoria of winning office after so long in the wilderness, overhauling a moribund ministry, ramming through a hefty raft of reform legislation, it was all bound to take its toll. I should have been looking after her, shouldering more of the burden.

When she'd cancelled the last two of our regular sessions at the electorate office, our fortnightly chance to catch up with each other, I hadn't even asked why. Preoccupied coping with Red, running maintenance on the house, and stewing in my own juices over Wendy, I'd even been relieved. Not that enquiring after Charlene's health would have got me more than a gruff affirmative. She took far too much pride in her reputation as a tough old chook to solicit sympathy. But that shouldn't have stopped me asking.

The whiskey and nicotine must have fired me up. The urge to do something, anything, gnawed at me. This Bayraktar business was a real piss-off. The last thing I needed to be doing right now was looking over my shoulder every five minutes for the boys from the Anatolia Club. But until Ayisha or Gezen turned up I was left hanging. Or was I?

I rifled the phone book. Fifteen Celiks were listed, ten in the immediate area, none with the initial A. There were no Gezens at all, and no listing under Anatolia Club. A gambling club, Ayisha had called it. Perhaps I was coming at the subject from the wrong angle, thinking about the car. Rational thought hadn't been getting me anywhere. Trying to second-guess the dark recesses of the right-wing Turkish mind could easily take forever. It was time for some direct action, even if it was a blind punt.

Under Police was a listing for the Gaming Squad. A machine answered and told me to leave a message. I hung up, collected my thoughts and rang back. Anonymous denunciation was a game two could play. My accent was terrible, more Bombay than Bosphorus, made even worse by the pencil clamped between my molars. Maybe I sounded like a crank, but I didn't imagine they got too many calls from a prisoner at the Anatolia Club, 636 Blyth Street, Brunswick, pleading to be rescued before he was castrated for his gambling debts. And like the man said, they were required to follow these things up.

The odds were long, but with a smidgin of beginners luck, Bayraktar's buddies would at least be getting an enquiring official knock on their glossy green front door within a day or so. Whether it would be enough to teach them a bit of road courtesy remained to be seen. Jesus Christ, I thought, as I hung up. What had started as a strategy to save the government from embarrassment was turning into a very bad vaudeville routine.

Branch meetings started at 8 P.M. As the product of two inveterate meeting-goers, Red had accepted from infancy the normality of spending at least one night a week under a table with his colouring pencils at some discussion group or executive committee or task force. At seven-thirty I told him to get his coat.

"I'm not going," he said, digging his heels in. This tough new haircut was going to his head.

I offered him a dollar. He was unimpressed. A dirty brown banknote and a glass of pink lemonade were lousy compensation for being bored out of your brain for two hours while your father massaged the grass roots.

But the options were non-existent. My old man was in Queensland, not that he would have been much use even if he was closer. Wendy's parents were getting on, lived in Camberwell and never volunteered. Besides, they voted Liberal. I couldn't see myself calling them up and explaining the urgency of chairing a Labor party branch meeting.

Red began to whine. Great. Here we were fighting on what was possibly our last night of bachelorhood together before Wendy arrived and started making trouble. There was no alternative but to put my foot down and take a firm patriarchal stance. "Five dollars," I said. "Plus a packet of chips."

Right then the front doorbell rang. Red, looking for an out, flew up the hall and flung it open. "It's a lady," he yelled.

It was no lady. It was Ayisha, draped nonchalantly against the verandah post in her quilted overcoat. "Sivan said you wanted to see me," she said, as though she had no idea why. "What's happening?"

This sudden materialisation on my doorstep set me back a pace. To be discovered like this — a tea-towel across my shoulder, hectoring a small child — wasn't going to do my image any good. How would I ever be able to pass myself off as a Gramsci-reading, internationalist sophisticate after this? Aside from which, where did she come off with this casual attitude? I tucked the tea-towel in my hip pocket. "What's happening?" I snapped. "You fucking well tell me."

My attitude took her aback somewhat. "You okay?"

"No, I'm not. I'm mightily pissed off. I don't appreciate being fucked around. You could have had the decency to tell me what I was buying into."

Red was all ears, alert to my tension, watching the way I responded to this strange woman. He tucked himself against my thigh, declaring prior possession.

Ayisha cocked her head to one side. "You've been to the police, haven't you?"

At the mention of the word "police," I felt an electric charge of excitement surge through Red.

"Where have you been all day?" I demanded, sounding like a jealous husband. "And what about your friend Gezen?"

"I've been at college," she said. "Why?"

"College? What were you doing at college?"

"Accountancy," she said.

Accountancy? Christ, what about the revolution? At least she was safe. "You and I need to have a serious talk," I said. Not with the child there, though. "But right now Red and I are running late for a meeting."

Red saw his chance. "No we're not," he piped up cheerfully. "Come in." Detaching himself from my leg he took off down the hall. Taking his cue, Ayisha shouldered past me and followed him.

"You have been to the cops, haven't you?" she accused. "I thought you said you'd help."

I tailed her down the hall. The draped laundry, so homey and efficient only minutes before, looked pathetic. Red had turned on the television and thrown himself onto the couch. Grabbing Ayisha by the elbow, I propelled her out of his earshot. She looked around the kitchen, summing up my domestic arrangements. I could see her mentally pigeon-holing me.

"My wife, well my ex-wife, sort of, well, she lives in Canberra and . . ." I was babbling, shifting from one foot to the other.

"Christ, Murray," she said. "What's got into you?"

"Don't come Miss Innocent with me," I said, recovering my indignation fast. "First Gezen disappears, then you take off, then I find out about Gezen's political background, then . . ."

She pulled me up short. "Gezen's political background? What do you mean?"

"The PKK, or whatever it is, the Kurdish guerillas. Sivan told me. Don't worry, I didn't tell him about the Bayraktar business."

"Sivan told you Memo was PKK?" That sly grin was spreading back across her face. "And you believed him?"

"Sure." But I knew then that I shouldn't have.

"Christ, Murray," she laughed. "Memo Gezen's got six kids and chronic back pain and lives in a two-bedroom flat in East Keilor. He's no more PKK than the man in the moon. Sivan's been pulling your leg."

Of course. So he had. And I'd fallen for it — hook, line and sinker. "Why would he do that?" I sulked.

"Jeeze, I dunno. Sivan's a born joker. Maybe he thought you were still playing that guess-the-name game you started him on yesterday. He probably thought you knew he was having you on."

"But when Gezen disappeared this morning, I thought those guys in the BMW . . ." To be perfectly frank, I could no longer remember exactly what I'd been thinking.

"Memo didn't disappear," Ayisha said. "He went back to work. When he first turned up, asking about getting a lawyer, he told me he was on his lunch break. Then you said for him to go to work like normal, not to draw attention to himself. So when we knew it wasn't the police parked out the front, I told him to piss off quick smart. Out the back door and back to work before he was missed."

"So why were the Anatolia Club guys in the BMW watching him?"

"Yeah," she said. "I've been wondering that myself all day."

"At college?"

"Yeah."

"But why did you take off so quickly? Sivan didn't say anything about you being at college."

"I knew he'd forget," she said. "Usually I go on Thursdays and Fridays. But end of year exams are on. I had a three-hour statistics test at midday. I hadn't exactly been expecting all that business with Memo, you know. And we had to go through that story of his twice, once in Turkish and again in English. By the time he'd finished I was running seriously late. Put me right off, it did. Wouldn't be surprised if I failed. Anyway, we all went off to the pub afterwards and I didn't get your message until I got home half an hour ago. How was I supposed to know you'd been looking for me?"

"Don't you want to know why I was looking for you?" I asked.

"Sure," she said. We'd sat down at the kitchen table by this stage. She didn't have anything better to do with her time. "That's what I'm here for."

I gave her the works, everything from disturbing the intruder onwards. I left out the bits about going to the Bell Street cop shop and calling the Gaming Squad. I felt enough of an idiot about having believed Sivan. For once she didn't interrupt or ask questions, but as I spoke she crossed to the stove, lit a cigarette off the gas jet and began pacing about like a caged animal. "So you see," I concluded, "I've been holding off going to the cops with the full story until I had a chance to talk to you. I want to do the right thing by Memo, but I've got a child to think about."

Through the door into the lounge room I could see Red entrenching himself deeper into the television. "Turn off that fucking telly this instant," I screamed. "We're late already." I considered ringing ahead, telling them to start without me. How could they? The agenda papers were on the back seat of my car.

"I can't believe it," Ayisha was saying. "Attacking you in broad daylight. It's crazy."

"You think I'm making this up?"

"No, no. All I mean is . . ." She brushed her hair back off her forehead, as though this gesture might better convey her meaning.

"We'll have to finish this later," I said. "I really do have to go." In the lounge room, Red had made no move.

Ayisha brushed past me into the other room and perched on the arm of the couch. Red's eyes flickered sideways, registering her presence, then re-attached themselves firmly to the screen. A man in a pair of blue rubber gloves was whispering to the camera in a stealthy undertone as he sidled through some shrubbery.

"This the part with the gorilla?" she said.

Red grunted in the affirmative, the mutual-recognition signal of the committed video-head.

"Can I watch with you while your dad goes to his meeting?" She moved onto the couch beside him, slipping her arms out of that inflatable overcoat of hers.

Could she what? "Uh-huh," he said. "The good bit's on next."

"You can wait a couple more hours before calling the you-know-whats, can't you?" Red moved aside to accommodate her. "Don't worry," she hastened to reassure me. "I know the drill. I've got five younger brothers."

There was no fighting it. I'd just been boxed in by the fastest coalition in history. A united front, irresistible force and immovable object.

16

THE LAKEVIEW HOTEL was a sprawling ranch-style beer barn in the middle of a residential neighbourhood half a mile from Sydney Road. At nineteen I had worked there in the guise of Fred Engels, pulling trays of jugs and the occasional barmaid. Across the road through a line of scraggy she-oaks lay Edwardes Lake, a flooded gravel pit landscaped with bike paths, coin-in-the-slot barbecues and adventure playgrounds.

The branch met in the Function Room. About the only useful function it served was to store a couple of derelict pool tables and provide a rent-free space for branch meetings. As usual Laurie the publican had laid a sheet of plywood over one of the pool tables, turned on the strip radiator bolted halfway up the wall, and set out thirty chairs on the Prussian blue Axminster. Laurie, a party member since before the Split, was an inveterate optimist. At that time of the year we'd be lucky to get a dozen takers, which was the exact number waiting when I bustled through the door at eight-fifteen. "Okay," I said. "Let's get on with it. We don't want to be here all night."

We did attendances and apologies first, me putting my hand up for Charlene, Greg Coates and half a dozen others. Thirteen attendances and fifteen apologies out of sixty-seven members on the books. It was the usual crowd — true believers, unreconstructed Whitlamites, reliable booth captains, handers out of how-to-vote cards, knife-sharpeners, has-beens and wannabees. Laurie's son Barry, a forty-seven-year-old bachelor draftsman at the State Electricity Commission, took the minutes on a concertina pile of computer paper salvaged from the SEC recycle bin.

The dauphin, Gavin Mullane, was there, keen to push his traffic safety barrow, and to keep a weather eye on the North West Progress Association, a childless couple in their mid-fifties who stole his thunder on local issues whenever they could. Our resident ex-Trotskyist was a teacher named Vernon Tibbett. Vern had squandered his youth selling *Direct Action* outside factory gates at the crack of dawn and was spending the rest of his life making other people pay for it. Behind him sat Sam Righi, administrator of the Broadmeadows Legal Service where Joe Lollicato worked. This was his first attendance in months. He'd be worth pumping later. A couple of fresh faces were paying their neophyte dues before they stuck their hands up for a job. The rest had always been there, nice old codgers who kept the faith, remembered the ancient enmities, and sat in wise silence as befitted tribal elders.

Mercifully, there were no Greeks. The local inventors of democracy had their own branch where they could engage in vigorous dialectics in their native demotic until the goats came home, sparing the rest of us the ordeal. "Item one." I moved briskly into the agenda. "Matters arising."

Tibbett leaped to his feet. "Comrade Chair. Point of procedure. I move a suspension of standing orders in order to bring forward agenda item number sixteen, a resolution pertaining to the federal government's flagrant overriding of party policy in respect of the mining and export of uranium."

"Fine," I said. "Seconder?"

Nobody moved a muscle except a rather jolly nursing aide called Maggie Alcott who was a shop steward with the Hospital Employees Federation. She sniffed and rammed her forearms deeper into the sleeves of her chunky-knit cardigan. I gave it a slow count of ten. "Motion lapses for want of a seconder. Now . . ."

We sped through the next fifteen items in an hour and three-quarters flat, including twenty brain-numbing minutes devoted to Gavin Mullane's hypothetical traffic lights, "not two hundred metres from where we are actually sitting at this point in time." Tibbett's motion was last up.

For all its outward efficiency, my chairing was driven by a growing sense of impatience and anxiety. After all that had happened that day, how had I been so willing to hand Red over to the first baby-sitter that came along? Ayisha's five little brothers, her childcare credentials, what were they but proof of her mother's fertility? You saw those immigrant families all the time, driving along with no seat belts, tribes of kids standing up on the back seat, only the slightest bump away from being catapulted head first through the windscreen. What did I really know about Ayisha Celik except that I was mad keen to pop her in the cot?

The meeting debated Vern Tibbett's resolution for a tedious half hour, amended it into grammatical incoherence, passed it on factional lines and directed me to convey its views to the national secretary and the relevant minister. By the time I thanked them for their attendance and closed the meeting it was twenty past ten on the Dewars Whisky clock above the bar.

After I'd helped Barry stack the chairs and turn off the heater, I went into the lounge bar to conduct the real business of the night. Mullane saw me coming, emptied his glass, nodded goodnight and ducked out the door. As if I'd want to drink with him. The old blokes were drinking in a school. I bought a round and asked after various grandchildren. No one volunteered anything about Charlene, so the word wasn't yet out. Sam Righi turned towards me and put two fingers up for another round, an unrefusable invitation. I excused myself and went over.

Laurie's beer was watered and there was urgent unfinished business elsewhere, but ever since Greg Coates' remarks earlier in the afternoon a question had been gnawing at the back of my mind. I hoisted the offered beer and once again lubricated my smoke-bruised throat. "How's life at the Legal Service? Joe Lollicato still running the joint?" I asked, just making conversation.

Righi grinned. "Not much gets past you, does it?"

I fired up a coffin nail. "Not if I can help it."

"That Lolly," he said. "Talk about falling on your feet. Good luck to him, that's what I say."

He said it, but he didn't mean it. Righi's bile was too close to the surface to hide. It seemed that Lollicato had had some kind of luck and Righi wanted to put his own spin on the story. "Lucky Lolly," I said dryly, as if to say I never liked him either.

Righi was warming up for a full-blooded bad-mouthing session. "The silly prick'll need a business card the size of a surfboard."

I egged him on. "Yeah?"

"He's been looking for a way out for months. Made no secret of it. Then, bang, out of the blue an offer like this." As he recited, he expanded his hands like an exaggerating fisherman. "Senior Lecturer, Intercultural Legal Studies, Faculty of Multicultural Disciplines, University of New England, Armidale."

I whistled and wiggled my eyebrows appreciatively. So Lollicato was planning on leaving town. Hardly the move of a man scheming his way into a local seat. "Look on the bright side," I said. "Fancy title, but those academic jobs pay shit money."

Righi hailed Laurie for another two beers, not his round. Lollicato was just for openers, there was something else on his mind, something he wanted. "Don't suppose you've had a chance to think about the by-election yet?"

"You've lost me."

"When Joe moves interstate, there'll have to be a by-election, won't there?" So that was it. Righi wanted Lolly's spot on Broadmeadows Council.

It was getting on for twenty to eleven. A frank and fulsome discussion of Sam Righi's ambitions would have to wait. I tipped my head back and let the bitter liquid wash across my tongue. As the glass came down, the public bar came into view through the servery hatch. It was deserted but for a solitary drinker wrapped tight around his glass at the far end, his back to the hatch. Something about the way he held himself tugged at a loose thread in my memory. Catching Laurie's eye, I pointed with my chin. "One of your regulars?"

The publican shook his head. "Been nursing that drink for half an hour. Better finish soon or I'll do my licence."

I stood up and laid a hand on Righi's shoulder. "If you have any ideas about likely candidates, let me know. They could do with some fresh blood up there at Broadie."

The guy in the drive-in bottle shop was shutting up, pulling the chains on the heavy roll-down door. I told him I wanted a bottle of white wine. "Something in particular, sir?" he asked, like he was the cellar-master at Chateau Lafitte.

"A bottle of Hope Springs Eternal," I said. "If you haven't got that, anything under eight dollars will do." The covered walkway to the carpark led past the public bar. I glanced in the window as I passed, but the room was deserted except for Laurie up-ending stools on the bar top. I shrugged and threw Barry's minutes into a Dumpster, planning to write them up properly in the morning. That uranium motion would need substantial rejigging. Buggered if I was going to have the federal Minister for Resources' office screaming its tits off at me because Tibbett thought his line wasn't sufficiently correct.

Righi's little jewel about Lollicato, coming on top of Coates, added to what I was beginning to glean about Agnelli, made it pretty definite that I'd been fed some monumental crap at lunch on Monday. As I crossed the carpark I tried to reconstruct exactly what Agnelli had said, but only fragments came to mind. On recollection, however, it was plain that Agnelli had been feeding me a lot of ifs, buts and maybes, leading the talk in the direction he wanted, encouraging me to put my reservations aside and jump to a lot of conclusions. Conclusions that were now looking pretty dodgy indeed. Clearly, Lollicato did not then have, and maybe never had, serious parliamentary ambitions. Clearly, there had never been any genuine likelihood of an industrial flare-up at Pacific Pastoral. So either

Agnelli had been misinformed, genuinely ignorant, or blowing a cloud of smoke in my eyes. The third option seemed most likely.

Agnelli was enough of a player to know that if he wanted Charlene's seat, he would need either to win me over or to keep me busy while he manoeuvred himself into position. He also knew the strength of my loyalty to Charlene and that any attempt to sound me out would have set off my alarm bells. So getting me out of the way while he lined up the numbers was the only real option. And what better way to get me to take my eye off the ball while the deals were done than to send me chasing a red herring? That's what this Pacific Pastoral cock and bull story had been all about. There had been more than one pigeon on the menu at the Mandarin Palace.

Christ, I'd been well and truly suckered. He'd probably even planted the story in the *Sun*. Agnelli hung around the Windsor Hotel, drinking with the political roundsmen, slipping them judicious leaks whenever the government wanted to fly a trial balloon on some contentious issue. Talk enough bullshit, he liked to say, and sooner or later it ends up in print.

The carpark shimmered, a shallow sea of puddles. I turned the Renault into the road. Its headlights found a break in the trees and fanned across the surface of the lake. A lash of wind stirred the darkness and a squall of fat raindrops burst across the windscreen. I headed up the hill and it began raining in earnest, heavy sluicing bucket-loads that whistled at the seams of the windows and buffeted the small sedan from side to side with a force that momentarily stalled the wipers in mid-sweep. The windscreen became a lustrous swarming blanket. I could scarcely see past the bonnet.

I turned the wipers up high and leaned forward, peering between their puny swipes. My knuckles were white as the wheel turned to mush in my hands. I was piloting a submarine up Niagara Falls. Slowing to a crawl, I inched forward. Up ahead was a roundabout, then the road dipped again, cutting across the bottom end of the lake where it overflowed across a weir and ran off into a creek so insignificant it had no name. This was where Mullane wanted his traffic lights.

The downpour was flash-flooding across the asphalt as the stormwater drains overloaded and backed up. As I neared the roundabout, the engine shuddered and it seemed I might stall, hubcap-deep. I changed down, slammed my foot down hard and felt the Renault shudder as the wheels threw great pounding jets of water up against the floor like fire-hoses turned on a rioting mob.

Just as I entered the curve, a powerful beam of light blazed suddenly on my right. Another car had come darting out of the cross street, its lights on high beam, apparently not seeing me. The idea flashed into my mind that I was driving without lights. I groped for the switch. Of course the lights were on, I realised simultaneously. How else had I been navigating? No, the other car must be able to see me. I was like a rabbit in a spotlight. What was the dickhead doing?

The dickhead was almost on top of me now, an advancing wall of white light, waves sluicing up from its front wheels. Mullane had been right about one thing. There definitely were some maniac drivers around here. I swerved left, pumping at the brake pedal, feeling it suddenly useless under my foot. The Renault glided forward, rudderless. There was a flash of blue and I recognised the Falcon just at the instant the Renault ramped up the sloping brick pavers of the curb and left the ground, surging forward into a gap between the crash barriers.

I rose with it, my backside lifting clear of the seat, snapping back into place at the strain of the seat belt. Then, as the Renault's front wheels slewed into the soft earth of the roadside verge, I felt myself rise again. The front end of the car had stopped so abruptly that the back was still going, its momentum carrying it into an end-to-end roll, pitching me into an acrobat's tumble, my hands locked around the wheel in a dead man's grip.

This is it, I thought, and screwed my face shut against the imminence of oblivion. The Renault flipped onto its roof, shuddered, and came to rest. The roar of the storm filled my head and luminous shapes bobbed on the edge of my consciousness. Something wet ran up my face, trickling into my nose and gathering in a pool at the nape of my neck. I sneezed, my eyes squirting open with the force of it. I was, I realised, suspended upside down by the straps of the seat belt, my head jammed sideways against the cold vinyl of the roof. Water was coming in from above, from the floor of the car. You can't be this uncomfortable and dead at the same time, I told myself.

My left hand groped for the catch of the seat belt and sprang it open, releasing me down upon myself, a foetal ball. My right hand searched for the door handle, and failed to find it. Gripping the bottom edge of the dashboard, I struggled to haul myself upright, my shoulders shucking themselves free of the seat belt. A scraping noise began. The car was moving, gathering momentum as it slid down the slippery incline of the bank. The steel shell of the roof screeched as it scraped across the concrete path that circled the lake. The Renault tilted abruptly, tottered for a moment, and slid into the water, rear end first.

The lake was enormously wet, enormously dark. It wrapped itself around the shell of the car and sucked it downwards. The door came open and water gushed in, frigid beyond my powers of description, filling the interior. I never felt more alive in my life. As water forced itself into my mouth, blind terror guided my feet against the dashboard.

Then somehow I was outside, breaking the surface, clawing at the air, my breath raspy and asthmatic, my testicles retreating before the icy onslaught. Sheets of torrential rain churned the surface around me. The bottom was somewhere in the darkness far below. My clothes were bonds, dragging me downwards. Breathing came in short hysterical gasps. Cold was crushing my chest. Looming above, dark on dark, was the embankment. Somewhere a light bobbed, moving closer. I kicked out towards the shore.

Some slimy thing brushed my face, then another, and another, triggering yet more spasms, panic and cold in equal proportions. What horror was this? A tendril swept into my mouth, scaly and stiff. I spat it out, but there were more, dozens of them, trailing their tentacles over my lips and ears. My arms flailed the water, swatting, grabbing, my fingers closing around one of the ropy lengths, slippery and elastic.

My upper body rose from the water and solid ground formed itself under my feet. I stood, amazed to find myself in less than a metre of water. The thing in my hand resolved itself into the dangling branch of a weeping willow. Over my shoulder, the Renault had disappeared entirely. My feet mired in unseen mud, sheets of torrential rain lashing my face, freezing water up to my thighs, I emitted an involuntary groan of relief.

The bobbing light approached, above on the embankment. A stocky figure, half umbrella, was braving the storm, sweeping the lake with the beam of a powerful torch. I opened my mouth to shout and nearly bit off my tongue, my teeth and jaws shivering into spasm. A thin, animal moan escaped from deep in my chest. It was all I could manage. The wind threw it back into the darkness behind me. Grasping the dangling ropes of the willow branches for support, I sucked my shoes up out of the mud and began shuffling ashore. The man with the torch, God bless him, would see me soon. Christ, I was cold.

The bank was a shoulder-high redoubt of slippery mud, cascading with rain water. I tried to cry out again, but still all that came was the same wounded animal noise, lost in the roar of the rain, and the castanet clatter of my teeth. One thing I knew for sure was that if I didn't get out of there soon I'd freeze to death where I stood.

The light was less than twenty metres away by then, almost close enough to touch. The figure holding it crouched low under the dome of an umbrella, and peered intently along the beam, methodically playing it back and forth across the roiling water. But it was pointed in the wrong direction, flashing uselessly across the place where the car had gone down. Whoever it was would pass without noticing me, half-drowned, virtually underfoot. I gathered a fistful of willow frond and hauled, dragging myself hand over hand upwards, into his line of sight.

My fingers were stiff with cold, my sodden clothes a dead weight. The branch bent low and snapped. I was back in the water, my feet kicking for the bottom, not finding it. My suit was a sheet of lead swathing my limbs, dragging me under. The light was going now, retreating up the embankment towards the road. I opened my mouth and pushed a yell up from deep inside my body cavity, but water filled my mouth and all that came out was a wheezing cough. Then the current took me.

Rain, flooding into the lake from every direction, had raised the water above the level of the containment weir. A foaming sheet was pouring over the lip of the spillway only yards away. I felt myself being swept along, the pull increasing. The smooth concrete lip of the rim reared out of the dark and struck my shoulder. Suddenly I was toppling over the wall, ricocheting down the open funnel of the overflow chute. White water buffeted me from all sides. Up ahead, at the apex of the funnel, the dark mouth of a stormwater drain yawned. There wasn't even enough time to scream before I was sucked into its swirling vortex.

17

TURBID WITH CRAP of every variety, the torrent surged through the culvert, hurtling me irresistibly, feet-forward into the void. My jaw was clamped shut against the water, but nothing could lessen the elemental roar that filled my ears as I barrelled the length of the stormwater drain, my head bang, bang, banging against smooth concrete walls.

Just at the moment my lungs seemed about to burst, I was spat out like an orange pip and deposited, flailing, into the bed of the creek with no name. My feet hit the rocky bottom with a bone-jarring impact and I immediately pitched face-down into the stream. Again I was swept helplessly forward, along with all the other crummy debris the storm was flushing away — a toxic minestrone of wormy furballs, slimy old Wagon Wheel wrappers, dog turds, all the dross of a thousand households. As I tumbled by, the blackberry bushes crowding the banks slashed at my clothes but failed utterly to slow my progress.

Several times I managed to struggle upright, but the creek bed was an uneven tangle of slippery rocks and lumps of masonry, and the pressure of the current was so immense that I was immediately sent flailing onwards, scrabbling to keep my head above the vile wash.

Then a glowing shape loomed ahead of me. An old white bathtub, upside down, its bottom perforated with rust like a colander, jutted into the stream. I threw my arms over its slippery enamel curve and felt the ground solidify under my knees as the tide fought to drag me back under. Staggering upright, I threw myself headlong up the bank and pitched into a thicket of blackberries. One, two, three steps and I hit a sagging chain-mesh fence. I scrabbled upwards, my fingers through the links, putting distance between myself and the eddying whirl behind me, until the dead weight of my body flipped over the top and toppled into a mound of green plastic garbage bags, soft and yielding.

As suddenly as it had begun, the storm was abating. Rain was still falling, but in an ethereal, almost benign mist. I rolled over and lay face-down, listening to my heart race. The slick plastic was smooth against my cheek. The cushioning softness yielded to my shape. My entire existence seemed to have been reduced to a dull pulsating throb that wobbled back and forth behind my closed eyes like a malignant octopus.

I was cold, I knew that from the chattering of my teeth — now a finer, more regular grinding movement than the out-of-control juddering of before. This was like a special machine, something for polishing stones. I could live with this sensation, as long as the ache in my head went away. Yes, I was cold, but first I had to rest, allow the terror to drain away. Every muscle felt bruised, every nerve teased raw.

Distantly, up the hill, I could hear the faint hum of traffic. I knew that if I looked up I would see a littered incline and the back of a row of small workshops and factories that ran along the ridge above the creek. But to do that I would have to raise my head. The view wasn't worth it.

I knew this place. On paper, it had long ago been slated for development as community recreation space, pending funding. I had seen the plans pinned to a board in the town hall foyer — thematic shrubbery, stick citizens at picnic tables. Submissions had been invited from the public. So far the only development had been the erection of a fence along the ridge behind the industrial estate and some signs prohibiting the dumping of rubbish. Ingenuity thrives on such obstacles. Uncivil garbage, rich in diversity, had insinuated its way over the chain link border and down the slope. Paint tins, twisted bike wheels, warped and splintered plywood, garden waste, trash and junk of all kinds littered the slope where I lay.

But at least it was dry land, drier than the creek anyway. And if not quite land then a squelching mattress, soft and warm against my body. I reached over and stroked the pliant, yielding cushion on which I lay, feeling warmth beneath my fingers as though the core of the earth had risen to comfort me.

Not just my face and fingers felt the soft heat, but my chest and thighs too, even through the sodden fabric of my suit. I snuggled deeper, drawing a filthy sheet of old linoleum over me as a blanket. Pain surged red behind my eyes with the effort of movement. Lie still, my brain commanded.

Smell, as well as warmth, enveloped me, the rich pong of rotting vegetation. Lawn clippings, I recognised. I poked a hole in the bag and it gave a fragrant sigh, a gaseous rush of breath. It was full of half-rotten grass, cut wet and packed down hard, dumped by some weekend gardener too lazy or too lousy to drive to the tip and pay his three dollars. Trapped in the airless plastic, the grass had begun to ferment and smoulder with the same febrile heat that causes haystacks to combust spontaneously.

Ignoring the shrill irritability of the poisonous octopus in my skull, I cradled the pillow closer and snuggled deeper into the bloated softness. Its embrace fused with the dissipating heat of my body and soothed the ache at the centre of my being. Shuddering, I groaned softly and drank in the steaming aroma of a hose-drenched summer lawn. Mother earth held me fast. "Mummy," I murmured.

The beer garden of the Pier Hotel had been my first proper lawn. Before that, living upstairs at the Carters Arms, I had envied the other kids their backyards, the space for balls and cubbies. As soon as I saw that lawn at the Pier I had claimed it, a mat of couch-grass just long enough for a run-up and a full toss. I hammered in the stumps as a claim of ownership and set the bails on top.

Fine, my father had said. You want it, you mow it. And he'd pointed into the shed, past the empty kegs and spare pluto hoses, to the rotary mower. At eight it had been all I could do to push the thing, its cylinder of blades and tractor-treaded iron wheels stiff with age and rust. Then, shaking off the months of disuse, it had darted forward, springing into life, tumbler whirring, and thrown an arc of green confetti behind, first rough and itchy on bare shins then soft and spongy under bare soles. A green rainbow in the summer sun, flecked with transient light like tail lights disappearing in the rain, like the sweep of a torch beam across freshly chopped water.

The police would be here soon. The helicopter would be thumping overhead, wompa wompa, sweeping its bloody great searchlight across the dark waters, following the line of the creek. Floodlights and generators. Frogmen, groping the mud, would attach chains to a tow-truck winch and haul the gushing Renault ashore. Orange tape stretched across the embankment, the traffic branch in their white raincoats going door to door. Did you see anything, madam? The Accident Appreciation Squad.

Told you so, I'd tell them. None of this would have happened if you'd pulled your fingers out earlier. A driver deliberately run off the road, a car on its roof in ten metres of water. Hardly a bit of harmless hooning around. Attempted murder, that's what. Questions in the House, there'd be. Charges laid. Red faces all round. Serves them right. Attempted murder. One for downtown, Russell Street. Well out of the local league, this one. Let's hear what Bayraktar's mates would have to say for themselves when the Homicide Squad came knocking on the door at the Anatolia Club.

Three days ago I'd never heard of Bayraktar, now someone in the guy's car was trying to kill me. What for? Crossing the street with intent to ask questions? What sort of fascistic bloody-mindedness was that? Shaking a fist in the street, hardly a killing offence. Talk about over-excitable wogs.

Gezen was the key. All this shit had started the moment Gezen had decided to make a clean breast of it. Double life Gezen. Timid little mop jockey Gezen, eyes that sucked you dry. What was it he had said? "I see everything." Maybe that was it. Maybe he had seen something he shouldn't have. Maybe somebody thought he had dobbed them in. Maybe they thought he had told me something he shouldn't have.

Bayraktar could not have been working alone. The man could hardly even sign his own name, let alone fabricate the contents of a tax declaration form. Was he just doing what he was told, someone else doing the thinking? Maybe it was all bullshit, Gezen's confession, the whole standover story. Gezen had Ayisha convinced, that much was sure. Or was she in on it, too? That rushed and hushed burble of Turkish before Gezen had told his story, what had that been all about? No, Ayisha wouldn't dud her pal Murray, would she? She liked me. Even though my head ached and I felt like shit, she liked me.

Why else would she be curled up beside me now, here on this rubbish tip, her rump tucked into the curve of my belly, her hair tickling my neck, the rhythm of her breathing rising and falling with mine? She wouldn't lie, she whose mouth was finding mine, the rubbery flesh of her lips nuzzling mine, the wet rasp of her tongue mashing my cheek, a whine of desire rising from her throat.

I opened my eyes. A black dog with yellow teeth — a foul-breathed, wet-mouthed, bow-legged roly-poly lump of an animal with an accordion button row of nipples down its belly — was slobbering over my face. I stumbled upright, throwing off the lino. My shoes squelched. My head felt as though it had been cast in some experimental material that would soon be recalled by the manufacturer. The sky was clear and bright and very high up. At the far horizon a few last cauliflowers of cloud raced ahead of the slight breeze. Through the broken glass of my watch I deciphered that it was just about to go one-thirty. Or had been when the watch stopped. I shook my head in disbelief, igniting fireworks behind my eyes. The searing jolt slowly subsided into mere pain.

Unbelievable. Run off the road, car wrecked, nearly drowned, swept away in a flood, and what do I do? I pass out like a baby, face down in a pile of compost for more than three hours. From somewhere uphill came the fading sound of a car engine. The dog licked my hand and stuck its muzzle in my crotch. It wasn't much, but I was grateful for the thought.

"C'mon," I said. The vibration of my voice triggered another chain reaction in my skull. I began picking my way through the broken glass and builder's rubble. Bile and old beer rose in my gullet. My trouser legs were rubbing the insides of my thighs raw. I shivered, that old spasm back again.

The double cyclone-gate at the top of the rise was locked, but there was enough slack on the chain to slip through the gap. The low row of brick workshops — a panel beater's, a printery, a tiler's yard — showed no light. Daytime places. In one direction the road curved away towards houses, in the other it ran back down towards the lake. I was a blinking neon of unpleasant sensation, sweating cold. The dog frolicked beside me, an imbecile.

"Easy, lover girl," I urged, needing to hear my own voice. It was high-pitched, all edge. I wondered where the energy was coming from. The lake came into view, a ruffled nap of black velour. I kept on down the empty road, past the bolted roller door of the Lakeview Hotel's drive-in bottle shop. The only sound now was the faint swish of the treetops.

No rescue squad. No nothing. Maybe, I thought, I'm still asleep. At the weir wall, a thin glaze of water curved gently over the culvert, no more turbulent than a blanket tucked tight at the end of a well-made bed. Down the embankment, the weeds flattened by the up-turned Renault's progress were already springing upright. The gashes torn in the earth by the impact were no more than a random string of muddy ruts. From the path at the lake's edge I peered into the water, willing the sunken car to reveal itself. Two grand worth of comprehensively uninsured frogmobile, vanished.

Not a single tangible sign existed that anything untoward had happened here. Maybe, I thought, I'm dead. Maybe I'm over there under the water watching myself, the sole witness to my own demise. The dog whined, clamped its teeth gently around my fingers and tugged. If I'm dead, I thought, who are you? Cerberus, watchdog of the nether world? "Not enough heads," I said, out loud. "You need more heads." I tried to remember how many, but it made my own ache even more.

Across the road, behind mute front gardens, houses slept dumbly on, substantial and warm. I considered opening one of the front gates, knocking on the door. "Excuse me for waking you. Someone tried to kill me, but I went to sleep. Mind if I use your phone. You couldn't spare a cup of coffee while I wait, could you?" A crap-encrusted madman, mongrel dog in tow. Just the thought of it was enough to make my headache worse. I turned to the lake and vomited, beery dregs and diced carrots. Where did *they* come from? How come when you chuck there's always diced carrots?

A car approached down the hill. I stiffened and hobbled into the shadow of the trees. A little Japanese number puttered down to the roundabout, turned, and disappeared between the houses, reeling its exhaust rattle in as it went. Paranoia, I thought. Proof of the existence of life. And why shouldn't I have been paranoid? Where were the fucking cops when you needed them? I paid my taxes, didn't I? Wasn't I as entitled as the next person to venture forth on the streets without fear for life and property? Hadn't the Gaming Squad got my message?

And what had become of the Good Samaritan, with his torch and his umbrella? What kind of person would see a car go hurtling into a lake, wander around in a storm searching for survivors, then pack up and go home without reporting it? Shit, maybe the police had already been. Come, found nothing and gone.

I felt my scalp, probing for hairline fractures, distrusting my memory. How could a man think in this state, beaten insensible, his head throbbing and surging? Tender lumps bulged at the nape of my neck. I vomited again, retching bile. I puke therefore I am.

Another car approached. It had a light on its roof. "Taxi," I croaked. The word hung in the air as if confirming my existence. I raised my hand and fumbled for the wad of notes and coins in my pants pocket. Five soggy dollars, ten, some change. Enough. I waved it above my head. The cab slowed. I saw myself reflected back in the driver's stony glance. A wild-eyed derro, standing in a pool of chuck, waving crumpled bills, a dirty dog. The cab kept rolling, picking up speed. He might as well have got out and kicked me.

"What's the matter with this country?" I asked the mutt. If the dog knew, she wasn't saying. This bitch was turning into a liability. I sprayed a handful of gravel half-heartedly in her direction. "Garn. Git." The dog skittered away, then cringed back, creeping forward on her belly. What have I done to deserve this? "True," I relented. "C'mon then."

C'mon where? When I'd started down the hill towards the lake I imagined myself being rushed by paramedics. I'd be wrapped in blankets. A steaming cup of tea would be thrust into my hands. A lady sergeant with a clipboard would sit beside me in the back of an ambulance. Well, it was pretty clear that no such thing was going to happen. I thought of Red and a spasm of anxiety gripped my stomach. I must call home. Call home then call the police.

Past the roundabout and up the hill was a little strip of shops — a chemist, a milk bar, an appliance repairer. And a phone booth. I began shambling along the footpath, the dog waddling alongside, forgiven and forgiving. The shivers were getting worse and my thighs were red raw. I was tempted to pee in my pants for thermal relief, like a surfer in his wetsuit. As we passed the neat front yards, their trees stripped of blossoms by the storm, I scanned the facades, wondering if I knew anyone hereabouts well enough to wake them up. The houses all but snored. No light showed, no television flickered behind venetians. Were there no insomniacs left in suburbia? There had to be someone. This was my territory, after all. It wasn't as though I was in a foreign country.

Fight the headache, fight the nausea, this was my mantra. Not far now. Think it through. Must call home, check on Red. Tell Ayisha. God, maybe whoever did this to me had also done something to Red. Calm down. They wouldn't harm a child. Why would they do that? But why do anything they'd done? None of it made sense. The Falcon in the rain, it was the same one, wasn't it? Visibility had been close to zero. There must be hundreds of big blue sedans on the road. Maybe it had just been a perfectly innocent accident. Ahead, a man on a horse tipped his hat at me. Marlboro man was riding the range on the billboard wall of the milk bar. I gripped the coins in my pocket and turned the corner. In front of the phone box, nose to the curb in the six-slot parking area, sat Bayraktar's Falcon.

A sheet of heavy-duty transparent plastic had been stuck over the missing rear window with blue electrical tape. It was billowing softly in and out like a lung. I went rigid and pressed myself against the cowboy's horse. Nothing else moved. Deep in the milk bar a row of bottles stood sentinel, back-lit in a refrigerated display. The Falcon was empty.

I grabbed the handle and threw the driver's door open, not caring any more. Nothing. No perfidious Turk waiting to spring. Not even any litter. Just the key in the ignition and the ozone smell of freshly wiped vinyl. The dog fixed that, bounding past me onto the passenger seat.

The dog was doing my thinking for me. Take the car and I could be home in ten minutes. I would know if Red was safe. If I called the police from the phone box, a prowl car might be twenty minutes arriving. Then would come the explanations, the questions, more explanations. I would have to take them down the hill, show them the vanishing skid marks, convince them I wasn't deranged. Fuck them. This was all their fault anyway. I'd call from home.

I walked around the car. I crouched, joints stiff, and peered underneath. I sprung the hood and peered into the oily pit of the motor. What was I looking for? A bundle of gelignite, a coil of wires, a ticking clock? The engine block was cold to the touch. I got in. The seat was too far forward, squeezing me against the steering wheel. The last person in this seat had been shorter. I bent forward and found the adjustment lever. A smear of drying mud covered the floor. The seat slid back and I turned the key. The big six-cylinder purred into action. Fingerprints, I thought, shrugged and gripped the wheel. Let the cops figure it out.

Streetlights flashed past overhead, a stroboscope that woke the epileptic octopus in my skull, made it real mad. A nauseating sickly-sweet detergent smell came up at me off the upholstery. Keeping off the main roads, I made it home in fifteen minutes. I parked halfway along the street and left the key in the ignition. "Stay," I told the dog. Dognapping. What would it be next?

The only other cars parked in the street were familiar. No BMWs. Ayisha's Laser was parked out the front where she had left it. Down the side of the house a light showed dimly at the kitchen window. I was standing on the verandah, patting myself down and asking the toxic octopus where I had left my keys when the front door opened. Out of some swamp deep inside me came the croak of a frog. "Red," it said.

Ayisha appeared, immersed in a pool of light. She swam towards me out of her halo. Our Lady of the Muddle Headed. "Fuck," she said.

Then nothing. Nothing at all.

18

SHE HAD ME on the bedroom floor and was pulling my trousers off. I felt a stirring in my underpants. Not now, I prayed, not now. Then I was under the covers, warm and dry. The octopus prised one eyelid open and Ayisha's face came into focus. "Accountancy?" I said, concentrating on getting my tongue to work.

"Takes skills to get things done." She was humouring me. She felt my forehead, all the while gnawing away at her bottom lip. "Program budgeting skills, mainly." She dispensed the reassuring grimace that passes for a smile among the caring professions. I'd have preferred a cuddle. "Lie still while I phone a doctor."

The wet clothes had been replaced by track pants and a windcheater. No undies, I noticed. I levered myself upright and swung my legs over the side of the bed. My mouth still wasn't working properly. "Pee," I made it say. Wee wees. Getting this much of me functioning made my head spin. Ayisha slipped a hand under my armpit. I shook her off, wanting to know how far gone I was. I was pretty far gone. At the door I turned not towards the bathroom but into Red's bedroom. An angular jumble of knees and elbows was breathing rhythmically under a familiar blanket. "I let him watch telly until he flaked out," said Ayisha defensively. "That okay?"

She stood outside the toilet door the whole time. I sounded like a brewery horse pissing in a tin bucket. "Where have you been? I've been worried sick." You'd think we had been married for years. I must have slept through the honeymoon. "You're covered in bruises. It's nearly 3 A.M. Your clothes are wet, torn to pieces. What happened, Murray? Tell me, for God's sake."

Even when the flush drowned out her voice, she didn't shut up, bless her. As I opened the door she put her palm back on my forehead and rolled back first one eyelid, then the other. Confidently, like she knew what she was doing. "You should be looked at by a doctor," she diagnosed.

"Look in the cupboard," I said, my mouth reluctantly responding to orders. "See if you can find some aspirin."

She put two tablets on my tongue and lifted a glass of water to my lips. I felt like I'd just played three consecutive Grand Finals at centre half-forward and we'd lost all of them. On the kitchen table the washing sat neatly folded in a laundry basket. The dishes had been done. I sensed the prospects of romance receding.

Ayisha fiddled with the kettle, poured tea. "I rang the hotel at eleven. They said you'd left. Can you remember what happened after that?"

The tentacles began mooching about irritably again, squeezing any stray brain cells they could find.

"I thought maybe it had something to do with that storm, an accident or something. Jeeze, it was bad. All this water started coming through the roof." Through in the lounge room I could see a row of saucepans lined up across the floor. "Anyhow, I rang around the hospitals, but nobody fitting your description had been admitted. I was beginning to think I'd better ring the police. Then I heard something out the front. It was you, collapsing on the doorstep. I thought you were dying, fair dinkum. Freaked me right out, you did."

Is it me, I thought, or does this woman take the cake? Softly, not enough to upset the octopus, I laughed. Ayisha's tale had filled me with enough strength to totter across to the cupboard and screw the top off the Jamesons bottle. I thought of the wine, nicely chilled at the bottom of the lake. Ayisha gave a cautionary shake of her head. Bloody Moslems, no appreciation of the tonic properties of the sacred waters. I added a tot to both our cups of tea and moulded a wad of her tobacco into a lumpy cylinder. All this physical therapy was doing me good. My thought processes were beginning to fight their way free. I did the attention-grabbing trick with the match again. This is why people smoke. So many clichés, so readily to hand.

"The aqua Falcon," I said. "Bayraktar's car. Ran me off the road. Right into Edwardes Lake. I ended up floating down some creek. Then spent half the night trying to get a cab to pick me up." I slumped back, exhausted from the effort of talking. I tried to get my thoughts into some sort of order.

"Jesus," she exclaimed. "This is getting right out of hand. You're gunna hafta call the cops."

I shook my head. It hurt. "No point," I winced. "Unless I tell them about Memo. And that's not going to do your, or the League's, credibility any good, is it? It was you who convinced him he could trust me, remember." Frankly, I couldn't give a shit about Gezen by this stage.

She looked at me like I was a gibbering idiot. "My credibility? Jeeze, Murray. Somebody's trying to kill you and you're worried about my credibility?"

Isn't she fantastic, I thought. The warm tea and whiskey were beginning to work their cure in the pit of my stomach. I started to unscrew the whiskey cap again. Ayisha wrested the bottle out of my unresisting grasp. "Call the police!" she ordered. What was it about me, I wondered, that brought out the bossy boots in women?

"I would," I said, "if I thought it'd do any good. But it's like your bloody petition. The cops won't act without evidence. And when they do move, it'll be too slow. Or too late." She didn't know about my earlier conversations with the constabulary, of course. "Shit, I don't even know why this is happening. You got any ideas?"

That shut her up. And thank Christ, too, said the octopus. On the table a saucer was piled with butts, hers and mine. If I survived, I'd have to invest in an ashtray. "In fact I'm beginning to wonder if it isn't Gezen driving the Falcon. Maybe he changed his mind about confessing and decided he'd eliminate the only other people who knew what had happened."

She thought I was serious. "Gimme a break." She leaped up and lit herself a cigarette on the gas jet. "Memo's a little flaky, I'll admit that, but you can't seriously think he's a killer."

I felt old eight legs shift, spread his grey gelatinous membranes and puff a slow balloon of darkness through the water towards me. A cool black cloud of ink, blotting out the light and noise and the jabber of voices in my head. The world was out there somewhere, moving distantly, glimpsed through a red-tinged slit. I made it go away.

Ayisha was shaking my shoulder. "You okay?" I jerked upright. I must have dozed off. This was fucked. How could I think in this condition? A sob story like Gezen's would have aroused every conceivable sympathy in someone like Ayisha. It was cruel to taunt her. "You okay?" she repeated.

I was okay. Red was okay. My constant companion the octopus was so fucking okay it was dancing a hornpipe with my frontal lobes. I had some thinking to do. The only tangible evidence of what had happened was the Falcon parked outside in the street. And in itself the car proved nothing. No doubt the only fingerprints it carried were mine, smeared all over the wheel, the doors, the hood. And I could guess why it had been abandoned with the key in the ignition. What better way to dispose of a car than to leave it where it was certain to be nicked by joy-riding kids who would dump it miles away?

No. It would take more than a dead man's car, a hair-raising tale and a half-baked story about extortion and revenge to get the cops fired up. I could be dead by the time they extracted their collective digit. The only thing I had going for me was that whoever ran me off the road probably thought I was already. "The Anatolia Club," I said. "I think I should pay it a visit. Let them know I'm on to them. See what I can find out." But not alone. "You reckon Sivan will come with me?"

"I'd like to see you try to stop him," Ayisha said, grinning. She was close, her presence overwhelming my senses. I could smell her, taste her. She yawned, no longer able to hide her tiredness. I made my play.

"You go home," I urged. "Thanks for minding Red. For everything. I'll talk to Sivan in the morning, speak with Memo again, sort something out." I cocked my finger like a gun. "No single fascist act must go unchallenged," I quoted from somewhere, unable to remember where.

It wasn't much of a plan, but she nodded approval. She was tired, resigned. The clock on the stove clicked over. 3:35 A.M. Then she was shaking her head. "But first you gotta see a doctor. What if you've got concussion? You could slip into a coma or something."

"First thing in the morning," I promised. The furry muck on my tongue mingled with the taste of tea and whiskey. I held down a retch. My timing was terrible, I told myself. I wasn't in a fit state for anything.

"It's nearly morning now. Got any blankets? I'll stay on the couch. Keep an eye on you."

"No," I insisted, wanting nothing more. Her hand moved, erasing the air between us, brushing my objection aside. Lucky I'd changed the linen. I led her up the hall to the bedroom, trying not to collapse on the way.

She stood with her back to the bed while I went through the motions of reaching up to where the spare bedding was stowed, stacked tight on the top shelf of the wardrobe. I tugged at the scratchy wool, high on tiptoes, dizzy from the altitude. The blankets broke free and I teetered before her, a man leaning into a strong wind. Then the wind dropped and I was pitching forward. Ayisha's arms extended effortlessly, receiving me, enfolding me. Her neck and my forehead, I observed as if from a distance, yielded a perfect fit. Motionless, cradling my eggshell head, she was a bottomless well into which I tumbled headlong into free fall.

"Oh, boy," exclaimed key sectional interests of my metabolism, sensing an advantage. "You can't keep a good man down." Actually you can, I'm grateful to say. I felt her warmth reach out and enclose me in its embrace. Warmth, yes. Heat, no. There never would be any heat, I comprehended. But even in the finality of that knowledge I could not bring myself to move, but stood there letting myself be cradled in her arms. What energy I had was devoted entirely to not weeping with gratitude.

Then Red walked into the room and I jumped about ten feet into the air. For a long moment he stood there, regarding me with heavy-lidded, vacant eyes. Then he gripped his pyjama pants by the elastic, gave them an upward tug, turned, and somnambulated towards the bathroom.

Nurse Ayisha, herself at the far extremity of wakefulness, scooped up the blankets and draped them over her arm. "That reminds me," she yawned. "Your wife rang just after you left. Said she'd be on the early flight. Said you'd know what that meant. She sounded very nice."

I'll bet she did.

"And someone called Angelo Annoletti or something. Said to call him urgently when you got home. Bit late now, I suppose."

Charlene! He must have rung about Charlene! God, she'd slipped my mind entirely since the branch meeting. Morning, first thing in the morning I would call. Later, later, much later. Sleep first. "Take the bed," I said. "I'm used to the couch." Shameless to the last.

Ayisha bustled me onto the couch, draped me with blankets, turned off the light and left me to die in peace. A blissful shroud of stillness settled over me. The darkness was good. Nobody would find me there. I could hide for a long time, nothing but me and infinite deep space and far, far away, the distant spiralling remnants of long exploded galaxies. The darkness was good. Darkness and the tick of molecular particles, hydrogen, oxygen, coalescing, swelling, tumbling, colliding, disintegrating. Tick, infinite pause, tick, infinite pause, tick.

The fucking roof was leaking. Very slowly, not much, but leaking drip after drip into one of the pots Ayisha had positioned across the floor. I screwed my ears as tightly closed as possible without disturbing the octopus and retreated into the soundproof maze of reason.

Somewhere my thinking had jumped the rails and taken a wrong turn. All along I had assumed that the nexus between me and Bayraktar ran through Gezen. The break-in, the stuff with the Falcon, it had all started after Gezen's confession. Therefore they were connected. But if this was not the case, then the chain of cause and effect I had constructed was missing some pretty crucial links. The longer I thought about it, the more it looked like a badly frayed string of dubious suppositions and unlikely coincidences. Get to the sharp end of the issue, I thought. Ask yourself the fundamental question. Who stands to gain from your death?

Those guys from the Anatolia Club, for instance. Even if they were a pack of right-wing psychos, why pick on me? Why not one of their own benighted compatriots? Had I witnessed something I shouldn't out at the cemetery? If so, were they also trying to bump off the two employees of the Martinelli family? That would be a serious mistake in anyone's language. Besides which, they hadn't even noticed me. And so what if I'd rushed out of the League's office shaking my fist at them? Hardly a killing offence, and it gave them no reason to connect me to Gezen. And even if they could do that, how had they connected Gezen with Bayraktar's death? In fact, I couldn't even be completely sure it was the same BMW I had seen parked under the carport at the Anatolia Club.

Gezen said they were following him, but Gezen also thought I was a copper, his bad conscience playing merry hell with him. Obviously they couldn't have been following him when only fifteen minutes earlier they had been playing parade-ground soldiers over their dead comrade at Fawkner Cemetery. Now that I thought about it, the idea that I had inadvertently stumbled into some sort of internecine ethnic warfare was less than plausible. Worse, I had been guilty of the most blatant kind of ethnic stereotyping. An old trap for new players. Christ, I'd be imagining the mafia after me next.

There must be a logical solution, I told myself. Could something other than Bayraktar's death be the issue? Something I knew but didn't know I knew? Something worth killing me to keep concealed. So who else knew of my interest in the Coolaroo plant? Who might be spooked by the sudden arrival of a snooper on the scene? Who might have access to the dead man's car?

Could Apps, the human jack-in-the-box, have found out that I dobbed him in to the boss for slack book-keeping and decided to get revenge? A drastic solution, but maybe. He was pretty highly strung, after all.

The boss himself, Merricks? He was out. For a start he had authorised the investigation. Mainly though it was the difficulty of imagining him behind the wheel of an aqua Falcon 500 in his Melbourne Club tie. Not his style at all.

There was Agnelli, whose idea it had been in the first place. Agnelli, who might well have reasons for wanting me out of the way for a while. Out of the way in hospital? Out of the way dead? Christ, maybe it was the fucking mafia, after all. And what about the drugs? Planting dope in my house had clearly been part of an attempt to discredit me. And that quantity of grass suggested a criminal connection, which took me back to the Anatolia Club. Shit, it was all too confusing. My head was spinning again.

Then there was the missing file. Had I merely mislaid it? Or had someone been worried enough to raid the electorate office, steal my notes, and leave a mess that made the break-in seem the work of artistically impaired vandals? But why? Unless somebody thought I had more information than I really did. There was nothing in the file. All it held was the list of Bayraktar's phoney names, a thumb-nail draft of the preamble of my MACWAM report, a bit of rough arithmetic and a scrap of paper with the name Herb Gardiner on it.

What was it that Gezen had said? "Then the other one comes. Gardening. I do not think he will come so soon." Meaning what? According to Gardiner's statement it was only by chance he had happened to be in the chiller at all. A spur of the moment decision to check the thermostat. "Six or seven minutes he is inside." How long does it take to check a gauge?

Old Herb knew I had the list of phoney names. He was interested enough in my activities to visit my office. In a strangely animated state, at that. He knew where I worked, where I lived, and my plans for the evening. His house wasn't a million miles from Edwardes Lake, either. Nor from the public bar of the Lakeview Hotel. And you don't have to be a gangster accomplice of a man to get hold of his car keys. You just have to take them off his key-ring when you find his body in a freezer. None of which explained why a man like Gardiner might want me dead. It was all too fantastic, too paranoid.

Then, in the interminable drawn-out vastness of time between two droplets of water, I heard at last the inexorable clunk of a penny dropping. And at exactly that moment the baying began. The long, full-throated, moon-mad howls of a captive dog.

19

THE SKY WAS CRYSTALLINE, utterly cloudless, miles high. The night had entered that great silence that precedes the birdsong. Apart from the pooch, that is, shut in the Falcon and yowling fit to wake the entire neighbourhood. The instant I opened the driver's door, she shut up. She just banged her tail on the vinyl a couple of times and sat there looking up at me. Wanted attention, then didn't know what to do with it. Just like some people.

I left the door open while I examined the patch-up job on the car's rear window. It was a work of art. The clear plastic had been cut to a precise fit. The waterproof seam of electrical tape was light blue, not quite a match with the paintwork, but a good try. A triple layer, the edges straight as a die. All very shipshape. I was thinking about a sailor, about fragments of conversation, things seen but not noticed, all rushing to reassemble themselves, like the film of an explosion running in reverse.

In a circle around me the rooftops were smudged with a flush of luminescence, mother-of-pearl buttons about to pop open and expose the daylight hidden underneath. Not everything was clear yet but, with every passing second, more and more details could be discerned, their blurred outlines coming more sharply into focus.

I could hold the pieces together only by the greatest effort of will. The story existed only as long as I kept telling it to myself. If I stopped figuring it out, even for the merest second, the whole thing would dissolve into an incoherent blur of suspicion and conjecture, the fantasy of a concussed brain. Relax, just for an instant, and none of it would make sense any more. I would no longer be able to convince myself, let alone anyone else. But if I plunged headlong into the morass, others would be forced to follow. No more the prey, I would be the one setting the agenda. Time to get pro-active. I turned the ignition key and felt the Falcon's power fill me with certainty.

Back in the house, pulling on a pair of shoes, I had caught sight of myself in a mirror. My hair had dried wet and sprang out on all sides, a tangle of grass and mud, a fright wig. The fright was my face, overgrown, wild-eyed, the welts peeling to reveal pink stripes. Saggy grey track pants, an old maroon windcheater flecked with paint. Le Coq Sportif. If the black lace-up shoes had been a little bigger, if I had a polka dot bow-tie, the clown outfit would be complete.

As I sneaked past the bedroom door I had glimpsed Ayisha, in my bed at last, dead to the world, guarding me against my coma. She lay there utterly vulnerable, totally impervious, her knees pressed to her chest under the covers. How I could ever have imagined her going for me was already beyond my comprehension.

But now I was heading north, my thoughts moving from darkness to light as inexorably as the widening band of grey on the horizon at my elbow. The dog was beside me, her paws kneading the passenger seat. After that piece of Gallic garbage I had been driving, that ride-on lawn-mower, the Falcon went like the clappers, a veritable limousine. Even the lighter worked. I rolled one-handed as I drove. The knack was back.

The radio worked, too, and the dawn shift announcer spoke in soothing nursery tones, which was nice of him. According to the five o'clock news, police and emergency service personnel were still mopping up after last night's record downpour. An empty caravan had been swept into the Elwood Canal. Big deal. The forecast was for clear skies at least until the end of the weekend. The worst was over, or so they said.

We drove in silence from there on, ruminating. Well, I was. The dog was still squeezing the upholstery. The details were hazy but, if you stood back far enough, the big picture could be discerned. The Rolf Harris method. What had happened was this, I reasoned, guessed, extrapolated.

Bayraktar was a semi-literate thug. A payroll scam, the faking of official paperwork, would have been beyond him. Someone who knew how the place worked must have shown him how to do it. Someone who knew the place well. Someone like Herb Gardiner. Every week, a couple of hours after the pay packets had been delivered, they each made separate visits to the same freezer. A convenient place for Gardiner to pick up his split of that week's bogus wages? But last Friday Gardiner changed the routine. He turned up early, and Bayraktar ended up dead.

According to Gezen, Gardiner was in the freezer a long time, six or seven minutes. More than long enough to read a meter. And when he arrived, Bayraktar had already been inside long enough to discover that he was locked in. If, as Gezen believed, Bayraktar was already dead of a panic-induced heart attack, why did it take Gardiner so long to emerge and sound the alarm? Something else had happened in Number 3 chiller. Some variation on the scam, perhaps? A falling out among thieves?

Whatever it was, Gardiner had succeeded in concealing it. Bayraktar had been carried out feet-first, successfully portrayed as an unlucky pilferer, a stiff stiff. The cops and government inspectors were satisfied and the payroll fiddle had gone undetected.

But not for long. All of a sudden there was a fly in the ointment. This Whelan character turns up asking a lot of silly questions. On the job five minutes and he trips over the one loose thread, Bayraktar's phoney pay sheets. He doesn't know what they mean, but he's asking a lot of silly questions. Christ alone knows what else he might discover, given time. He needs to be flummoxed, discredited, scared off. Got out of the picture, one way or another. And the evidence he has already turned up, the list of names Bayraktar has been using, has to be retrieved before he realises its value.

Fortunately, the guy is an idiot. A trusting soul who volunteers his home address and his planned movements. First his office is broken into and the list taken. Then drugs are planted in his house. Then, after a pretty serious effort is made to scare him, he passes up an offer to talk. So things get deadly.

But where did the drugs come from? And why up the ante to homicide? So what if this Murray Whelan got a bit snoopy? Why were the stakes so high? Charges of fraud would be difficult to substantiate. Even more so with manslaughter. Why go to so much trouble to eliminate someone who wasn't even a witness? Why not sit it out, see what develops? Sit it out while taking in the Pacific from the balcony of your Broadbeach condominium. Sit around soaking up those Queensland sunbeams? Why try to kill a man? Why risk the prospect of spending the rest of your retirement in a ten by twelve cell in HM Pentridge with a view of the handball court?

These were questions best put in person. Bang on Gardiner's door, ask him loud, in front of the neighbours. Make a mess in Tidy Town. Put a rocket up the collective arse of the constabulary. And if I was wrong? If good old Herb was no more than he seemed? What then? Then Murray Whelan too could be no more than he seemed — the dazed and delirious victim of a car accident, concussed, confused and in bad need of a few hours sleep.

It was nearly day. Gardiner's house slept in the stillness behind its For Sale sign. Further along the street a solitary window showed the lights of an early riser. I stepped over the wrought-iron gate and into the space between the house and the cream brick of the garage. Behind me on the nature strip, the black dog did what dogs do on nature strips.

Through the slatted glass of the louvre window the garage interior was matt black. I cupped my hands around my face, adjusting my eyes to the gloom. Floor, walls, work-bench emerged out of the darkness. Shapes floated above the bench, dark silhouettes against a white background — a hacksaw, the descending Gs of a row of clamps, the outlines of tools on a shadow board. No car. The tan Corolla was gone. Across the floor a glint of diamonds caught the pale light of the new day.

The door was locked. I kicked it open with my heel and threw the light switch. A pile of glass fragments, the remnants of a shattered car window, had been swept into a neat pyramid beside the cutdown drum of a rubbish bin. Off-cut strips of clear plastic, precise straight edges, lay heaped in the bin. On a ledge above the bench a row of jars held screws and bolts and nuts — self-tappers, countersunk, round-head. Above the jars rolls of electrical tape hung on nails, red, green, blue. A damp umbrella leaned against the wall. Beside it, drying on a sheet of newspaper, was a pair of muddy brogues. Tidy Town, Tidy Shed, Tidy Man.

Up until then I had been a tightrope walker, teetering on a thread of conjecture. Now the ground felt solid beneath my feet. Here was evidence. There would be more evidence out at the plant, of the fiddle at least. Then would come motive.

I sat the ball of my thumb on the doorbell and wiggled, waking an electric Quasimodo, sending it into spasm in the darkness inside. "Come out, Gardiner," I yelled. "I want to talk to you." The palm of my hand came down hard, rattling the aluminium frame of the screen door. Yapping exploded behind the door, answered from the nature strip. My dog sounded tougher.

A carriage light above the door went on and the Nextdoor's head and shoulders appeared. She tugged at her dressing-gown cord and held herself back in the shadows, torn between curiosity and her mortification at being caught out in Gardiner's bed. "What do you want?"

The dogs were going at it hammer and tongs. I had to raise my voice. "Where's Gardiner?" I bellowed. It felt good, from the pit of my stomach.

The merry widow recoiled from my certainty. "He's gone to work."

I rattled the handle. The door was locked, but the woman drew her collar around her throat defensively and stepped back, receding even further into the protective dark. This wasn't what I'd had in mind, scaring old ladies. Her hand was on the white telephone. "I'll call the police."

"You do that," I said.

As I started the Falcon, the dogs were still going at each other through the barred door. Snap and snarl and gotcha. Lights were coming on all the way up the street. I swung open the passenger door and whistled. Red had been on at me for ages about getting a dog. I liked this one. I liked her attitude.

20

SEEN DISTANTLY from the highway, the smoke was no more than an oily grey smudge on the baby-blue face of the new day. It was only as I neared the dozen or so semi-trailers marshalling on the asphalt apron that I could see where it was coming from. Above the tangle of huge refrigerated rigs moving in and out of cavernous apertures, a guttering black snake was uncoiling itself from the roof of Pacific Pastoral.

I left the Falcon in the carpark with the dog on the seat and loped past the deserted gatehouse. Thin grey wisps were beginning to curl around the upper edge of the entry nearest the office. As I passed through the great door, alarm bells erupted, tripping each other off deeper and deeper into the building, loud, serious, metallic. The acrid smell of burning paint filled the air. The bundy clock read 5:23. Gardiner's card in its alphabetical slot showed a clock-on time of 5:01.

Apps was hopping about at the bottom of the office stairs, a spluttering fire extinguisher dangling upside down from his hand. His Adam's apple was doing the cha-cha, and other parts of his body looked like they were trying to secede entirely. The upstairs landing was belching smoke and through the windows of the lunch room I could see tongues of yellow licking the walls.

"I told the stupid cow that radiator was a menace," Apps whined at the top of his lungs.

First law of management, I thought. Find a scapegoat. On the periphery of my vision, figures were running everywhere. Shouts and engine noises set up a counter beat to the unfaltering scream of the alarm bells. Apps, registering my identity, turned away from the smoke and grabbed my sleeve. "What are you doing here?" he demanded.

For a moment I wondered if Apps, not Gardiner, had set the blaze. It couldn't have come at a more convenient time for both of them. No, Apps didn't have that much imagination. "You said I'd find it more interesting at this time of day," I said. "You were right." I jerked my arm free. Apps cocked his head, straining for meaning, scandalised by my costume. He lunged for my arm again. "I can't be held responsible . . ."

I danced out of his reach and took off into the plant. Apps could go to buggery. It was Gardiner I was here to see. But where was he? High above, an oily black haze was gathering, rubbery and noxious. The fire was spreading rapidly. An ominous hissing could be heard below the high-pitched frenzy of the alarm bells. God alone knew what lethal gasses were poisoning the air. I jogged away from the fire, deeper into the complex, straining down corridors for a glimpse of Gardiner's stocky figure.

Herb Gardiner was not only methodical, he clearly had a lot of energy for a man of his age. You had to hand him that. At this rate not just the records in the office but half the plant would be a charred ruin before the fire brigade had backed their shiny red appliances out the station door. He should have put up a sign. Herb's Braised Beef. The arson squad would need barbecue aprons and long tongs to make any sense of this.

I jogged on, dizzy from the effort, getting disoriented. This wasn't how I had pictured it. The idea had been to confront Gardiner, shirt-front him with accusations, create a scene. Instead, Gardiner was one step ahead, putting distance between himself and the evidence. With the records gone up in smoke, it would take a confession to convince anybody of anything. I realised Gardiner would probably be making his way to one of the exits, joining in the confusion and excitement of his fellow workers. He would mingle with them on the apron to watch the spectacle, a mask of plausible surprise on his face.

I turned towards the pale rectangle of one of the doorways. A group of figures in overalls, some white, some blue, was moving in the same direction. One of them had a lamb carcass slung over his shoulder. The things people think to save in a fire. I broke into a trot to catch the last of them up. The acrid smoke began to burn my lungs. Abruptly it started to rain. Somewhere far above, the red tracery of the overhead sprinkler system had kicked in. I bent my head and hurried forwards, concentrating on keeping my balance on the now slippery floor. I'd had more than enough soakings recently, thank you very much.

Just ahead of me, Gardiner came out of an access alley and headed towards the exit. I fell into step beside him. He glanced around. "Hello, son," he said, his self-possession never faltering.

"Something I've been meaning to ask," I said, raising my voice against the unearthly din. "Where does an old bloke like you get his grass?"

Gardiner slowed and looked at me quizzically. I suddenly felt that I had made a serious mistake. The gap to the hurrying crowd ahead widened. Gardiner said something. I leaned forward. "What?"

Gardiner put his hand on my elbow and his mouth up to my ear, as if he was taking me into his confidence. "That prick Bayraktar," he said. "He was using the place to shunt the stuff around." As he spoke, he shifted his grasp to my wrist and stepped behind me, twisting my right arm all the way up behind my back. At the same time, he whipped a long heavy-duty screwdriver out of the thigh pocket of his overalls and pressed its blade against my throat.

I felt a flash of pride at having my assumptions proved correct, but the vanity was short-lived. For a man his age, Gardiner was as hard as a rock. The old bastard sure must have been giving the All-Bran a nudge. He jammed the tip of the screwdriver into the soft flesh between my jaw and windpipe. One hard shove and ten inches of drop-forged steel would be sticking out the top of my skull.

The pain in my shoulder forced me into a forward hunch, pushing me down harder on the screwdriver and bringing tears welling into my eyes. Through the artificial rain I could see the last of the workmen vanishing through the exit. I punched wildly sideways and failed to connect. The sharpened metal bit emphatically into my skin. "A word in private, if you don't mind, son," said Gardiner.

He angled me sideways and frog-marched me forward. At every attempt to struggle free or grab at him with my left hand, he twisted my arm to the extremity of its socket until the pain subdued me. "This is crazy," I gasped, my carotid artery thumping on cold steel. Gardiner shut me up with a jab and propelled me onwards.

Abruptly, with a sideways sweep of one leg, he knocked my feet out from under me. My arm strained at its socket as I went down, and I cried out in agony. As I hit the ground I felt the screwdriver disappear from my throat. It instantly reappeared behind my head, probing the tender spot at the top of my spine. My forehead was jammed hard against the wet floor, my lips kissing the cold concrete, tasting the tomb. Gardiner's foot was in the small of my back, pinning me down. "Hasn't anyone ever told you that nobody likes a smartarse, son?"

I struggled feebly, immobilised by the pain in my shoulder and the threat of being skewered. The octopus was back, sorely pissed off. This is not what I had expected. But what exactly had I expected, running around a burning building like a chook with its head cut off, not knowing what I was going to do next, all dumb-fuck cunning and rampant glands?

Gardiner on the other hand knew exactly what he was doing. He worked methodically, the necessary materials readily to hand. Pivoting on the screwdriver, keeping its pressure constant, he jerked my arm downwards. The relief was immediate but temporary. He transferred his foot to my neck and I felt the full weight of his body bear down. Then he lashed my wrists together with tape, his movements sure and agile.

"You're a lucky bastard, I'll give you that." Gardiner liked to chat genially as he worked. "When that heap of yours went into the water I was convinced you were a goner." He hauled at the tape, dragging me to my feet and propelling me forwards again, the screwdriver back against my jugular. We continued down the line of freezers, both now soaked to the skin. Gardiner didn't seem to mind. I was shivering miserably.

At one of the freezer doors Gardiner again forced me to the ground and planted a foot firmly between my shoulder blades. Keys jingled briefly, then I was hauled to my feet and pitched into the cavernous interior. I stumbled, hit a wall of cartons and spun around. The door was sliding into place behind Gardiner. He already had one arm in the sleeve of a padded parka and was holding the screwdriver in front of him like a bayonet. His eyes never left me as he transferred the weapon to his other hand and zipped the jacket closed. Icy air wrapped itself around me, sending a chill through my damp clothes. At a very minimum I was going to come out of this whole thing with a severe head cold.

I teetered precariously back into balance, tugging at the tape. I succeeded only in digging it deeper into the flesh of my wrists. Apparently unconcerned at my mobility, Gardiner began to tug on one fur-lined glove then another. As he did so he stamped his feet, dancing about in a little boxer's jig, and waving the steel shaft in small circles, as though inciting me to charge him headlong. I half expected him to suggest I have a go. And so we faced each other, stamping and steaming, dancing partners in a macabre frug.

"Freezing, eh?" Gardiner said without malice, the words propelled out of his mouth on puffs of white haze. "Thermostat's all the way down. Turn a carton of boned beef into a slab of granite in twenty minutes flat. Fit young fellow like you, all his juices flowing, a bit longer maybe. But you'll be out cold well before that. Didn't take Bayraktar any time at all. But then he was in shocking shape."

Freezing wasn't the word for it. The gust of air that had entered with us was a shroud of vapour swathing our feet. We'd been in there less than a minute and already the sodden front of my sweat-top was white with hoar-frost and I was shivering uncontrollably. Shouting would be useless. Even if anyone remained outside to hear above the din of the fire alarms, the freezer walls were thick with insulation.

Gardiner's intentions were now abundantly clear. Keep me prisoner in the freezer until I passed out from the cold, remove the tape and leave me to die. Or even drag my body out to thaw, closer to the fire. Do that to a chicken and you end up with salmonella. Frozen, baked or bombe Alaska. What a choice.

I glanced about. Aside from being even colder, the freezer we were standing in was identical to the one Apps had insisted on showing me. Corridors of waxed cartons led off into the interior. Nowhere to run, nowhere to hide.

"Oh, don't worry," Gardiner went on, his mouth pursed against the biting air. "You won't feel a thing, though I daresay it'll be a little nippy at first."

As he spoke he unzipped his jacket far enough to thrust a gloved hand down his front and pull a pack of cigarettes and a disposable lighter from an inside pocket. He mouthed a stick from the pack, fumbled the lighter into action, lit up, and zipped himself closed. His eyes never left me. "Sad what can happen to someone who doesn't know what he's doing when he goes wandering around a place like this."

I stared at the glowing tip of the cigarette hungrily. It occurred to me to ask for one, a dying man's request. But breathing was hard enough. Each intake of air was an icy flame, searing my lungs. "You won't get away with it." The shivering was close to uncontrollable, my voice a pathetic reed trembling behind clenched teeth.

Gardiner shrugged indifference, clapping his gloved hands together around the screwdriver, making a muffled, decisive sound. "Don't see why not. I did last time."

My legs jerked spastically under me. The front of my pants was a crackling sheet of ice, a good case for never going out without underpants.

Gardiner was droning on, the words hypnotic. "Even if you made other copies of those names Bayraktar was using, they won't mean anything without the payroll records. And this little bonfire should take care of those quite nicely. Tell you the truth, I've been meaning to get round to disposing of them for some time. I suppose I should thank you for hurrying me up."

This was what Gardiner wanted, I realised. To keep me standing here, listening, until my legs gave out underneath me. If I went down, I wouldn't get up. I pleaded through the wa-wa pedal of my juddering jaw. "Please. I don't want to die. Not for some lousy little fiddle."

Gardiner stopped jogging on the spot and drew back in mock outrage. "Lousy little fiddle? That any way to talk about a man's life work? Best part of a million dollars I've pulled out of this place over the years, I'll have you know. Call that lousy, do you, son?"

I shook my head, or rather it shook me. It was jerking uncontrollably as the intensity of the shivering increased. I was thinking of the escape hatch, wondering how far I would get with my arms tied back, which way to go. It took all my muscular control just to force words out. "I'll do anything you want." Except die. I swivelled on my heels, back and forth, preparing myself. If I was going to go, I might as well go going. Swing right, I decided, and see how far I got.

"You should have thought of that before you tried putting the squeeze on someone like Lionel Merricks," Gardiner said.

My instruction to my legs faltered halfway down. Excuse me. What had the man just said?

"You've got some moxie," Gardiner went on. "I'll give you that much, son. Ringing up, bold as brass. Off the record. Confidential. That will be fifty thousand dollars, thank you very much, Mr. Merricks. Bloody cheeky all right. But stupid. Lionel doesn't like being stood over, especially not at the moment. Fix it, he told me. Tidy up all the loose ends. But what do you do when I come around to try to sort something out? You send me packing. Not very civil of you, was it?"

Below the waist I danced on the spot, my legs half rubber, half braced to sprint. The shaking was getting worse. In contrast, my thought processes were slowing down, trudging step by tipsy step across an endless plain of snow. It would be nice, I mused dreamily, to hear the end of Gardiner's story, hear where this latest twist led. Then lie down and sleep. I gathered a breath from my diaphragm and pushed it out my nose. "Wool ship."

This pleased Gardiner greatly. "Bullshit, is it?" He examined me afresh. "I knew it," he declared gleefully. "I told Merricks you were just flying a kite. Fifteen years we've been working together, him putting in lame-duck managers, me handling the day-to-day details. Not a hint of a problem. Even the Yanks thought it was just an innocent mix-up. Buggered if we could figure out how you'd got onto us so quickly. Turns out you hadn't, after all." Then he chuckled, a terrible laugh of self-congratulation, and I knew how far gone he was.

My brain struggled through a blurring haze to make sense of what I was hearing. The only bit I understood was that I was being killed because of a misunderstanding. "Let me go," I pleaded. "We can deal." My words were a string of staccato grunts, like a spluttering engine about to stall. "Why Merricks fiddle own payroll?"

Gardiner was contemptuous behind his glowing cigarette, like it was all my fault that he was being put to the inconvenience of having to murder me. "Christ, son, you really don't know anything, do you? Merricks isn't tickling the till. That's just a private little sideline of my own. Except I picked the wrong man to go into business with, didn't I? My trusty fucking sidekick Bayraktar got greedy and decided to branch out into drug distribution. Had the stuff coming in from the bush by the truckload. Put our whole operation at risk, the silly cunt."

I wanted him to know I wasn't completely ignorant. "And extortion."

This was new to Gardiner. "That so?" he said thoughtfully. He threw his cigarette to the floor and ground it out with his heel. "Not any more though, eh son?" He bent at the knees, his gloved fingers pinching uselessly in an attempt to gather up the scrap of mangled butt. His eyes flickered downwards.

I took off. My legs, loyal lieutenants, jerked me to the right and begun to pump. Skidding on icy soles, I veered into a slot between two mountains of stacked boxes. The cold was viscous and resisted my efforts to push my way forward. I moved in slow motion, the air tasting of wet tin and searing my lungs. Wobbling erratically, trying to find my balance, I bounced off the walls.

Somewhere behind me Gardiner laughed. "Go on, son, run," he shouted. "That greedy pig Bayraktar had the same idea. Go ahead. Burst your heart, just like he did."

I lurched on and turned deeper into the maze of cartons. Muffled applause tracked my progress. As I stumbled forward I sawed my wrists numbly back and forth, dimly aware they had no feeling. Had the tape cut off my circulation, I wondered, or could this be frostbite so soon? The effort of movement brought dizziness. Careening full-tilt against a wall, I pirouetted through 180 degrees and came to rest. Gardiner was at the far end of the aisle, genially ambling towards me.

Jacking my hands up between my shoulder blades, I pushed my elbows outwards with as much strength as I could muster, quivering with exertion. My pulse roared like the ocean in my ears. The octopus reared. Gardiner advanced, the screwdriver circling casually at his thigh, impatience beginning to crease his natty, bedroom-bandicoot face. My arms exploded outwards and sent me reeling. Tape dangled from my wrists. Gardiner showed irritation then disappeared from view as I turned and shuffled through a dangling curtain of beef carcasses, setting the whole rack swinging.

A dead end blocked my path, the back wall. I cast about for the hatch, hearing Gardiner's footfall moving closer. The hatch was there, chest high. I fell forward and clutched at the handle. The catch sprang open and the hatch swung wide, wrenching my palm with it, super-glued to the metal. Outside was an oven of smoke and noise. Balmy air, thick with smoke and chemical stench, hit me in the face. I sucked at it hungrily, feeding on its warmth.

Gardiner's arm came around my neck and dragged me backwards. My hand tore free, raw flesh, and I hit the floor. Gardiner kicked me hard in the ribs, one, two. My knees came up protectively, curling me into a ball. Gardiner loomed above, framed demonically against the square of the hatch, blocking the blast of heat from the fire outside. "Good idea," he grunted, catching his breath. He half turned and made a facetious show of warming one gloved hand. "At my age you really feel the cold." Hunching down, he risked a glance outwards. He was impressed by his own handiwork. "Spreading pretty fast. No time to waste." He turned his attention back to the job at hand.

Never once taking his eyes off me, he transferred the screwdriver to his left hand and reached back with his right, searching for the handle of the hatch. The little door had swung right back on its hinges. He swiped at the air with his gloved hand, the handle just beyond his grasp. "You certainly take a lot of looking after," he grumbled, demonstratively jabbing the screwdriver towards where I lay.

Rivulets of condensation were already beginning to stream down the wall. Gardiner bobbed swiftly at the knees, ducked his head and shoulders out the hatch, and grabbed the hatch handle. As he did so, I came out of my cringe and jerked myself up into a runner's starting stance, all my weight on the tips of my splayed fingers. Gardiner twisted at the waist, hauling the trapdoor inwards, half-turned in profile.

That's when I killed him. Head-butted him in the nuts.

I rammed my skull into his groin with all the force I could muster. The impact caused his whole upper body to jackknife sharply forward. His forehead smashed hard against the outside edge of the hatch. "Ommfff," he went, and his head whiplashed back towards the fire. By then I had my arms wrapped around his knees and was lifting him up, shoving him backwards out the hole. I don't know whether he was dead already then or not, because I was too busy anticipating a punctured lung from the screwdriver. But he was already going limp and when he landed on the top of his skull I heard his neck crack, even over the sound of the alarm bells. I stuck my head out the hatch and saw the screwdriver clatter to the floor.

Then I looked up and saw Memo Gezen. He was just standing there, tight-lipped, staring at me. Water ran off his white shower cap and down his long morose face. Gardiner was an inverted L, hanging from the sill of the hatch like an oversized child on a monkey-bar. I grabbed his ankles and dumped him out into the access alley. His head twisted sideways and his tongue flopped out of his mouth. All the way out. It lay there beside him, twitching on the wet concrete.

I took a couple of deep breaths and climbed out after him. "Here," I said. "Hold this." I handed Gezen the screwdriver, slammed the hatch shut and turned towards the exit, stripping the remnants of tape from my wrists and tossing them in the gutter as I went.

21

OUT IN THE CLEAR LIGHT of day it was all happening. There were fire engines everywhere. Officers were shouting instructions through breathing apparatus. Hoses had been run out, bulging and writhing like engorged pythons. A trio of ambulances sat side-by-side with their double-doors swung open, stretchers at the ready. The paramedics were doling out blankets to sprinkler-soaked refugees. Nobody paid me the slightest attention.

The big rigs had been pulled clear of all the fuss and formed a solid wall along the far side of the road. Their drivers stood around in groups of three and four, arms folded across their chests, watching the show. I slipped between two of the semis, heading for the carpark. A heavy-set figure swung down from the driver's cabin and blocked my way. "You'll catch your death," he said, and thrust a pair of oil-stained jeans and a scrappy navy-blue windcheater into my hands.

I mumbled thanks and began to strip off on the spot. The driver looked modestly away, told me I could keep the stuff, and sauntered back to his mates. The pants were a good three sizes too big, and there was no belt. Breakdown gear. Not that I was ungrateful. I stuck my head through the windcheater, hitched up the daks and waddled across the road. The carpark was deserted. I started the Falcon and headed for the highway. A line of squad cars was coming in the other direction, spraying gravel and flashing their lights.

I steered one handed, my left palm stripped back to a nasty little stigmata by the super-frozen metal of the hatch handle. I'd never killed anyone before. I wondered what I should be feeling. I rolled down my window and let the cool air buffet my face. The day was turning out to be a bobby-dazzler. The night's storm and everything that had happened in it was already receding into ancient history. On the far horizon the towers of the city were just visible. The highway was an arrow pointed straight at the tallest and most dazzling of them, the Amalfi, shiny and freshly washed.

Some of the picture was clearer now, but the picture itself kept getting bigger, the canvas widening and widening. I wasn't sure that I would ever be able to see it all, let alone make sense of it. Merricks, according to Gardiner, was behind all this. "Fix it, he told me." So said the dead man. And dead men tell no tales, do they? But what had he meant? That was a question, I decided, best put to Merricks in person.

But not now. Not like this. Not arriving in a stolen car with a rubbish-tip mongrel farting away on the seat beside me. Not in a pair of fat man's dungarees held up with a bleeding hand. Not in a cast-off jumper, not even one with "Police Co-Operative Credit Union" printed on the front. Not with a three-day growth and wet shoes and compost in my hair. If this keeps up, I thought, I'll end up looking like Jimmy Barnes.

Merricks was not a man I could see making an impromptu confession. My ill-considered phone call to him had not only very nearly got me killed, it had put him on the defensive. Merricks had more resources at his command than I could possibly imagine, someone to be approached only with the greatest care and planning. Assuming I was in a position to do anything of the sort. Assuming I was not in police custody myself. From now on, spontaneity was out. No more bull-at-a-gate stuff. Aside from which, I had more immediate worries.

I punched the radio on, got the time, punched it back off. I was in no mood for breakfast cheer. It had just gone seven. Ayisha, I prayed, would still be asleep. I could be back on the couch before she woke. I parked a few blocks short of the house and left the keys in the car. There was a high school nearby, and with luck the Falcon would be three suburbs away by the end of morning recess. The mutt got out and followed, her nails pitter-pattering along the footpath behind me. They needed clipping. She'd need a decent wash, too. And a worming. And a distemper shot. I'd have to knock up a kennel for her, too, or Red would have her sleeping in the house. A name would be useful as well. I was still alive, so Cerberus was definitely out. Red would want to do the choosing. Voltron, or something like that, no doubt.

Up ahead I could hear a banging noise, hollow and reverberating. As I turned into my street, Ayisha came out of the house in her big quilted overcoat and crossed the road to her Laser. I picked up pace, shuffling towards her as fast as I could, both hands hoisting the waistband of my pants. She opened her bag, fishing for keys, and saw me coming. The noise was getting louder, a demonic bashing and crashing, and I realised it was coming from my house. Ayisha found her keys, got the door open, and slid behind the wheel.

Just as I got to her, the banging reached a frenzied pitch. The whole of my roof was rearing and pitching and seemed about to break up into its constituent parts. Abruptly the noise ceased. The sheets seemed to settle. A low metallic screech began. One by one, the iron sheets started to slide downwards, gathering momentum, catching and dragging each other, until the entire skin of the roof was an avalanche pitching towards the yard below. There was a moment of near silence. Then, with a great crash, the whole lot tipped over the guttering and landed on the garden, burying the prostrate boobialla under an ugly midden of twisted, rusting iron sheets.

Ant appeared on the ridge beam above. He gave a lunatic whoop and waved a pinch-bar triumphantly in the air. He was wearing a blue singlet, tattered jeans, heavy work boots and wrap-around sunglasses. He looked like the original speed-crazed bikie from hell. When he saw me, he waved, pulled his top lip back to display his new choppers, and gave me the thumbs-up. By then, old Mrs. Bagio had come out her front door and was standing at her gate with a broom in her hand. Other neighbours were coming outside for a look, too.

Ayisha wound down her window. Her hair was dishevelled and wide black smudges of mascara circled her tired eyes. She looked like a bad-tempered panda. "You okay?"

"Yeah," I said. "I guess."

She turned on her engine. "From now on," she said, "I think we should keep everything on a strictly professional basis, don't you?" She was looking right through me.

"I, um," I said. Across the road, the front door opened and Wendy appeared. She was got up in her corporate amazon outfit — full war paint, shoulders that would scare the shit out of a rugby forward, and, of all things, a double string of pearls. Considering she looked like her mother, she'd never looked better. She appeared pleased to see me, too. But only in the sense that a tiger might be pleased to see a tethered goat.

Ayisha was waiting for me to finish. Wendy came out onto the porch. She had Red by one hand and was carrying his overnight bag in the other. A taxi turned into the street and cruised slowly towards us. "I, um," I said again. It seemed to be the best I could do. Wendy began clomping across the pile of corrugated iron with Red in tow. She waved to the taxi. The Laser began to move. "See you later," said Ayisha. I doubted it.

Wendy was on the footpath by then. "Hi," I said. "I see you got here nice and early."

Wendy went straight for the throat. "Don't bother trying to talk your way out of this one, Murray." She brushed past me, wrested open the taxi door and hurled the overnight bag inside. "I get the early flight down especially so I can take Red to school myself. And what do I find?"

Ant came around the side of the house, took one look at what was happening and ducked back out of sight. Wendy let go of Red's hand, grabbed hold of her own little finger and shook it. My crimes were about to be enumerated. "For a start, you're not here. You've left Red in his bed and disappeared. And where you've gone is anyone's guess. Nobody knows, including" — she moved on to the next finger — "the strange woman I find asleep in my bed."

Poor Ayisha. Talk about *Wake in Fright*. And I thought the emphasis on the "my" was a bit unfair considering Wendy hadn't slept there more than six nights in the previous six months.

"Ayisha," said Red, exasperatedly. "I told you her name is Ayisha."

"Yes, sweetheart." She laid a proprietary hand on the child's head, then snatched it back to tug at a third finger. "Banned from school with nits, he tells me. And what do you do? You get him butchered." Red, the little traitor, made no attempt to contradict her. Worse, he went all waifish, averted his eyes and fiddled with a plastic model he was holding, something halfway between a stegosaurus and an armoured personnel carrier. I remembered the dog and looked around. It was nowhere to be seen.

This lack of attentiveness compounded my dereliction of parental duty. For a moment Wendy looked like she was about to rip my arms off with her bare teeth and beat me to death with them. Then her expression turned to one of genuine hurt. "And my beautiful rug. I carried that thing all the way back from Srinagar."

"The roof was leaking," I pleaded lamely.

That just made things worse. She let go of her finger long enough to jerk her thumb back over her shoulder. "If you think I'm paying for any of this you've got another thing coming. No expenditure without consultation." Then, having run out of fingers, she propelled Red into the cab, got in beside him, and fiddled with his seat belt. She pulled the door shut decisively and wound the window down. "Haven't you heard of passive smoking?" she said. "There are cigarette butts from one end of the house to the other." Then she touched the driver on the shoulder and they were gone. She hadn't even asked about my face.

I stood on the footpath and watched them drive away. Wendy was right, of course. Leaving Red like that had not been a good idea.

Things did not augur well for the tussle to come. Ant slunk out of his hiding place and stood beside me. "Christ," he said. "What a fucking dragon." Up close, his teeth looked like he'd gone to the wrong address and ended up at the veterinary college.

"I'll thank you not to speak that way of the mother of my child," I said.

A flat-bed truck pulled up, driven by a dopey-looking teenager in a Collingwood beanie. "This is Trevor," said Ant. "My offsider." By the look of him, Trevor was on day-release from a youth-training institution. But as far as I could tell he didn't have a single tattoo. Considering I was paying him twenty-five dollars an hour, cash, I took this as a reassuring sign. He and Ant began slinging the old iron onto the back of the truck and I went inside.

Ayisha must have been nervously lighting cigarettes while waiting for me to return from the branch meeting. Lots of her butts were only half smoked. I squeezed one back into shape and fired it up. The smoke hit the pit of my stomach and instantaneously I was ravenous. I poured myself a bowl of Wheaties and ate as I smoked. Then I ate another two bowls. Pretty soon I would have to report the Renault running into the lake. There must have been quite a few accidents during that storm. Talk about lucky.

I turned the shower on full-bore and used the last of the nit shampoo to wash the mud and grass out of my hair. The blood on my hands was mostly metaphorical, so I couldn't do much about that. But I kept scrubbing anyway. The real dirt was what Gezen had on me. I wondered how much he had seen, and decided not much. Not that I could imagine him rushing to the police. If he was nervous before, he'd be shitting himself now. Aside from which, we were even. We knew each other's secrets.

Shaving hurt like hell and a couple of the scabs came away and started bleeding. I offered it up as a penance for my own stupidity. Ant and his offsider were back on the roof somewhere above me, stripping the last of the guttering away and pitching it to the ground. They were working to the sound of a radio tuned to some God-awful top forty station. The nine o'clock news came on, and the fire was the lead story. The blaze had taken three quarters of an hour to bring under control. Damage was estimated at more than a million dollars. But that information came later. First up was a police statement to the effect that an unnamed man was dead. Traffic on the Tullamarine, Eastern and South-eastern freeways was smooth. Nothing about Charlene. We were heading for a top of twenty. Wake me up before you go-go.

My ninety-nine-dollar del Monaco special was a write-off. I found a pair of tan cords, a white shirt and a clean jumper. Just as well nobody had ever been run out of the Labor party for being badly dressed. At least I wouldn't be stalking the corridors looking like a werewolf. The plan, if you could call it that, was to discover as soon as possible what was happening with Charlene. Then I would pin Agnelli down for a full and frank exchange of views. I assumed that Charlene's bad turn would put a temporary dampener on Agnelli's little scheme. And if he hadn't already worked out that stabbing a sick woman in the back might not be good for his image, it would be my pleasure to draw his attention to the fact.

The soggy bills in my suit pocket would just cover a taxi into town. I rang one and went out the front to survey the damage. The roof had been stripped as bare as a departmental budget the night before the end of the financial year. Ant, Trevor and the supply-yard driver were unloading new sheets of iron off the back of a truck. The garden was fucked, but that was the least of my troubles. The dog had reappeared and attached herself to Trevor like a limpet. I whistled and she ignored me. A car pulled up behind the truck, some sort of public service fleet vehicle. Agnelli got out, smoothed his lapels and waited for me to come over. He looked decidedly un-happy.

"You've really fucking fucked it this time, you fucking little fuck," he said. With a command of the language like that it was a wonder he wasn't in the federal Cabinet. "Get in. Charlene wants to see you." As he drove away, Agnelli tooted. His idea of solidarity with the working class. I closed my eyes and slumped down in the seat.

Agnelli had woken up the octopus. It had gone and now it was back. It put its suckers on my eyeballs and started dragging them backwards into my cranium.

As Agnelli drove he reached into his inside jacket pocket. "You seem to have forgotten just how close to the bottom end of the political food chain you are, sport. Talk about Whelan the Wrecker. A trained chimpanzee could have done a better job." He had a piece of paper in his hand. My report to MACWAM. "No immediate cause for concern . . . Press reports having no basis in fact." He quoted my concluding paragraphs snidely and flapped the page in my face as he changed lanes. "You're deliberately trying to make me look like an idiot in front of the committee, aren't you? 'No cause for concern.' Shit, yesterday there was only one dead body, now there's two and for all I know the count is still climbing."

He stuffed the paper back in his pocket. I took it that I was supposed to be impressed by all of this. The car was overheated and stuffy and I'd had a hell of a night. I closed my eyes, let a gentle torpor settle over me, and concentrated on getting the octopus to go back to sleep. I guess I must have yawned. This did not go down well.

"You think it's a joke, don't you?" Agnelli screamed. "I've got Merricks on the phone at the crack of fucking dawn screaming government incompetence at the top of his tits, and you think it's a joke. Half the fucking joint burned down and the other half is out of commission indefinitely. If you had one iota of decency, you'd resign on the spot. You'd order me to stop the car, right here and now, and get out. You'd resign and spare Charlene and the rest of us any further embarrassment." He slowed down, as if I might take him up on the suggestion and throw myself out of the moving vehicle. "You, mate, are in more shit than a Bondi surfer."

A sticker on the front of the glove box thanked me for not smoking. I reached over and tried to peel it off. The sticker was made out of some sort of paper that tore when I pulled it. Thank You for Not, it now read. "One thing I don't understand," I said. "The story in the *Sun* on Monday. How did you do that part?"

Agnelli didn't miss a beat, I'll say that for him. "I don't know what you're talking about."

"It's all been bullshit, hasn't it?" I said. "Lollicato was never planning a challenge at all. You've been feeding me crap from the word go, keeping me busy chasing my own tail."

Agnelli was suddenly deeply intent on the traffic. He seemed to find it hard to speak while getting his mouth back down below melting point. "Why would I want to do that?"

"Because you're lining yourself up to challenge Charlene."

"Ah," he said, a long, upwardly-inflected exhale. It was, I knew, as close as he would come to an admission.

"And Charlene?" I said.

"Charlene?"

"Yeah, the woman you're busy trying to shaft. How is she?"

He shrugged. "Ask her yourself," he said.

We were in Royal Parade by then, going down the long tunnel of shade cast by the avenue of big trees. I closed my eyes, feigning sleep. After a while the silence got to Agnelli. He snapped on the radio. It was the ABC. Crap, crap. Blah, blah. Then we got the ten o'clock news. The Reagan re-election campaign was entering its final phase. The word Armageddon was mentioned. Marcos had ordered the trial of suspects in the Benigno Aquino killing. I couldn't see much coming of that. The Maralinga Royal Commission had commenced. The British High Commissioner was bitching that Britain's name was being dragged through the mud. So not all the news was bad, then.

After five minutes of this, I had almost fallen asleep for real. Then the local bulletin came on. The fire had already been overtaken by more current stories. In a joint state-commonwealth police operation, illegal gambling equipment had been seized from an address in Brunswick overnight. It was also believed that charges relating to immigration offences would be laid in the near future. After that I must have dozed off properly, because the next thing I knew Agnelli had pulled into a vacant space outside the Peter MacCallum

Institute. That woke me up quick smart. The Peter Mac is a cancer hospital. "What are we doing here?"

"Talking to Charlene." That was as much as I could get out of him.

"She's okay though, isn't she?"

"You're so fucking smart," he said. "You tell me." He led the way along halls that smelled like the 1930s, all wax and boracic soap. Outside her room he softened a little. "She wants to tell you herself," he said.

Charlene was in a private room, in a bed with too many pillows, a view of the back end of the Titles Office, and ominous plumbing fixtures. She was propped up with a tube sticking into her arm and another one coming out of her nose. It was the first time I had ever seen her without make-up. Her complexion was parchment, as if her face had ceded priority to more demanding parts of her metabolism. Her customarily rigid helmet of a perm had flopped into a lifeless mat. She looked a hundred. Whatever was happening to her was happening fast.

She was studying a document. Her reading glasses had slipped down to the end of her nose and she looked out over the top of them. A major display of gladioli had been shoved to the back of the bedside table to make way for dispatch boxes. Arthur, her driver, was standing at the foot of the bed scrutinising his shoes.

"Lovely," she whispered. "Beaut." She signed the page, handed it to Arthur, and sank backwards. Arthur nodded to us on the way out, far too emphatically.

Wordlessly Agnelli and I parted and stood one on each side of the bed. Charlene took off her glasses and put them aside. She winced at the effort and tried to hide it. "Sit down," she ordered. Her voice was a tremulous echo of what it had been.

The visitors' chairs were made of tubular metal and plywood and had been painted cream sometime during the battle of Balaclava. Mine shrieked when I dragged it across the floor. I cringed and sat down as quietly as I could.

"It's just a few tests," Charlene said. "Not the death of Napoleon." Paradoxically, her fragility made her seem all the more powerful. "Angelo told you?" she asked me.

"Told me what?"

"Good," she said. "Didn't want you getting any wrong ideas."

"What's wrong, Charlene?" I said. "You look terrible." I thought I could tell her that because it was something she would already have known.

"Bit of a growth," she said. "An opportunity to reorder my priorities."

One of her hands lay on top of the bedclothes, like a chook's claw with rings on. She let me pick it up. It was cool to the touch. As she spoke, I rubbed it between my palms. It didn't seem to get any warmer.

"I've decide to retire," she said. "The Premier knows. One or two others. Now I'm telling you." To my eternal shame my first thought was of myself. Charlene read my mind. "It's all been taken care of," she said. "Angelo."

Agnelli leaped up, strode to the foot of the bed and gripped the metal bed-end. Rehearsing, I realised as he spoke, his new role. "Charlene and the faction leaders have agreed that I should take on Melbourne Upper," he announced, pausing long enough for Charlene's silence to constitute a confirmation.

I assumed she would have some pretty good motives for going along with this caper. She lay impassively, giving me no hint what they might be.

"As you know," Agnelli went on, addressing the chart above Charlene's head, "there are always those at the local level who find it difficult to reconcile these sort of decisions with both traditional practices and their own personal agendas."

Charlene fidgeted impatiently under the sheets. "Cut the cackle, Angelo. You're not in parliament yet," she said. She inclined her head in my direction and spoke so softly I had to bend closer to hear her. She did this, I realised, to stir Agnelli. "The truth is, Murray, this close to an election we can't afford another factional brawl over pre-selection. Angelo is what you might call" — here she paused and made a minor show of looking for the right word — "acceptable to both the left and the right."

"Acceptable?" I said. "This is quite a surprise." Agnelli couldn't conceal a look of triumph. "And it's bound to be messy." Agnelli temporarily shelved his hubris. I went on. "Parachuting in some heavy-weight with high-level connections and expecting the local branches to endorse him. It won't go down very well."

"Quite right," said Charlene ambiguously. "That's why we want you to smooth over the transition. Help Angelo garner the support he'll need in the electorate. That sort of thing."

Do Agnelli's dirty work for him? Like buggery I would. "Ange has just finished telling me how little confidence he has in me," I said.

"Ah, don't be so thin-skinned," said Agnelli. "You think I'd want you if I didn't think you could do the job?"

"Aside from which," said Charlene, more to the point, "some-one well regarded in the electorate will need to be right there beside you all the way through the process."

An immediate answer seemed to be required. I didn't know what to say, so I didn't say anything. Perhaps Charlene took my si-lence for a rebuke. She pretended, at least I hope she was pretend-ing, that it was a negotiating stance.

"Angelo has agreed," she said, "that in return for my support, and as a personal favour to me, that he will retain you as his electorate officer for at least the next parliamentary term, whether or not we are in government. His agreement is a matter of record. Isn't that right, Angelo?"

"Absolutely," said the fucking snake who little more than half an hour before had been trying to get me to jump out of his car.

The temptation to tell Agnelli to shove it was strong. But Charlene had obviously gone to some pains to see me looked after in whatever deals Agnelli was busy cutting. And, truth be known, it was hardly an ideal time to be looking for a new job. The Family Court did not look kindly on the custody claims of unemployed fathers. Aide-de-camp to Agnelli wasn't exactly Ambassador to Ireland but it was a job. And a boy must have a job. I couldn't bring myself to say yes, so I just nodded.

"Good boy," said Charlene and squeezed my hand. "Forgive me?"

I never found out what she meant by that. A hippo-faced specialist in a white coat had barged through the door with a clutch of chinless interns in tow and turfed me and Agnelli out. That's what you get for not going to the right schools.

If she meant, did I forgive her for leg-roping me to Angelo Agnelli's political fortunes, the answer was yes. The decision was mine and I've accepted responsibility for it.

If she meant, did I forgive her for conniving with Agnelli to send me on a wild goose chase, the answer is I don't know. I don't know because I could never bring myself to ask the prick if Charlene was party to it, so I'll never know if there was anything to forgive. Nor could I ever bring myself to enquire too fully into the intricacies of the deal that saw Agnelli become the party's endorsed candidate for Melbourne Upper. The fact is some things just don't bear too close examination. Sometimes it's enough just to know that you're still on the team. I held my hand out to Agnelli. "Congratulations," I said. "Comrade."

22

THE REST IS, as they say, ongoing context. Let me parameter the specifics for you.

Charlene was out of hospital the next day just in time to usher the workplace insurance legislation safely into law and see the end of the spring session of parliament. Three days later she announced her resignation and a week after that writs were issued for a state election. While all this was happening, I was having a few sleepless nights waiting for the coppers to come knocking on my door. When they hadn't turned up after a month, I knew they probably never would.

We won the election, despite the best efforts of the *Sun*, with an increased majority. We even picked up a marginal gain in Melbourne Upper, but only at the booths in the heaviest Italian areas. Five months later Charlene was dead. We gave her a wonderful send-off and she's buried out at Fawkner Cemetery. Eternally committed to the electorate is probably the way she'd put it. Keeping in touch with the grass roots.

Going out there again, past those rows of tombs lined up like a miniature set from some sword and sandal epic, reminded me of those weirdos with the military salutes standing over Bayraktar's coffin. By then I knew what had been going on, or thought I did. Coates and I had pieced the basics together, and I fleshed the rest out from incidental titbits that Agnelli picked up on the legal grapevine when the Anatolia Club gambling case came up.

Appearances can be deceptive. At first sight the fact that the Anatolia Club looked so much like a small private casino blinded me to the fact that it essentially was just that. And as such had certain requirements in the way of personnel. That's where Bayraktar came in, initially at least.

The proprietors, including the two bozos I'd seen at the cemetery, had imported Bayraktar from Turkey to act as their debt collector. They were former military officers and Bayraktar had once been an NCO, so they might have known him from the army. Perhaps he'd merely been well recommended by their crim colleagues in West Germany. In any case, he turned out to be a bit of a liability, inclined to shake down the clientele on his own account. Rather than grasp the nettle in the way that Gardiner ultimately did, they suggested he find employment elsewhere. But they let him keep his little flat out the back, a sort of implicit threat to any of their customers tempted to welsh on their commitments.

Temporarily forced to work for a living, Bayraktar had fallen on his feet. First he was recruited by Gardiner to front the payroll scam. Then he began putting the squeeze on likely fellow employees. Eventually he worked out that Pacific Pastoral provided the ideal set-up for shifting drugs about the countryside. When Gardiner eventually got fed up with all these extracurricular antics and gave him the big chill, the crew at the Anatolia Club were probably as relieved as anyone else.

But he had once been a fellow soldier, and honour required that his death not go uncommemorated. His former associates at the club signed for the body, chipped in for a medium-priced Martinelli walnut overcoat and stood in the rain at attention for two minutes. I can only hope someone does as much for me when the time comes.

Not that any of this came out at the inquest. No new evidence was presented to counter the original supposition that the fat boy had taken a heart turn in the midst of laying in his weekend supplies of scotch fillet. The coroner came down on the side of natural causes, and took the opportunity to comment broadly on the importance of maintaining safe work practices in the cool-storage industry. The Department of Labour responded with a press release pointing out that it was in the process of amending the regulations regarding mandatory aisle-widths and expected to gazette them in the not-too-distant future.

The one minor hiccup in the coronial hearing was the unavoidable absence from the witness box of the man who had found the body. Herb Gardiner was, of course, the subject of his own inquest barely a week after Bayraktar's. Based on the fact that he was wearing protective clothing, and on the testimony of the fireman who found the body, as well as the medical evidence, it was concluded that Gardiner had been inside one of the freezers when the alarm went off. Making a late run for the exit, he had slipped on the wet floor, broken his neck, and been asphyxiated by the smoke as he lay unconscious.

Frankly, that last bit was something of a surprise. I'd honestly thought he was already dead when I left him lying there. Misadventure, the coroner said. I couldn't agree more. More proof, if any is needed, that you can't help bad luck. The cause of the fire was attributed to a radiator accidentally left burning all night in the administration area. Speculation that arson was involved was dismissed by both the company and the police as groundless. The insurance was paid out in full.

Herb Gardiner left an estate worth the best part of two million dollars, including a Broadbeach condominium, an Adelaide motel and part shares in a macadamia nut plantation. It just goes to show what hard work, a bit of thrift, and a remarkable fifteen-year-long winning streak on the horses can achieve. His punting record was all carefully documented in papers found in his bookcase — date, course, race, horse, dividend. In case the tax man ever asked, I guess.

With no one to lay claim to the estate, it all went to the Public Trustees Office, which will meticulously administer it down to a zero sum over a period of 150 years.

On the way back from Charlene's funeral I drove past 636 Blyth

Street. It had already changed hands twice since the Anatolia Club was shut down and was being refurbished as a Maltese wedding reception centre. For all I know that's what it still is. I must check next time I'm out that way.

That could be some time. These days Melbourne Upper is just one small part of the territory I cover in my capacity as adviser to the Minister for Ethnic Affairs, Angelo Agnelli, MLC. Fortunately, for me at least, Angelo is also Minister for Local Government, a demanding portfolio that leaves him with insufficient energy to do serious damage to the interests of those valued members of our community who derive from the more non-English-speaking parts of the planet. In fact Local Government is so unrewarding a portfolio that I'm beginning to think poor old Ange must have trodden on a few important toes on his way up the ladder. Mullane senior for one. Apparently Ange promised my job to young Gavin in return for the old man's support on pre-selection. Right now Ange is off in the bush somewhere trying to convince some quasi-autonomous local instrumentality to voluntarily sacrifice itself on the altar of efficiency.

As for me, I try to keep my head down and my tail up, but I'd be lying if I said I was overextended. Ethnic Affairs is mostly about trying to find ways to give a bit of a leg-up to government supporters with funny surnames. Speaking of which, I saw Ayisha Celik the other day at the Ethnic Communities Council Conference. It was the first time we'd spoken since the big event. Somebody started to introduce us. Ayisha cut in, laughing with her eyes, gorgeous as ever. "You seen a doctor yet?"

"No need," I said, "now that the swelling's gone down."

"Murray had terrible rash last time I looked," she explained to our host.

"I see," he said knowingly. "Like that, is it?" It wasn't, but she didn't seem to mind if he thought so. Then we all stood there silently rocking on our heels for a moment until the other guy got the idea and made himself scarce.

"I dunno what happened between you and Memo Gezen. And

I don't want to," she said. "But whatever it was, it did the trick. He's gone back to Turkey. Wife, kids, the works. Thanks."

I said it was no trouble and all for the best and she said congratulations on my new job. Then the coffee break ended and we had to rush off and chair our respective workshops. For a brief moment there I considered pressing my suit with her, but in the end I decided against it. Keeping secrets is one thing that Ayisha is good at. Best not muddy the waters.

Word is she's on the short list for Co-ordinator of the Migrant Resource Centre. She's got the advocacy routine down pat, and that degree in Public Administration she's got should set her in good stead. So if anyone asks, I'll tell them I can't think of a better person for the job, even if she has got herself engaged to some Macedonian mother's-boy from Pascoe Vale.

Gezen's not the only one to have moved. Red lives in Canberra most of the time now. Very good for kids it is. He can walk to school and Wendy even lets him ride his bike to the shops. The woman Wendy is living with has a girl two years older, so he's not short of family life. He flies down one weekend a month, which is all I can afford at the moment, and as much as his social life permits. I get him on the school holidays too, although last time he went to Samoa instead because Wendy was speaking at a conference there on Women and the Future of Work in the Pacific, and it was too good a chance to pass up.

We'll probably get round to formalising the divorce sometime soon. It's not as if there's any great reason to rush. Wendy eventually saw reason on splitting the cost of the roof job, even though it turned out that Ant had charged five hundred dollars above the going rate and was ripping the materials off as well. What decided her was the capital gain of twenty-five grand we made when we sold the old place. I put my half down as the deposit on a nice little fully-renovated zero-maintenance terrace in Fitzroy. It's handy enough for me to be able to walk to work, which is just as well, as it's murder trying to find a parking space around here.

Of course it's quieter here in Victoria Parade than it was out at the electorate office. We don't get much passing trade. Just to get to see me, you have to sign in with the commissionaire in the foyer, take the lift eight floors and negotiate two secretaries and an administration officer. Not that I don't make an effort to keep my finger on the pulse, mind you. It's all No Smoking up here, so whenever I want a quick puff I have to pop down to street level and mingle with the other desperados. There's always a little crowd steaming away in the foyer of the Resources and Technology Department next door, and it's amazing what little tit-bits of info you can pick up. And sometimes this woman from Information and Publications on the fourth floor is there. Antoinette Aboud her name is. Lebanese, I guess. Fascinating people, the Lebanese. So much history, so little space.

And you never know, do you? There's this safe seat out Springvale way that might just possibly be on the market before the next election. It's right across the other side of town and I'll probably have to learn a word or two of Vietnamese, but at this stage I'm confident of enough factional support at the centre to warrant throwing my hat into the ring. Naturally the locals will have to be squared off. The electorate officer is apparently quite a handful. But I do feel that I do have a certain amount of expertise in these matters. And expertise is the name of the game these days.

Or maybe I'll stick to my snug little office here on the top floor. I've got my own window now, and I can see right across the treetops of the Fitzroy Gardens, past the spire of the cathedral, to the city with all its cranes and new office towers. Almost every day there's something brand new on the skyline. The way this city is going, by the end of the eighties the place will be unrecognisable. For the past few months one high-rise tower in particular had held my attention, a combination media centre and hotel being put up by a consortium headed by Lionel Merricks.

These days Lionel is not nearly so critical of the government as he was in the first few days after the fire. Not after I found the opportunity for a conference with him. I rang for an appointment a couple of times, all very civilised, but never got past the ice queen. I supposed that Lionel wasn't too keen to start taking my calls again.

So I hung around outside the next meeting of the City Revitalisation Committee and caught him in the hallway during a coffee break. Rather than face a scene, he agreed to a private chinwag in the stairwell. He tried to browbeat his way out of it, of course. But I felt that this time I had the edge on him, what with my new suit, my face all healed up and a few well-researched facts up my sleeve.

The folks at the Department of Agriculture had been particularly helpful. They explained just how much illicit money you can make if you've got a meat works, an export licence, a low-key, long-term approach, and a certain amount of contempt for the law. You just stick your boneless beef labels on something else. Donkey meat is a big-margin item. Kangaroo, too. But they're a bit risky. You can still make a pretty penny using lower grade beef.

Naturally, it doesn't pay to get caught. The trick then is to pass it all off as a mistake. It helps if your plant manager is convinced it really is one. And since this sort of thing can do a lot of damage to the reputation of a nation's export industries, the official inspectors are loath to come down with a finding of systematic abuse. Fortunately for Pacific Pastoral, the issue never arose. The fire gave them a much-needed pretext to divest themselves of their entire commodity export operations. They flogged the works off to a Japanese feed-lot enterprise based in Queensland, and used the proceeds to finance their move into tourism, media and real estate development, all of which have been a real boon to the state economy. Not that the issue of finance raised its ugly head in my conversation with Merricks. I was very careful about that.

"Herb Gardiner told me everything," I said first up, my back pressed against the door. "He felt the need to unburden himself."

"I didn't even know the man," Merricks blustered. "We've got thousands of employees."

"True," I said. "But how many of them were with you on HMAS *Wyndham*?"

Another thing Agnelli was right about was how insulated the leaders of big business are. I was probably the rudest person Merricks ever had to deal with. He employed others to deal with ill-mannered oafs like me. He lacked the skills required. "A frigate," I said. "That's not a very big boat, is it? Not like an aircraft carrier or something."

"The *Wyndham*'s not a boat," he bleated. "It's a ship." That's when I knew I had him.

Which was just as well, since I was only guessing about him and Gardiner having met in the Navy. The Office of Naval Records doesn't give out personnel information and I'd got the name of the ship Lionel served on from the journalist who'd written the profile for the *National Times*. I'd taken a punt and rung her up, telling her I needed some background for an award the government was thinking of presenting to Merricks. It turned out that he'd mentioned the *Wyndham* in the course of the interview and I put two and two together. It was sheer quantum mathematics that I got four, since I hadn't been able to find out anything about Gardiner's service record either.

With the *Wyndham* bobbing about in front of us, Merricks' memory suddenly improved and he was prepared to allow that there may have been a mechanic named Gardiner aboard. And he couldn't definitively discount the possibility that the same man had been employed at Coolaroo at the time he was an up-and-coming line manager out there. But I'd have a lot of trouble proving he'd had any direct dealings with the man subsequently, he told me. And the suggestion that the two of them had in some way been co-conspirators in criminal activity was a preposterous idea. One that, if repeated in public, would land me in court.

I didn't doubt that for one minute. But it was a hollow threat. I had no intention of taking on Merricks. The laws of libel are designed to protect the rich, and the idea that Pacific Pastoral might allow its internal records to be used to implicate its own chairman in protracted and systematic fraud was ludicrous. This little chat was just something I felt was needed by way of clearing the air. A personal matter. The last time I had spoken to Merricks, he thought I was trying to blackmail him. In the light of what had happened since, I just didn't want him thinking he had the moral advantage on me.

"Meat substitution isn't really a crime, I guess," I told him.

"More just a bit of sharp business practice, eh? *Caveat emptor,* and all that. But what about the payroll fraud, the extortion, the drugs? You and Gardiner were diddling the consumers, Gardiner and Bayraktar were ripping off the corporation, and Bayraktar was screwing the employees and dealing dope off the loading-bay. Nice sort of company you keep, Lionel."

I think he was so genuinely scandalised by then that I omitted dangerous driving and attempted murder. I left him standing on the stairs and shut the door behind me.

And to give Merricks the benefit of the doubt, I think it unlikely he actually suggested killing me when he delegated to Gardiner the job of sorting me out. Perhaps he had a generous cash settlement in mind. Lionel is a broad brush-stroke man, and not, I think, by nature violent. As distinct from Herb Gardiner, who had clearly been driven barking mad by the prospect of fifteen years' slow surreptitious graft in the arsehole of the universe disappearing down the gurgler two weeks before he retired to enjoy his illicit earnings. A person can hardly be blamed for the things done in his name by over-zealous subordinates.

Merricks, in fact, is so tractable these days that Agnelli has been able to wangle some very substantial donations out of him to offset the rising cost of elections. The outcomes of which have ensured my continuing employment. So I guess that pragmatism is not merely a civic virtue, it is also a personal grace. In tending the Garden State, one must always be mindful of the serpents.

And it's not like I have anything to complain about. Not since the bruises healed up, anyway. As I say to Angelo Agnelli on those rare occasions he asks for my advice, *"Bir tesselli ver."*